CAMP
SCOUNDREL

Doing what it takes to
survive paradise.

First Published in Great Britain 2018 by Mirador Publishing

A copy of this work is available through the British Library.

ISBN: 978-1-912601-04-2

Mirador Publishing
10 Greenbrook Terrace
Taunton
Somerset
UK
TA1 1UT

Camp Scoundrel

Doing what it takes to survive paradise.

By

David Luddington

~ *Chapter One* ~

The security guard closed the door behind me and leaned with his back against it.

"So, you're that squaddie that nicked five million from the Minister for Disability and stuff, what's his name? Oh yeah, Stephen poncy Lethbridge." He nodded thoughtfully. "Respect to you."

"Ex-squaddie," I said. "And I didn't actually nick it." I settled onto the hard wooden chair by the radiator and stared at the walls. Drab cream with highlights of institutional grime, broken only by the odd poster explaining various rights to which I was entitled. I wondered if this was the last I was going to see of the outside world for a while.

"They're all innocent in here." He wriggled his back against the door as if trying to scratch an unreachable itch. "I've been working in these courts for ten years now and I've yet to see a guilty man."

"No, seriously, I didn't steal anything. I just made it go away."

The guard pondered that piece of information for a moment then, "What, magic, like Derren Brown? How did you do that then?"

"I hacked into his bank account. Money is only ones and zeros in an electronic box these days. I just poked around in the box and turned all the ones into zeros. It all went away. It can't be stealing if I didn't actually take it."

"Did the jury buy that?" He nodded his head towards the courtroom across the hall.

"No."

"You should've kept it for yourself and buggered off to Marbella. That's what I would've done."

"That wasn't the plan," I said. "He's the self-serving prig who cut all the benefits to the disabled. I wanted him to feel what it was like to have to live on the pittance he voted for."

"And now you're facing a spell inside and he's back to swilling down the Moet on his yacht. Makes ya' think."

A knock on the door jerked the guard upright. "Here we go," he said and opened the door.

My solicitor, Eric Hansard, nodded his thanks and headed for the little desk against the wall where he placed two cardboard cups. "Coffee," he said.

I looked at the muddy brown liquid. "I'll take your word for that. Any chance of a cigarette?"

"Not in here, sorry." Eric looked at the guard. "Thank you, Jim. Can we be alone for a moment?"

Jim shrugged and left the room, closing the door behind him.

"Well?" I said. "What's happening?"

"You know the Crown Prosecution want your blood, don't you?"

I nodded.

"Look, Mike –"

"It's Michael."

"What? Oh, right. Look, Mike, I have to be realistic with you, you're in quite a lot of trouble here. The CPS is requesting a custodial sentence. They're calling for an example to be made and for what you did, you could get up to five years."

"Five years?" I did a mental calculation. "That'd make me forty-four. That can't be right?"

"What makes you think the justice system has anything to do with rights and wrongs? You've offended the Establishment and now they want blood. Remember what they did to the Great Train Robbers?"

"Five years though?"

"At least it's a roof and a dry bed." Eric took a sip of the coffee and flinched slightly.

I pondered the thought of a guaranteed bed and roof. No, it wasn't going to happen, I'd go crazy. Crazier.

"You did point out that the money went straight back the next day, didn't you?" I queried. "Five million, straight back, no problem yet it took *my* bank six months to refund me when they screwed up my rent payment. And then they went and added charges for going overdrawn. That's how I lost my flat."

"I do understand; it must have been very difficult for you. However, we may have an option. I happen to know Judge Carrington; he's a member of my lodge. He's a retired colonel from the Fusiliers and served in the first Gulf War, so he does have a modicum of sympathy for ex-services personnel."

"There's a chance of probation?"

"Hmm, not quite that simple, I'm afraid. Probation is a non-starter if you don't have a fixed address."

"What then?"

"Carrington's old-school and he's taken to thinking that the rot in society started when conscription finished. He's long nurtured a belief that the cure for all society's ills is a military style boot-camp training programme. You know, teach offenders how to survive off nothing and they'll stop thieving from the rest of us."

"But I've already been through Boot Camp once," I said.

"The army are not likely to let me have a second go. Not after this."

"Bear with me. Have you ever heard of Approved Premises? They used to be known as Halfway Houses or Bail Hostels. Sort of a Not-Quite-Prison for those who Don't-Quite-Need-Prison."

"And you think I might be sent there instead of prison?"

"Sort of. He's finally managed to persuade the Department of Justice to allow a pilot Boot Camp linked to one of these A.P.s and they need an ex-military type to run the pilot for him." Eric went to take another sip of coffee but his face crumpled in resistance before the cup arrived at his lips. He shook his head and replaced the cardboard cup on the desk. "Basically, he wants somebody with survival skills to take a group of villains off to some God forsaken spot and teach them to be self-sufficient. He had Wilderness Jack lined up. Do you know Wilderness Jack? He was in your lot. Anyway he's the chappie who parachutes into random jungles or deserts then has to walk out. He was all set to do it but he was offered a celebrity reality TV show at the last minute and went off to do that instead."

I gave my coffee cup a little swirl. The liquid didn't seem to move in quite the way I expected coffee should. I replaced it on the desk. "I'm still not sure how all this helps me?"

"You're ex-Special Forces aren't you?" He leafed through my file. "Ah, yes, here we are, I knew I'd seen it somewhere. Electronic Warfare Operator assigned to Special Forces units in various locations 2012 through 2015. Perfect."

"Oh, I see. I think I might need to explain."

Eric placed his pen on the papers with a degree of precision and care I'd not seen since I'd watched Jacko Williams disarm a roadside IED in Helmand. "Go on," he said.

"I was a Signaller, *assigned* to 22 SAS. The key word here is *assigned*. Not actually *in* the Special Forces. You see?"

"No, not really, but please elucidate."

"Well, you know when James Bond abseils over the side of the desert stronghold and blows the doors off with an explosive concealed in his Rolex?"

"Yes."

"And then he kills five bad guys with his hat before opening the case which holds the nuclear detonator?"

"I'm familiar with the tropes."

"And when he looks at the timer on the control panel and talks through his radio ballpoint pen to a geek sat in the back of a van twelve miles away and asks him to crack the password?"

"Yes."

"Well, that's me. The geek in the van that is, not James Bond."

"I see. But..." He leafed through my file. "Your nickname was 'Bomber' Purdey? Why Bomber?"

"Hmm, Bomber, it's army humour. I used to destroy Taliban IT systems using a sort of virus bomb. Quite clever really, it delivers an infinitely rotating zero-day packet..." I watched his eyes drift. "Never mind."

He thought for a moment. "Well, it doesn't really change anything, I suppose. I mean to even get close to the SAS you had to pass some sort of survival training, surely? As long as you can catch a rabbit or two, that's probably all that's going to be needed."

"Um, well. Not exactly. You see, it all started with a bet with an old mate that I could get through the SAS selection so I hacked into their systems to record that I'd previously completed the survival course. And the Combat Medic module. Oh, and the Escape and Evasion training."

Eric let out a long sigh and I felt my chances of avoiding a prison sentence expiring with it. "Why on earth would you do that? I mean, you're fit, so surely survival training wouldn't have been that bad?"

"It is for a vegetarian. I don't eat meat so catching a rattlesnake with a spoon and turning it into a soufflé was never something which really appealed."

"How on earth does a vegetarian survive in the military?"

"Hitler managed okay," I said.

"Hitler? What's he got to do with anything?"

"He was a vegetarian."

"Hmm, perhaps we won't mention that to the judge. It might not help your case."

"Now, do you have any teaching qualifications?"

"Teaching?"

"You're not allowed to supervise offenders without something called…" He referred to a file he had on the desk. "PTLLS, it's a sort of basic teaching certificate. Apparently you can be issued with one if you've ever done any teaching."

"I taught basic computer skills to OAPs for a while when I first came out. Clapham Community Centre on Wednesday nights. Does that work?"

"I think we can make it work."

"I did mention that I know bugger all about survival training, didn't I?" I said. "I'm not sure how I'm supposed to teach something I know nothing about."

"Just do what everybody else does. Look it up on Wikipedia."

"I'm not allowed access to a computer," I reminded him. "Part of my bail conditions."

"I'll clear that for you. Judge Carrington is in his last year and wants a notable achievement to smooth his path to a knighthood. And short of Andy McNab turning up in front of him, you're his only hope."

"I'm to be his path to a knighthood?"

"And he'll be your path to avoiding prison."

"I guess I've made worse deals."

~ *Chapter Two* ~

I'd been assigned to a group of several Approved Premises known as Newstart Houses, each located in quiet residential suburbs of Bristol. Apparently this group had already been earmarked as a candidate for the project which was now known as Camp Newstart. Julie, the Project Co-ordinator and one of the House Managers, showed me to her office and indicated a chair opposite her desk.

"These are generally some of the lower security Aps," she said.

"Aps? Oh yes, Approved Premises." I settled into an old armchair which threatened to engulf me.

"That's right. They used to be called Probation Hostels. We're a halfway house for offenders but this one focuses on lower risk clients, you know, drugs, petty theft…"

"And computer hackers."

"I suppose. Not had any before. We had a TV repairman once but I suppose that's not quite the same thing."

"Not quite."

"He was very useful though. He fixed up my Nan's old Binatone a treat. The only trouble was it kept picking up next door's home video channel. You wouldn't believe what they got up to. I tried to get him back to fix it again but Nan wouldn't let him touch it again."

A young man in jeans and white T-shirt brought a couple of mugs in and set them on the desk.

"Tea?" Julie asked him.

"Dunno," he mumbled. "Jo made it."

"Thank you, Jerry. Close the door on your way out."

I reached for a mug.

"I wouldn't," said Julie. "Not if Jo made it."

I looked at the mug in my hand then sniffed. It smelt like tea. "Jo?"

"One of our regulars. He has a bit of a predilection for experimental chemistry."

I very carefully placed the mug back on the desk. "Do you know who's going on the camp yet?"

"No, I don't have a say. The only person I know of is Simon Reeves; he's your Camp Colleague."

"What the hell's a Camp Colleague?" I asked.

"He's your... um... support. He's just retired from Shapham High Security Prison. He was Senior Officer there."

"I see."

"The Department of Justice regulations. You didn't think they were going to let you all go unsupervised, did you? Judge Carrington's had to pull enough strings to let you all travel abroad; you're hardly going to be allowed to wander round the backwoods of Spain on your own."

"Spain, huh." Things were looking up. "Any idea whereabouts?"

She reached behind her to an overstuffed shelving unit and pulled out a map book. "Southern Spain," she said as she leafed through the pages. "Andalucía. Somewhere called the Alpujarras. Mostly mountains and..." she pushed her glasses up off her nose and squinted closely at the pages. "Nope. Just mountains." She pushed the open map book across the table.

"Don't know exactly where until we have the right permissions from the local authorities there."

I took the map. It was fairly low scale and really only showed major topographic detail and a few major roads. Very few.

"Why there?" Any hope I'd been fostering of a nice beachside location was fading fast.

"I think one of Judge Carrington's old service friends knows somebody out there, somewhere. Apparently it's very… original. Not too much chance of the little rascals causing mischief when the only other inhabitants are mountain goats."

"When do we start?"

"You're flying out in the next few days to set things up, until then, you'll be staying here."

I was shown a small room on the top floor, not much more than a badly converted loft, but at least the small window showed me the outside world. My possessions these days fitted neatly into a rucksack so unpacking wasn't too much of a chore. I'd managed to secure a new laptop from Eric as part of the deal on the condition I only used it to send in a daily blog from the camp. I opened it up, hacked into the Wi-Fi network, downloaded a full set of programmes I kept hidden on a web server and disappeared off into cyberspace for the rest of the day.

The day before I was due to fly out to Malaga, I met with my newly assigned Probation Officer, Pauline. She took no time making it quite clear that she really didn't approve of the deal I'd been given and that it certainly wasn't normal to have her clients running around the continent wherever they pleased. She also explained in great detail that the first sniff of a transgression and she'd unleash the Hounds of Hell to hunt me down and drag my backside straight to a waiting prison cell on a small rock just off the Isle of Skye. I thanked her very much for her faith in my rehabilitation and dutifully signed the mountain of paperwork. I tried to read it but my eyes glazed over by page two. I did manage to glean however that I was under some sort of extended Community Service Order, which, I assumed, was how they had managed to set up this particular project.

***

The Departure Hall floor was cold and hard and having to sit on it did nothing to lift my mood from the Gatwick Airport school holiday mayhem. Over my years in the army I'd certainly spent more than my fair share of hours in airports, both civil and military. On balance, I always preferred the military versions. Despite their Spartan nature, one could usually find a seat and there were certainly fewer screaming babies, stag party rowdies and badly driven luggage trollies.

A family of seven, in disturbingly matching tracksuits, passed by in a cloud of argument and discarded crisp packets, completely oblivious to the fact their overladen trolley had just run over my foot. I pulled my feet in closer to avoid further injury and once more scanned the departures waiting area for a vacant seat.

I spotted the man through a crowd of milling holidaymakers. He was a young man, Asian and maybe early twenties. The small rucksack on his back was what first alerted me; it seemed too new and out of keeping with his clothes. His head moved, checking out the departure area in all directions. I looked around. Crowds of tourists, families, children, business types. Far too many people, far too close together. I stood slowly, flexing the cramps from my legs. The adrenaline flushed my system. Should I alert the police? Shout a warning? I could reach the man in about three or four seconds. What then? Snatch the bag and run? Where?

He raised his arm in the air and just as I was about to sprint I spotted a young woman. She had clearly caught eyes with the man and moved towards him. I hesitated. They both looked at each other, waving their arms, they were smiling. They closed on each other and embraced. I let my breath go as I watched them take each other's hands and head for one of the departure gates.

My heart banged in my ears and the excess adrenaline took the strength from my legs which threatened to collapse under me. I pulled a cigarette from the pack and fumbled it to my mouth. I was about to click the lighter when I heard a voice.

"You can't smoke in here, sir." The policeman had come from nowhere.

"Sorry," I said. "I forgot."

"There's a designated area just past the gates over there." He pointed to the far distance.

"Thanks." I hoisted my rucksack on my shoulder and he wandered off.

I needed a drink more than a smoke so I headed for the nearby Happy Burger Eatery, searching the tables for a space. My eyes caught the signs of movement as a young mother decamped her ketchup-laden child from highchair to buggy. I moved quickly to the table.

"You going?" I asked.

"I will if this little sod stops wriggling and lets me strap him in." She nodded to the buggy. "Hold it still for me will you? He's like a bleedin' octopus on meth when he don't want to go nowhere."

I obligingly held the buggy still while she fastened the

straps so tight I was sure the child's head had actually started expanding.

With a, "Now get out of that, you little toad," she wheeled the child off in the direction of the departure gates.

I turned to the freshly vacated table to find a young woman had just settled herself down at it. She looked to be in her late thirties. Her short, sun-bleached hair, sharply defined features and deep tan told of an active lifestyle.

"Oh, I was going to sit there," I said.

"You still can," she said, pointing to a vacant chair. "I don't take up much room."

"Thanks." I settled down and moved the empty burger boxes and escaped fries to one corner of the table. "It's chaos today, school holiday isn't it?"

"Probably." She pulled a paperback from her rucksack. I couldn't see the title but it looked like a Game of Thrones.

I took a serviette from the holder and wiped ketchup from the table. "Going anywhere nice?"

"Depends how you feel about an overcrowded rock in the Med full of drunken Brits and Matelots."

"Ah, not keen on Gibraltar then?" I dropped the soggy serviette in the burger box.

"It's work." She leafed through the book to find a turned down corner which marked her place. I repressed a shudder.

"I didn't think there was much work on Gib. You're lucky," I said.

She closed her book and placed it on the table. "Ah, you want to talk."

"What? Oh, sorry. No, carry on reading."

"We can talk if you like?" she said.

"No, it's just that I was there for a while."

"That's nice." She opened the book again.

I glanced up at the departures screen. My flight wasn't even listed yet. This was going to be a long wait.

"Could you keep an eye on my bag?" I asked, nodding towards my rucksack.

"Is this the bit where you want me to take your bag through security for you?" she asked.

"No, I promise. I'm just going to get a beer; do you want anything from the bar?"

"A coffee would be good, thanks. White."

"Just white?" I stared across at the Planet Costa outlet and although it was too far away to read properly, it looked like the coffee menu ran over three chalk boards. "Only they seem to have lots of different options. Café Latte Skinny Dipper with Mocha?"

"Just coffee, thanks."

"It's all a con anyway," I said. "Mostly they're just cups full of bubbles with made-up Italian names." I glanced back at the woman but she'd already returned to her book.

The price of the beer almost made me contemplate going without. Almost. I ordered the beer and searched the chalkboard for something resembling plain white coffee but that option didn't seem to exist. I had to go for a black double espresso grandé and take the milk from the jug supplied for tea drinkers. I got a helpless glance from an elderly woman as she tried to extract a teabag from her scalding cup with something that resembled a toothpick but I think was actually supposed to be a planet friendly, disposable stirrer. I took a plastic knife from the cutlery tray provided for the Danish Pastry eaters and retrieved her teabag.

"Thank you, young man. It's bad enough they make us tea drinkers stand in the corner here like naughty children for not drinking their frothy rubbish, the least they could do is give us a proper spoon. You can't make a decent cup of tea with a twig. It's not right."

I dropped the teabag in the bin. "It's all American, they don't understand tea anyway."

"That will be that dreadful president they've got." She picked up her cardboard mug in its little cardboard sleeve. "I'd box his ears if he was my grandson." She headed off in the direction of the tables.

I carried our drinks back to the table and placed the coffee in front of the woman.

"I think it's coffee," I said. "But it might equally be beef soup, I don't speak Planet Costa."

"Thanks," she said without looking up from her book.

The beer went down way too easily and I tried to make it last but failed. My eyes drifted to the departures screen for what was probably the twentieth time. My flight was at least now on the board although there was no gate attached yet. I thought about pulling out my laptop and looking at the Earthview of the Alpujarras once again. Why had they chosen such a remote area? I'd rather hoped that when they'd told me I'd be heading to Spain for this farce, I'd at least be close to a beach and a bit of nightlife. But as far as I could see from Earthview this was just mountains and forests.

The woman sipped at her coffee without moving her eyes from the page. I could see now it wasn't Game of Thrones but an Arthurian Fantasy and, going by the cover image, with a definite LGBT twist.

"Good book?" I asked.

"I don't know yet." She studied her cardboard coffee mug. "Mike?"

"Michael, actually." I looked at the name the lad behind the counter had scrawled on my paper cup. "I guess they didn't have enough room to write Michael on the cup, or they were trying to be chummy in a sort of vomit inducing way. Anyway, everybody calls me Bomber."

She glanced at my rucksack. "Are you telling me I just looked after an abandoned bag in a busy airport for somebody who goes by the name of Bomber?"

"Hmm, you can call me Shotgun, that's what they called me in school. It's a play on my surname, Purdey. Although I'm not sure that would help much." I grinned.

"Let's hope my new employer doesn't find out." She took a sip of coffee and wrinkled her nose. "You sure this is coffee?"

"That's what Jason told me, he's my personal barista and new best friend. What's the problem with your boss?"

"I'm due to start work tomorrow as a contractor for Blacklance Security."

"Ah, I can see how looking after a bomb in an airport might look messy on your CV. I promise not to tell. They offered me a job once. Mostly ex-service personnel, were you in?"

"Yes." She opened the book again.

"I did ten years." I looked again at my beer glass but it was still empty. "Signals mostly but attached to 22 SAS at the end."

"I'm impressed," she said without looking up.

"Don't be. I was an Electronic Warfare Specialist and I only got hooked up with them by accident."

"How does one accidently end up in the SAS?"

"It was a bet. I bet my mate five quid I could pass selection then I hacked their IT systems. I got top marks."

"Well done."

"Yes, well, I didn't expect them to actually assign me though. That came as a bit of a shock."

"Ah yes, I can imagine. I think I heard about you." She

folded a page and closed the book. "When you got out, didn't you go on and steal all the money from that politician's bank?"

"I didn't steal it. I just got inside his bank's systems and made it all go away."

"Why would you do that?"

"I wanted him to see if he could live on the benefits levels he voted for."

"How did that work out?"

"It didn't. Somebody just pressed a button and made it all come back again and I'm now having to nursemaid a bunch of thugs on a 'Personal Development Course' in some god-forsaken wilderness in a forgotten part of Spain that looks to me to be impassable to anything other than a hyperactive mountain goat."

She pushed her coffee cup to one side. "Wasn't that tried some time ago? I seem to remember a huge outcry in the Daily Mail because the courts were paying for groups of young hooligans to go on holiday in Ibiza."

"Yes, I know. But some retiring judge wants to make his mark on the system in the hope of bagging himself a gong and they needed a fall-guy to blame it all on when everything goes tits-up and the Dirty Dozen make off with the Spanish Crown Jewels."

She smiled and glanced up at the departures board. "Are you sure you're the right person to be taking that job? Only, if you don't mind me saying, you don't seem to be fully on-board with the philosophy."

"I'm not. I think it's insane but if it keeps me out of nick… Anyway, Wilderness Jack, the guy they had lined up to do this, changed his mind and he's gone off to do Celebrity Death-Camp somewhere in the Kalahari Desert."

She stood and threw her backpack over her shoulder and

nodded towards the departures board. "That's my flight. Have fun."

"You too," I said. I watched her as she disappeared into the throngs around the departures gates. Quite cute, in a boyish sort of way.

I pulled out the folder Julie had given me which contained all the project details. Pages one to forty-eight gave the background to the project. I'd tried to read that section on a couple of occasions but never got past page three which went into Judge Carrington's philanthropic nature and how he believed even the worst recidivists could be rehabilitated as long as they were given enough tough love.

I opened the folder and turned to the section detailing the resources at my disposal. This section ran to one and a bit pages and gave an outline of the location, telephone number for a Fernando Hernandez, my local contact, and the list of equipment waiting for me. I read through the list again, even though I could remember it clearly. Saws, axes, a machete, two tarpaulins, a hundred metres of rope, fire starting kit, three water purifiers and miscellaneous cooking utensils. There was also a starter box of 'Basic Rations' to keep us going until we'd shot, grown or gathered enough to keep us fed. Not much to support a group of seven people for six months. She had also thoughtfully provided the numbers for the full range of emergency services, including SASEMAR, the Spanish Coastguard. I wondered just how badly screwed up things would have to get before we needed the coastguard halfway up a mountain. Although I hadn't yet been given the exact location, I knew it was in the Alpujarras, a region in the southern Sierra Nevada mountain range in Spain. There was also a field plan included which clearly showed which parts of the area we were allowed to use, where we could cut wood, set up camp and where we were permitted to light fires. The appendix referenced the various local regulations relating to fires, tree felling and permitted constructions along with the penalties for transgressions. It looked like I would be better off copping to the full sentence for my crime in England than getting caught lighting a fire in the wrong place.

"Is this seat free?" I heard a voice and looked up. Three young women stood facing me, they wore matching pink onesies and penis shaped hats. One wore an L-plate around her neck.

"Yes, I'm just leaving," I lied. Returning to sitting on the floor would be preferable to sharing a table with a hen party.

"Don't leave on our account, lover." They all giggled and I hoped they weren't going to Malaga.

As it happened, my flight was called as soon as I started to move so I headed straight for the gate. Time for my new life.

~ *Chapter Three* ~

The flight was smooth and we landed in Malaga two hours late.

"We apologise for the delay," said the hostess over the P.A, as the plane taxied. "This was due to a suspect device being identified and disposed of at Gatwick. We do hope this didn't affect your enjoyment and look forward to welcoming you back on board for your return trip."

After clearing passport control, I followed the directions in the file to the meeting place in the airport where I was supposed to find Simon Reeves, my minder, or Training Camp Colleague as they insisted on calling him.

I lit my much needed post flight cigarette and settled at the bar just outside the arrivals hall, watching the constant tidal wave of humanity pour through the doors. A wash of sun-starved faces blinking into the bright sunlight, all desperately trying to re-connect their phones before social media starvation turned them into zombies.

After two beers, one coffee and an overpriced salad baguette I called Julie, the Project Coordinator back in England. The phone went straight to voicemail. I tried again a couple of times with the same result.

After another ten minutes of watching the tourists and business types swarming through the doors I was on the point of trying Julie again when my phone rang. I glanced at the screen. It was Number Unknown. I answered it.

"Hi, Michael?" a man's voice asked.

"Yes."

"It's me, Simon Reeves. Your Camp… co-colleague… partner… um… host. Are we supposed to be meeting somewhere?"

"I'd almost given up. Where are you?"

"Malaga Airport. Isn't that where I'm meant to be? Where are you?" Simon sounded slightly panicky.

"I'm just outside the main door," I said.

"At Malaga Airport?"

"Of course," I said.

"That's a relief."

"Where are you?"

"I don't know it's all so big."

"Do you see the main doors?" I scanned the area. I'd never met Simon but I hoped I might see somebody looking vaguely lost. My first glance proved the futility of that idea as half the people here were looking vaguely lost.

"There's some big doors just over there," Simon said. "Are those the ones you mean?"

"I don't know," I said. "I can't see you so I don't know which doors you're pointing at."

"Oh, yes. Silly me. Those ones there, near the bar."

I took another glance around. Malaga Airport had no shortage of doors, or bars. "Can you see the taxi ranks?" I asked.

"No. Where are they?"

This was hopeless. I'd been told that Simon was some powerhouse of discipline and efficiency; he really shouldn't be having this much trouble navigating a medium sized airport. I looked around again. "Can you see a row of buses?"

"No. Are they anywhere near the luggage carousels?"

"The luggage carousels?" I asked. "Why are you near the luggage carousels?" Then it dawned. "Are you actually inside the airport?"

"Yes."

"Why? I thought you'd been sent to meet me. How did you get inside the airport?"

"No, I've only just got here. Flew in from Gatwick an hour ago and been waiting here for you."

That would have meant he'd probably been on the same flight as me. This didn't bode well for the smooth planning of the rest of this project.

"Right," I said, feeling the need to take charge of the situation. "Just follow the signs to the exit and I'll be waiting right outside the doors. I'll put my jungle hat on so you can spot me."

"What colour is it?"

"It's green. It's a jungle hat."

"Okay."

I continued to wait by the bar from where I had a good view of the endless exodus through the doors. Still no sign of anybody who in any way complied with my mental image of a newly retired prison officer. My eyes caught two men who seemed to be about to have a row. One was wearing a Lacoste shirt, smart grey chinos and a blue baseball cap. The second man was shorter and slightly built and wore a thick grey sweatshirt which I guessed must be very hot in this weather. The man in the cap was clearly getting more irritated with sweatshirt man.

My instinct for trouble kicked in and I felt my body readying without conscious effort. Even after leaving the army well and truly behind, some things never fade. I calmed my breathing. This was no time to let things get out of hand. Deep breaths; hold each one a moment.

The man in the cap pushed at the chest of the smaller man. That was more often than not a precursor for violence and I felt the adrenaline kick in my stomach. I wondered if I should intervene but noticed two Guardia Civil officers moving towards them and I forced myself to relax. Leave it to the professionals. The man in the cap spotted the two men closing on them, pointed his finger at sweatshirt man as a last warning then disappeared into the crowd. The Guardia officers paused momentarily then resumed their patrol.

I lit a cigarette and returned to watching the doors, briefly annoyed with myself for being distracted and wondering if Simon had slid out unnoticed. Another five minutes passed with still no sign. I rang the phone again and Simon answered.

"Where are you?" I asked.

"I'm here," he said.

"Okay, but where is here?"

"By the doors. Where you said."

I looked around, still no sign of him. I noticed sweatshirt man again, he looked lost. He was talking on his phone. It couldn't be?

"Simon," I said. "Wave your arms; I'll see if I can find you."

Sure enough, sweatshirt man started waving his arms. I walked over to him and tapped him on the shoulder.

Simon turned to face me. "What? Speaky on telefony," he said and waved me to go away. "No comprende, no dinero. Manana."

I pointed at my hat. "Green jungle hat?"

Simon paused and stared at my hat. "Ah, I see. You meant a *real* jungle hat. For wearing in the jungle."

"As opposed to...?"

"I thought you meant Jungle hat. You know, Jungle, the fashion clothing brand? With the tree logo? They do some kicking dance wear, like Tees and Baseball caps which glow emojis under black light."

"Do I look like the sort of person that wears glowing dance wear?"

He looked me up and down. "No, of course not. That's why I thought he was you." He pointed vaguely in the direction the man had gone.

"But he was wearing a blue hat anyway."

"I thought you'd made a mistake."

"About the colour of my hat?"

"It happens all the time. Especially if you have a lot."

"I don't have a lot of hats. I have a green jungle hat. This one. You are Simon Reeves?" I asked.

He paused and stared up at me. "Yes. Why? Don't I look like him? Me?"

I studied the man. He was around five eight or nine and probably no older than mid-forties. I wondered at what age prison officers retired. "I've never met you before so I don't know," I said.

"That's okay then." Simon held his hand out and we shook. "Where's the camp?"

"I haven't the faintest idea," I said. "I thought you were here to take me there?"

"Really?"

"I think there's been some sort of cock-up." I took my phone out. "I'll ring Julie and find out what's going on."

"You sure we can't find it ourselves?" He stared around the airport buildings as if expecting the camp to suddenly appear. "I mean, I'm sure Julie's very busy."

I stabbed the office number and listened as it rang out again.

"Which prison were you at?" I asked.

"Shapham," he replied without hesitation.

"And you've just retired?"

"Ill health. Bad back from all the… picking up stuff, murder on a back. Slipped a whatsit apparently."

"Disc?" I offered.

"Yeah, that one. All over the place. I think we should go." He looked around the concourse.

"Well, I know it's in somewhere called the Alpujarras," I said. "So I guess we could start out in that direction and keep trying to ring Julie."

"There, you see! Knew you'd come up with a plan." He hoisted his bag over his shoulder. "Where's your car?"

"I don't have a car. I thought *you* were meeting *me*."

"But I did."

"We'll have to rent a car. Did Julie give you a credit card?"

He pulled a wallet from his pocket and thumbed through the contents. "No. I don't know. Maybe in my bag," he said. "I've got a tube ticket to Clapham."

"I don't think they take those here anymore. Not since they went over to the Euro."

We spent an hour dragging through queues at various car hire desks only to be given the same answer each time we reached the desk. "None available unless pre-booked. Unexpected period of high demand due to the school holidays."

I'd noticed several slightly dodgy looking car-rental touts plying for business amongst the arriving tourists so we intercepted one of them and ten minutes later we were in possession of a set of keys and more insurance forms, waivers and indemnity notifications than I had ever seen in my life. Even joining the army hadn't resulted in this much paper, just a few forms to say basically I'd do what I was told, didn't object to being shot at, that I was good at keeping secrets and I was on a plane to Iraq.

The car hire man had tried to explain it all but I'd lost the will to live halfway through the list of exclusions, which for some bizarre reason included the wheels. It seemed I could pretty much trash the car completely but as long as I returned the wheels in good condition everything would be just fine. I wasn't too concerned though as I wasn't the one paying the bill. Somewhere in the pile was probably a receipt for the D.O.J. credit card on which I'd paid for this and I should probably separate it out and email it to the office in triplicate. However, as at that moment we lacked any email facilities, I simply passed the pile of paper to Simon who promptly stuffed the whole lot in the glove box of the little Fiat Panda.

I searched for the Alpujarras on my satnav and located what seemed like the central town in the area, somewhere called Torvizcón with a population of around 800. In the absence of anywhere else to go, I programmed it in and a pleasant voice informed me the time to my destination was one hour and fifty-one minutes. So that was the time to beat. I wound the Fiat up through the gears which went from rumbling rattle all the way up to a gentle whine and we settled in to the drive.

The first thing I learned about this little car was exactly that, it was little. At just over six foot, I'm not huge but I certainly fell outside of the design team's project specs. I soon discovered that changing gear necessitated shifting my body slightly to the left to avoid my knee jamming against the steering wheel and that frequent stops were probably going to be required in order to straighten out my joints. The second thing I learned was that this little car can spot hills that no human eye can detect. What to me, seemed like a gentle incline, forced our little vehicle into the crawler lane to allow a convoy of fully laden super-trucks to pass by. At one point I really thought we were going to be swept up in the riptide of a massive low-loader carrying a giant wind turbine arm as it cruised past us.

"Let me know if you fancy taking a shift," I said after about an hour.

There was no reply and a quick glance showed that he was fast asleep, his face squashed against the side window.

I pulled over into a service area. Simon didn't stir so I left him there and went in search of coffee. Although the little car was lacking in power and space, the air conditioning was faultless but I only realised quite how good it was when I stepped outside. The heat hit me like opening an oven door on the Sunday roast and my shirt was a sodden mess by the time I'd covered the twenty metres to the bar. I changed my mind about the coffee and ordered a beer instead. It arrived promptly, along with a plate of olives.

I tapped redial on the phone, expecting to hear the endless ringing once more. I didn't notice at first when Julie answered.

"Hello? Hello? Newstart?"

"Oh, hi, Julie. It's me, Michael. I'm in Spain."

"Michael? What the hell are you doing in Spain?"

That wasn't quite the response I'd been hoping for. "The project? Camp Newstart? Sort of a big thing only a couple of weeks ago."

"Didn't you get the text message? It went out to everybody."

"If that was the one telling me not to be in Spain, then no. I think I'd have recalled that."

"Oh, shit. Sorry, you were on the Priority List but we've had a bit of an emergency here."

"What happened?"

"One of our clients has disappeared."

"Why does that stop the Camp Newstart project?"

"What? No, that's something different. We had to put Camp Newstart on hold when Simon Reeves confirmed he was pulling out."

Today was making less sense by the minute. "Okay, can we start there? Simon Reeves has pulled out?"

"Yes, he changed his mind at the last moment. Did you not receive that email either? That was over a week ago, just after the one about car parking allocations. Before the one we sent about putting the project on hold. He was offered a job as Technical Adviser on that TV show, Celebrity Prison Break. You ever seen that? They had that blonde from Mayfair Posh on the last series, you know, what's her name… Oh yes, Tyarra Starlove, the one with that unusual piercing."

"I can't say I've ever seen it," I said.

"You must have done, everybody did. When she got tangled up in the rope ladder and popped out of her top. All over YouTube it was."

"I'm sure it was unmissable. So Simon has pulled out?" I peered through the bar window to where the little Fiat sat on the edge of the car park. I could just make out the figure of Simon Reeves slumped against the window. "What happens now?"

"Well, that's a bit complicated. You see, technically you've broken your licence conditions and I should report that."

"How have I broken my licence conditions?" I picked at the olives, they were especially tasty.

"You're not supposed to be out of the country unsupervised."

"But that's not exactly my fault. So what do I do?"

"To be honest, your absconsion is the least of our worries right now. As you're there, just keep your head down until we find a replacement for Simon and hopefully the DOJ won't notice. Your group isn't due to be arriving for another week anyway, so plenty of time. Look on the bright side, you never know, we might even manage to persuade Bear Grylls by then."

I noticed Simon climbing out of the car. He stretched like he'd just come out of hibernation and stared around, a puzzled look on his face and clearly wondering where he was. "Tell me more about this client you've lost. I thought your hostel was supposed to be a secure place?"

"Bob Cyrankiewicz, but everybody calls him Bob, or Cranky. It is secure, reasonably. We don't lose that many. Well, not as many as G4 anyway."

"Is he dangerous?" I watched Simon, or Bob, or Cranky, amble across the car park.

"Dangerous? Bob? Oh, heavens no. He is a bit... um... eccentric though. He's a serial Identity Thief. He doesn't mean any harm; he just likes being somebody else. He first came to us because he'd been convicted for impersonating a priest. He'd been in the parish for two years and it only came to light when one of his parishioners complained to the bishop about all the pet funerals. Apparently he'd cancelled somebody's christening to conduct a goldfish burial. It was all quite embarrassing for the church. Oddly though, most of the people there loved him. They even organised a petition to get him to stay. Why are you interested in Bob?"

Bob drifted in through the door and gave a casual wave in my direction as he headed for the bar.

"I think I might know where he is."

I gave Julie a hurried description of my passenger and she

confirmed it was indeed Bob. Julie decided it was best not to say anything to anybody, especially Bob. She didn't want him to disappear again until we had some sort of plan. Bob arrived at the table, two beers in hand, so I ended the call quickly.

"Who was that?" Bob asked as he sat down.

"Just Julie," I said. "I was trying to sort out where we were going."

"Where's that?"

"I don't know. We got cut off." I lifted the beer in acknowledgment. "Thanks."

"No worries. Did she say anything else?"

"Like what?" I asked.

"Anything? Nothing really." He pulled on his beer. "They know how to make beer in this country. So, we still don't know where we're going?"

"Nope, bit of an adventure!"

We left the motorway after another twenty kilometres and snaked through a valley following the signs to Torvizcón. The road twisted and climbed and with each increase in gradient, the little Fiat lodged its protest. Spanish driving consisted of mostly avoiding things. Lumps of rock in the road, the odd ibex or two, cyclists and a steady stream of little white vans that seemed to think the white line was their own personal route to their destination. For a while at least, I was grateful for the diminutive stature of the Fiat as it enabled me to tuck in close when faced with hurtling white vans driven by aged, bearded dwarfs with phone in one hand and the other hanging out of the window. I was sure I heard one of them yell, 'Woohoo!' as he flashed past.

My phone rang just as we left a small tunnel near somewhere called Órgiva. I pulled into a gravel cut and answered it.

"Hello, Mike," said Julie's voice.

"Hi, Julie."

"Can he hear me?" she asked.

I glanced at Bob; he was busy trying to take photographs of the mountains on his phone.

"No, all fine."

"Good. I think we're beginning to put together a plan," Julie said. "Bernard, sorry, Judge Carrington, has been in touch with an old army mate of his who runs a security company, they think they can supply a substitute for Simon at short notice. They're fully accredited so that should satisfy the DOJ."

"So the project is still on?"

"Of course, it has to be, Bernard's banked his reputation on it."

"And his knighthood."

"No. No… but if he *was* called it would be ungracious of him to turn it down."

"Ah, the burden of the ruling classes. Are you allowed to tell me where this camp is supposed to be yet?"

"I'm texting you the full details but I'm having a spot of trouble finding you any transport though. Are you still at Malaga Airport? Only it seems everything's booked up. School holiday holidays and all that. Any chance you can catch a bus? They're quite good in Spain I think, they've even got toilets now. Put it on the credit card but be careful, funds are tight; the government have cut their payments again. Reasonable expenses only."

"Don't worry," I said. "It's all sorted. I found a car hire firm at the airport. I put it on the card."

"Oh, wish you'd said. How much did that cost?"

"I can't remember," I said. I wasn't even sure I remembered asking.

"Well. I suppose it was a sort of emergency. Try to be careful though, we have to account for everything. You know, since… um because…"

"You mean, on account of me being a convicted felon?"

"Well, you know how picky accountants can get. I'll let you know as soon as I have any more details on your new Camp Colleague. And do try not to lose Bob."

The phone went dead and I dropped it in the centre console.

"Problems?" Bob asked.

"No, just telling me she's sending details of where we're going."

We sat and waited a moment then my phone bleeped to announce the arrival of a text message. I read the brief directions.

"Heard of a place called Virriatos?"

"Nope. Is that near Benidorm?"

"No. Why Benidorm?"

"It's just that I've been there before. Would've been cool if we were going there. There's a great Cockney pub that does 60's karaoke and chicken in a basket."

I stared at him. "Chicken in a basket?"

He looked at me with soulful eyes. "I happen to like chicken in a basket."

"We're not going anywhere near Benidorm, thank God. It's a bit of nowhere called El Valle del Pastor where the closest attempt at civilisation is this place called Virriatos."

Bob pulled out the map which came with the pile of car paperwork. "Nothing on here," he said after a moment's study. "Mind you, it doesn't show that other place we were going to, Torvizcón?"

I called up Maps on my phone and searched for Virriatos. Nothing. Fortunately, Julie had included the GPS coordinates of the camp location so I entered those. Maps showed a mostly green screen with only two towns visible, Capileira and Trevélez. The little cross identifying the camp location lay roughly equidistant between them.

"Have you found it?" Bob asked.

"It's about a mile above sea level and halfway between the Middle of Nowhere and Fuck Knows." I tried to expand the scale on the screen. A small grey blob resolved into a slightly larger grey blob. "Hope you packed your oxygen bottle."

"So, where are we going?"

I pointed at the huge mountain rising up behind the town of Órgiva. "Up there."

~ *Chapter Four* ~

The route took us through the town of Órgiva, which brought a whole new level of crazy. Random stopping and reversing seemed to be so much a part of normal driving here that I wondered if they were actually included in formal driving lessons. Tooting at your mate across the other side of the road was good, as was tooting at the car in front if it failed to respond to a green light within the required nano-second. Tooting at the lights themselves apparently forced them to change colour though of course if one didn't like the current colour then they could be ignored completely anyway. Dogs had right of way on the roads but pedestrians were considered fair game even when on zebra crossings. I found avoiding the dogs somewhat easier than avoiding humans as at least they were reasonably predictable in their randomness. After dodging a cloud of hippies, a huge German coach on a mission to take all before it and several over-laden donkeys, we finally cleared the town and I could relax a bit. Or at least as much as one can relax when coaxing a baby car up a relentless climb while being driven at by the ubiquitous white vans with a total disregard for their own, or anyone else's well-being.

As we climbed higher, the views became more spectacular and the villages more touristy. Huge coaches dominated each village we came to like conquering behemoths disgorging their armies of souvenir hunters upon the local populace.

Once past Capileira, the tourist busses and white vans diminished, as did the road conditions. The one constant was the interminable climb upwards. Even with the low gearing of the Fiat, we still rarely moved beyond second and fourth would be a treat only savoured on short downhill sections. The road became more uneven and the surrounding area crowded in with fir trees and a few stubborn patches of frozen snow clinging to the shade. The potholes and badly repaired sections of road increased steadily until I realised that the tarmac had actually ended some while back and we were driving on compacted earth and gravel. Each time satnav gave instructions to turn this way or that, the road deteriorated more.

Eventually we spotted a small cluster of buildings ahead and as we approached, they resolved into a small community. A battered sign announced 'Bienvenido a Virriatos'.

"We going to stop?" Bob asked. "I could do with a pint, my nerves are a mess."

"No, I want to find where we're supposed to be setting up while it's light. We'll see what's there then come back here for supper. It can't be much further now."

The village of Virriatos consisted of one main road, recently, and rather randomly, tarmacked and a handful of side streets. Some tarmacked, some cobbled and others just compacted gravel. As we passed through, I noticed a couple of bars, a hairdresser, general stores and a shoe shop. A few other non-descript shops littered the road but it was difficult to make out what they sold. Our passage through the village was soon over as houses gave way once more to fir trees and our route continued upwards over increasingly difficult terrain. Satnav announced we were only a half kilometre away from our destination when the trees suddenly gave way to open land and we were driving along a gravel track which undulated across endless grassy meadowland.

A short dip downwards between two hills led to a small river running across the track. I stopped the car and got out and Bob followed.

"What do you reckon?" he asked.

I studied the water. "I don't think it's very deep. No more than a foot." I found a stone and tossed it in. The short splash confirmed my guess. "I'm more worried about the slope the other side."

We both looked at the track as it continued through the little ford and upwards over the next hill. This was significantly steeper than anything we'd encountered so far.

"Will she make it?" Bob stared at the little Fiat. "She's not really built for this sort of stuff. Why didn't you get a four-by-four?"

"Well, firstly, choice was somewhat limited, if you remember and secondly, I did think that wherever we were going was still going to be connected, even if just vaguely, to some part of civilisation."

Bob looked around. "This reminds me of Dartmoor," he said. "That was remote and deserted too. Well, there was a pub just over there," he pointed to a slight rise in the landscape. "And a Visitor Centre with a gift shop just that way." He pointed ninety degrees from the imaginary pub. "And of course where we are now, that would be the A30."

I stared at him for a moment to be sure he wasn't trying to wind me up. "So, nothing like this place really then?"

"Well, not exactly. It rained a lot there, I do remember that. It never stopped, so I suppose this is quite a bit different now you come to think of it."

"Right," I said. "Here's the plan –"

"Great, a plan. Knew you'd come up with something."

"Here's the plan," I tried again. "You're going to drive and I'm staying just behind to give a bit of an extra shove if you get stuck. There's not much weight to this thing, especially if we off-load the luggage first. We could almost carry it up the hill."

We placed the bags just off the track and Bob revved the engine. "All ready," he yelled above the engine noise.

"Not so much throttle," I shouted back. "Gently."

"What?"

"Gently."

"I can't hear you. Shall I go now?"

I gave up trying to make myself heard. It wasn't my clutch anyway. I waved my hand to indicate he should go.

Bob screamed the engine to the point I thought it might actually drop out of the bottom. He gave a big grin through the window then dropped the clutch and hurtled through the stream, showering me on the way. By the time I'd cleared my eyes of stream water he was already halfway up the hill. Looking good. I set out to follow. If it stopped, I didn't want to be trying to start it again against this slope.

The car slowed and I'd nearly caught up with it when I noticed it was struggling. Damn, I should have been waiting halfway up instead of trying to follow.

The little car fought bravely against the slope but all of a sudden there was a loud bang, the bonnet bounced free of its catch and a cloud of black smoke billowed out. The Fiat rolled backwards down the slope and came to rest in the stream. Steam rose from underneath the engine compartment and mingled with the black smoke already belching out from under the bonnet.

Bob pushed the door open and jumped clear of the car. "That doesn't look good," he said.

"You think?"

"Probably blown a pipe or a belt or something."

"Seems like you know about as much about cars as I do," I said.

"It'll be alright," Bob said. "We'll just let it cool down then take a look."

There was a gentle 'woompf' sound and orange flames sprang up from under the bonnet.

"We might have a bit of a wait on that one," I said.

"Do you think we should call the car hire company?"

"Probably an idea. Details are on the paperwork I expect. Do you want to get them?" I nodded towards the burning car.

We stayed and watched the little car in its final hours until the flames died and the car cooled enough to get close. The driver's compartment was just a blackened mess but I did notice a sticker on the rear window proudly advertising. 'Lucky Car Hire'. I telephoned the number and explained there'd been an incident. We were transferred to a breakdown service who wanted to know in great detail what the problem was. It seemed that spontaneous combustion halfway up a mountain didn't fit their standard question/answer sheets and necessitated much transferring and holding. Eventually I was informed a recovery vehicle would be with me within the hour.

Given our current location. I wouldn't have taken bets on the timely arrival of the rescue truck, or come to that, even turning up at all. As it happened, the breakdown lorry was with us in twenty minutes. The driver informed me he'd just been on a breakdown the other side of Trevelez which was why he'd been so quick.

"Usually it would take one maybe two hours up here," he

said. "The company I work for are in Granada though the nearest rescue centre is Órgiva. But they are always very busy, they cover a huge area."

I gave him a full description of events but the state of the car pretty much told the story for me.

The driver wanted to make small talk as he winched the remains of the Fiat on the back of the rescue truck.

"You are living here?" he asked.

I explained we were here as part of a self-sufficiency project and he wanted to tell me how this area had changed over the years.

"I remember this road before it became a proper road," he said. "Once there were only horses and goats here then they built this road and tourists came for spiritual retreats and the goats moved further up."

I looked at the track that had just killed the Fiat. A road?

"A spiritual retreat?" I asked.

"They built a temple up there." He waved his arm towards the hills. "Buddhists or Hindu or something. All hippies anyway, these mountains were full of them. They all went away when the busses stopped coming this far and then the village died. The local men went to work in the city." He pushed a clipboard at me. "Sign here and here."

I signed his forms without reading them and handed the clipboard back to him. He went round the vehicle and made some final checks on the straps holding the husk of the little car firmly in place. It had been a brave little car. I consoled myself that the wheels looked to be in good condition so at least the policy excess should be safe. Perhaps that might go some distance to placating the DOJ accountants.

We accepted his offer to drop us off in the village where he said there was a good small hotel.

"They have rooms there," he said. "And the food is the best in Las Alpujarras."

***

The Casa de Pastores was a rambling hotel which had probably once been a rather grand bodega. We were greeted like long lost family and presented with glasses of beer and a plateful of indeterminate meat. I managed to explain I was a vegetarian and the owner's wife disappeared for a few minutes to return with a huge plate of cheese, tomatoes, olives, bread and ham.

Bob peered at my plate. "Is that ham?"

"Yes, it's a local delicacy apparently."

"But I thought you told them you were a vegetarian?"

"I did, but I think jamon is a product which defies normal culinary classification. At least as far as the Spanish are concerned, they seem to treat it as a food group all on its own."

Bob looked around the room. "It's not much like Benidorm."

"More like Sidmouth," I said. "Same feeling of the world moving on without telling anybody it was going."

"Bit like my ex, she pissed off without telling me." Bob forked at the meat. "This is good, you'd like it."

"No, I wouldn't."

"I meant, if you weren't a vegetarian of course. You'd like it then." He dipped a piece of bread in the orange coloured sauce. "How come you're a vegetarian anyway? Isn't that a bit odd for a survival expert? You should try this sauce, that's not meat."

"No, thank you. Not odd at all, I've always found carrots much easier to catch than rabbits."

He paused with a forkful of meat halfway to his mouth, a

slightly confused expression playing across his face, then, "Good point." He waved the forkful of meat in my direction before popping it in his mouth.

"Tell me about your time at Shapham nick," I said.

"What? Oh, nothing much. Just the usual, you know." He stared at his plate.

"Did you ever come across Fingers McGee?" I placed a slice of tomato on a piece of bread and drizzled it with olive oil. "Big guy, about six five, built like a tank."

"Don't recall him." Bob continued to avoid my gaze. "Probably on a different wing to me."

"That's probably just as well. Do you want this ham? It's supposed to be very good, as far as bits of dead animals go."

"Thanks." He held his plate next to mine and I pushed the ham across. "Why'd you say that? Just as well?"

"Oh, nothing really. Just that he's one of the attendees on this project and I happen to know he's got a bit of a thing about screws."

"Bit of a thing?" Bob was looking decidedly worried.

"Didn't you know? That's how he got his nickname, Fingers. On account of the fact he made a habit of breaking fingers of people he didn't like. Mostly prison guards."

"Really?"

"Yes, and then there's Gnasher Hodges. He's an animal that one. Did you hear about the time he took down four officers in the Scrubs? That's why they sent him to Shapham."

"He's coming as well?"

I nodded and popped the last bit of cheese in my mouth. "Surprised they ever let him out of the psyche unit."

"They're both coming here?" He looked nervously around the bar as if they were about to make an entrance that very moment.

I nodded. "You alright?" I asked. "Only you're looking a bit peaky."

"I think I should probably tell you something," he started.

"What, like you mean you're not Simon Reeves and you're not really a prison officer?" I raised a quizzical eyebrow.

"Yes. How the… You bastard, you're winding me up."

"Sorry." I grinned. "No actually, I'm not sorry; you should have seen your face." I waved towards the bar for more drinks. "I wasn't supposed to say anything but who's going to care round here and you're not very likely to disappear on me. Not after setting fire to our only means of transport."

"What now?"

"Nothing. I'm hardly one to say anything. They think I'm the love child of Crocodile Dundee or Tarzan." The drinks arrived and I thanked the barman. "Why Simon Reeves?"

"I saw he was due to go here and I fancied a holiday."

"A holiday?"

He looked at me like I'd said something strange. "Sure, don't you like holidays?"

"Yes, of course but I usually just take a kitbag, not somebody else's identity."

"Oh, you should try it. It's very easy, I just emailed KwikJet and they were very helpful and changed the name on the tickets without any trouble."

"But why do you do it?" I asked. "I mean, it's not for money or you'd pick a banker or a politician, not a prison officer."

"It started at school. My real name's Robert Cyrankiewicz. You can imagine the names I got called and have you any idea how many times a day I had to spell that? By the time I left school I calculated I'd spent eighteen days of my life just spelling my name to people. The most popular kid in our class was John Smith, I always envied him. He never got asked to spell his name."

"You started stealing people's identities just because you got fed up spelling out your surname?"

"There's a better reason?"

"Well, stealing an inheritance? Escaping prison? Secret agent? Annoying ex-wife?"

We finished our drinks then headed for our rooms. Mine was a family double room and surprisingly modern considering the rest of the building. It had a small but functional shower room, air conditioning and a flat screen television. I leafed through my Project Folder and found the telephone number of Fernando, the local contact, and arranged to meet him in the Casa de Pastores at ten the next morning. He had a grumble about the early hour but conceded.

After a quick shower, I tried watching television for a while but the exuberance and frequency of the advertisements drove me to give that up. I read a few pages of my book before falling asleep.

***

The morning brought brilliant sunshine and a sky of the clearest blue I'd seen in a long while. Bob was already partway through his breakfast of scrambled eggs and what looked like black pudding when I arrived downstairs.

"What's the plan for today?" he asked.

"I thought a dip in the pool first, couple of rounds of golf then a massage and take in a show for the evening."

"Huh?"

"Or we could go to the camp location and see what we're up against."

"Okay." He returned to his breakfast.

I ordered eggs and mushrooms which arrived before I'd had chance to butter my bread. I spent the next few minutes picking diced ham out of the eggs and passing it to Bob.

The owner, whose name I discovered was José Felipe, offered to hire me his Suzuki four-by-four until we could get alternate transport sorted. He didn't seem fazed by my lack of cash and said any day was as good as another.

"How do you know you can trust me?" I asked.

"Where are you going to go?" he said.

"I might steal the car and head off down the mountain."

"I think not. It is probably best to go nowhere near the mountain roads in that." He laughed and patted me on the back. "The brakes are, how would you say, not quite as convenient as they once were. Okay up here where we have more space for leisurely stopping, but not down there," he waved his arm in the general direction of the main road. "Too many loco drivers, too many big drops."

We finished our breakfast and took charge of the little Suzuki. It proved to be remarkably nimble across the uneven track and we were soon back to the point where the Fiat had expired, a blackened area of grass a testament to its final moments. The Suzuki breezed up the slope that had proved so fatal to the Fiat and as we crested the hill we saw what was destined to be our home for the next six months. I stopped the car to take in the view. A huge open area of rich green grass, finely kept under control no doubt by frequent visits from the sheep herders. Fir trees flanked the area to the left and right and in front of us, about two hundred metres away, the ground dropped away creating a false horizon and giving a view across to the Mediterranean with glimpses of North Africa just beyond.

"Now, that beats Benidorm," I said as I tried to take in the full beauty. "If you're lucky, you might even be able see it from up here."

"No karaoke though," said Bob.

"Karaoke?"

"I won an award for my Tina Turner. Well, it was a round of drinks at the Tatler's Arms but all the same."

The spectacular views had quite stolen my thoughts from our reason for being here. I climbed out of the car and stared across open land, beginning to realise the implications. "There's fuck all here," I said.

"Yup, cool isn't it?"

"No, not cool. I was expecting a bit more than an empty field. How are we supposed to spend six months here? Look at it."

Bob walked round the car towards me. "You're the SAS man, aren't you supposed to be building us a forward base or something?"

"Where did you get the idea I was SAS? I never told you that."

"Your file," he said.

"You've been nosing around in my file?"

"It was when I was deciding who to be. Obviously I couldn't be Julie and yours and Simon's were the only other files I could find."

"You were planning on stealing my identity? I don't believe this."

"It's not identity stealing that would be wrong. It's just supplemental, an alternate version of somebody. Sort of in addition to the original."

"So why Simon?"

"He left a gap."

"A gap?"

"He wasn't there, not where he was supposed to be. Everybody was expecting Simon to be there and he wasn't. It was a gap, you see? He left a gap which I could walk into and nobody noticed."

I stared around the field. "Pity you couldn't have chosen to be somebody a bit more useful. A builder would've been good."

"So you're not a survival expert then?" Bob said. "How are we going to find food now?"

"Well unless I can hack into Sainsbury's Home Delivery Service and persuade them to extend their home delivery round to the Alpujarras, I'd say we're in a spot of trouble."

"We could just stay in the hotel," Bob said. "We've got credit cards."

"They won't let us get away with that for very long and anyway, there's a group coming out in a week and they'll be expecting some sign of life here. Even if it's only a basha and a campfire."

"Where do we get one of those?"

"A basha? We build it out of bits of trees and stuff."

"Like a tree house?" Bob's eyes lit up with childish enthusiasm.

"Nothing like a tree house."

"Oh, I always wanted a treehouse."

"We're not building a treehouse."

***

We arrived back at the Casa de Pastores just a few minutes before ten. Fernando wasn't there so we waited outside. At about twenty past, a little white van pulled up. The driver opened the window and a cloud of cannabis smoke billowed out.

"Fernando?" I asked.

"Si. Señor Miguel?"

"Michael, yes."

Fernando indicated for us to get in the van. I took the front seat and Bob clambered in the back in amongst a collection of buckets, paint pots and a step ladder. The air cloyed with the scents of paint and cannabis. I wondered for how long I could hold my breath.

The short journey through the village was punctuated by a series of sudden stops as Fernando spotted people with whom he needed an emergency catch up. My Spanish was good but the Andaluz version spoken by the locals round there was almost impenetrable. The best I could make out was that most of these sudden exchanges centred on the previous night's football, deliveries of olives to the local mill or his wife's feet. One exchange, in the middle of the road, seemed to consist of nothing more than noises.

"Hey, José."

"Hola, Fernando."

"Que pasa?"

"Nada."

"Oi."

"Woa."

"Wer."

"Bleh."

"Hasta."

"Venga."

Only the repeated horn blowing of a butane bottle delivery truck behind us cut short the reunion and we proceeded down the main road for another twenty-five metres before parking on the pavement. The total distance we had covered from the Casa de Pastores was no more than a hundred metres.

"I leave the key here." He pointed at a small overflow pipe above the garage doors. "You come when you want." He pulled open the wooden doors and flicked a light switch.

A dim bulb dangling from an ancient wire made a brave but ultimately fruitless attempt at pushing back the gloom. My eye caught a large canvas bag that appeared to be stuffed full of a huge tangle of rope.

"That's yours," Fernando confirmed. "And those tools," he indicated a cardboard box with various knives, saws, hammers and other basic construction items. "And there." He pointed at some folded plastic tarpaulins in the corner. "But if you need anything else here, you can use it if you replace anything you break or lose."

I scanned the garage and failed to see anything of much use. Certainly no marquees or Portaloos. Lots of paint pots and brushes. So whatever we built with our rope and tarpaulins we'd be able to paint it white if we wanted. I thanked Fernando and told him we'd be back when we needed equipment. He grunted and climbed back in his van. I pulled the garage doors shut, hid the key in the pipe and turned to watch Fernando reversing back up the main road towards the Casa de Pastores. He only needed one stop on the return journey.

"Is that it?" asked Bob.

"That's it. Glad you came?"

"I'd still rather be in Benidorm. Any chance we can bunk off and hide there for six months?"

"Come on, let's reccy the village then find a coffee."

There wasn't much to reccy. A handful of small shops sprinkled the main street. Two butcher's shops, a baker and a greengrocer so at least we wouldn't starve. There was a small hardware shop which, from the look of the window display, sold everything from tins of nails to washing machines. The shoe shop seemed to specialise in high fashion women's shoes and boots and next door, a clothes shop which appeared to only sell bras, big pants or men's hats. A few more shops littered the narrow side streets but we could save exploring those for another day, no point in using up all our adventures at once.

We headed into the other bar in the village, the Venta Pastor. We ordered coffee and tostadas and settled on the small patio overlooking the main road.

I checked my phone, five bars and no messages. Rural Spain always seemed to have impressive mobile phone and internet coverage. Whereas in England, dare to venture outside of the M25 and telecommunications are immediately back in the stone age, yet here, three quarters of the way up some remote mountain, I had five bars and blazingly fast 3G internet.

I called Julie.

"Ah, glad you called," she said. "I've got some good news."

"The project's been cancelled and I'm being given a full pardon and an MBE?"

She ignored my flippancy. "We've found a replacement for Simon so it's all systems go and full steam ahead."

"Oh good. What do you want me to do with Walter Mitty?" I ignored Bob's quizzical look.

"Who? Oh, you mean Bob? You haven't told him you know have you? Only he's likely to do a bunk."

"Yes, it sort of slipped out. He's okay." I winked at Bob.

Bob waved towards the phone as if he could be seen. "Hi, Julie."

"Bob says hi," I said.

"I heard. And I'm not impressed. We're going to officially transfer him onto Project Newstart so he can stay there. Of course that can't be properly official until you have an approved supervisor there, so don't lose him in the meantime."

"Who've you got to replace Simon?"

"A chap who used to be a sergeant in the Parachute Regiment, he's just come out. Nick Brewer, ever heard of him?"

"Oddly, no. I know the army is getting smaller, what with all the cuts but it's still a bit too big for me to remember everybody by name." I sipped at my coffee. "When's he coming?"

"Not sure yet. A couple of days, I think. I'll let you know. Anything you need?"

"We've broken the hire car; well Bob set it on fire, so we'll need a new one of those."

"You won't need a car. We'll arrange a pickup for you at the end of the project. Anything else?"

"A cement mixer and a couple of bricklayers would be useful, or even a caravan might do. I'm just not feeling it for the field."

"Jolly good. Glad you've still got your sense of humour. Anyway, don't want to keep you from building your camp, must be great fun for you. Bit like being back with your chums in the army."

I closed the call and slipped the phone in my pocket.

"All alright?" asked Bob through crumbs of tostada.

"Just wonderful. We have an ex-sergeant from the Paras coming out to keep an eye on us. That buggers our chances of turning this into a skive." I tapped a cigarette out of the packet and lit it without thinking. I studied it for a moment, contemplating tossing it but decided what the hell.

~ *Chapter Five* ~

We spent most of the next day with a tin of white paint marking out on the field the locations of the shelters, kitchen and latrines. We'd had several goes at the job and had changed our minds about where things were going so many times we ran out of paint and the field resembled a Jackson Pollock. We had to go back to Fernando's lock-up for another pot of paint.

"Are you sure the kitchen should be next to the toilets?" Bob asked as we stood and surveyed our latest attempt.

"Well, where else are we going to put it? I mean, the kitchen needs somewhere to drain off the waste and stuff. No point in digging more holes than we need. We can just make a little channel to join them up."

"Yeah, but isn't it going to whiff a bit?" he asked.

"Course not. We're outside, aren't we?"

"I suppose. Are we going to dig the hole now? Only we didn't bring the spades."

I checked my watch, getting on for three o'clock. "No, I think we've done enough for one day. Need to take things more slowly at higher altitudes."

"Is that why nobody seems to do much here?"

"Probably. That and the dope. I've not smelt this much cannabis in the air since Afghanistan."

We headed back to the Casa de Pastores for a late lunch.

José Felipe provided us with large plates of something called Migas Alpujarreña, a sort of couscous with a variety of vegetables, fish, black sausage, chorizo and the ubiquitous ham. I picked out the meat and fish and dumped it on Bob's plate. I was pleasantly surprised at how tasty the meal was.

"You don't know what you're missing." Bob waved a skewered piece of black sausage at me. "We had a butcher in our town who used to make his own black pudding. People came from miles for it, famous over three towns he was, but it weren't a patch on this."

"I'm so glad. Can you please not aim that thing in my direction? I might be forced to kill you."

He popped the sausage in his mouth. "Wonder if they use wild boar's blood?" he mumbled around the mouthful.

When we'd finished, José Felipe brought a selection of local cheeses which were absolutely delicious. I looked around the bar, apart from a couple of older men playing dominoes and chewing on pipes the place was deserted. Somewhere serving food of this quality in London would have been packed all day. The trendies would love it, especially with the views up there.

"So, what do we do tomorrow?" Bob poured himself another glass of wine.

"I think we should build a shelter. It's coming in to rain on Friday."

"How did you know that? Do they teach you that stuff in the army? I bet you can read the cloud formations or the way the birds move or something. Wish I could do that."

I pulled my phone from my pocket and placed it on the table. "Weather Watch."

Bob looked disappointed. "That works too," he said. "What do we build the shelter with?"

"We have tarpaulins, we have rope and there's plenty of wood. Can't be that difficult, Boy Scouts do it all the time."

***

The morning brought clear skies and piercing sunshine. My initial optimism at shelter building became somewhat tempered by my first attempts to cut down timber for the construction. A big pine tree had proved impassive to my assaults with both axe and saw, so a rapid reassessment of the potential scale of our shelter was necessary. Rather than coming at the project from the position of what type of shelter would be comfortable living in for six months, we modified our vision to that which we could create with timber we could actually cut down. This realignment of vision and practicality brought with it a decided feeling of deflation.

I stared at the meagre pile of mangled twigs and branches which represented our morning's work.

"This is going to take longer than I thought," I said.

"Is this how you did it when you were in the SAS?" asked Bob.

"I keep telling you, I wasn't actually *in* the SAS. I was just *assigned* to them for a while. And by the time I arrived anywhere, there was usually a base already set up and a pot of tea on the go."

"Oh, so what did they build their bases out of?"

"Tents, mostly." I kicked at the pile of branches. "There's not enough here to build a rabbit hutch."

"We could try again tomorrow."

"No, we really ought to try and least make a start." I pointed towards a group of saplings. "If we can get a couple of those down we might be able to make a sort of frame."

Another hour with saw and axe yielded another few branches to add to our collection. We'd still been unable to bring down anything of any size, certainly nothing with which to build a secure frame. The main problem was one of boredom. Ten swings with an axe or five minutes of sawing was about the limit of my capacity for boring, repetitive physical labour. The collection of still proudly standing saplings testified to that, despite several of them now bearing the scars of our aborted attempts.

"Okay," I said. "Let's see what we can do with what we have."

Tying several short branches together at least partly compensated for our inability to cut down anything of any useful length. After another hour, we had a small collection of makeshift poles made up of shorter branches. We'd stripped off most of the smaller twigs but further confrontations with my boredom threshold had resulted in much straggly twiggy stuff being left attached. I reasoned it would add to the general structure in some yet to be discovered way.

By the time the sun was tipping the trees at the eastern side of the meadow we had a passable shelter. Okay, it was much smaller than we'd set out to build, measuring only about two metres long, one wide and one high, but one person could crawl inside and shelter under the tarpaulin we'd staked across it.

I stood back and surveyed our handiwork. "Well, it's a start."

"How many people are coming?" asked Bob.

"Seven, in total. Including this new Camp Colleague, what's his name, Nick Brewer."

"So we need another six of these then?"

"Plus a kitchen and eating area."

"Don't forget the toilets," said Bob.

"We'll do those tomorrow. That's mostly just digging holes. It'll make a break from tree chopping."

By the time we returned to the Casa de Pastores, the sun had already set and the early evening showed signs of becoming distinctly chilly. José Felipe already had a welcoming fire burning in the huge hearth. We ordered a couple of beers and pondered the menu. Today's Menu del Dia offered pork, meatballs or omelette. A choice I suspected added for me. We ordered and relaxed into our drinks. The soothing alcohol and the warming fire soon eased the aching muscles and by the time the food arrived I was feeling quite mellow.

The omelette was primarily potato and onion but touched with some added flavours I couldn't recognise. The chef was wasted here, he should be in Chelsea, he'd make a fortune.

After we'd eaten I took an evening stroll and marvelled at the number of stars in the sky and the clean, sharp air. I settled down to watch Spanish television just to reassure myself that I still understood Spanish after twenty-four hours struggling with Andaluz.

***

We met downstairs for breakfast then headed off for day two of the construction phase of our operation. As we crested the hill which bordered the meadow I realised immediately something was wrong. The little shelter we had fought all day to construct had disappeared and in its place was a tangle of sticks loosely tied together with bits of rope. I parked the Suzuki near the little pile and climbed out.

"What happened?" Bob asked.

"I don't know. It's completely trashed."

"Do you think somebody came and smashed it up?"

"Looks like it, but why would they? Where's the tarp?" I scanned the field and eventually noticed the remains of the tarpaulin tangled high in some trees at the far end of the meadow. I pointed it out to Bob.

"How the hell did that get up there?" he said.

"Wind, I think. Can't be anything else. Nobody in their right mind would come out here, trash our base and climb a tree just to hang the tarp from it."

"How do we get that down?"

"We don't," I said. "Look at it, it's shredded."

The plastic tarpaulin looked like it had been torn apart by Edward Scissorhands in a temper tantrum. We weren't going to be using that one again.

"That must have been a fair wind up here," Bob said.

"It looks like we're going to need to build something a bit more substantial." I scanned the meadow. I hadn't realised quite how exposed the site was, I could see now that if the wind turned to the southwest it would funnel through there like a tornado. "We need some bigger logs."

A quick phone call to Fernando confirmed we could borrow a chain saw for a day in return for a pile of logs. We agreed to meet up at his lock-up as I needed to pick up another tarpaulin and some more rope anyway.

Fernando gave me a quick lesson in chain saw usage and he actually laughed when I asked if he had gloves and a facemask I could borrow.

"This is just a baby." He fired up the saw and handed it to me with the same casual air with which one would pass a bottle of wine. "Just don't touch this bit," he pointed at the whirling chain. "It bites." He laughed again.

I tried it out on an old beam and the saw went through it like it wasn't there. I'd handled all sorts of weapons in my time but this was the scariest thing I'd ever wielded. It reminded me a bit of my first handling of the Minimi machine gun when it seemed to want to jump out of my hands and kill everything within a fifty metre radius. A couple more practise cuts though and the chain saw and I came to a sort of understanding. I'd let it find its own way through the wood and in return, I could keep my fingers.

We headed back to the field and identified our target, a nice straight fir about ten metres high. I started up the saw and cut into the tree. For the first couple of centimetres the saw sliced into the wood with little effort then all of a sudden the saw kicked in my hands and came to a halt. It was stuck fast in the trunk. It took me a moment to realise what had happened. Unlike sawing a beam in a horizontal position, the tree was vertical and once I'd created a slight cut, it had compressed into the gap under its own weight and trapped the saw solid. I tugged and pushed but it wouldn't move.

"That's a bit of a problem," I said.

"Can't you just cut it out?" Bob suggested.

"Won't start. Blades locked solid under the weight of the tree."

We stared at it for a moment then Bob said, "I'll get the axe."

"Really? You're going to hack a chain saw out of a tree with an axe?"

"You got any better ideas? We can't leave it there."

I looked at the chain saw and gave another futile tug. It was stuck fast. "Let's go and have lunch and a think."

We settled at a table outside the Casa de Pastores, ordered beer and let José Felipe bring tapas. Bob and I had settled into a sort of routine where we divided up tapas into meat and nonmeat rather than constantly trying to persuade the kitchen that ham and black sausages aren't vegetables.

"What we need to do is pull the tree in the opposite direction," said Bob. "That way the saw would come free."

"How do you propose we pull a tree of that size?"

Bob pondered for a moment then, "We could tie a rope to the Suzuki and pull it."

I thought about that as I supped my beer and picked at olives. It seemed an insane idea but it might just work. We only needed to take the pressure off the cut just enough to free the saw.

The Andalusian system of bars providing free food with drinks is a wonderful idea but does encourage the drinking of slightly more at lunchtime than is probably wise. Especially where chain saws and Suzukis are concerned.

An hour later we were back in the meadow with a rope lashed round the highest part of the tree we could reach and the other end tied to the Suzuki's towbar.

"Will it hold?" I asked.

"Should do." Bob gave the rope a testing tug. "Baggsy driver."

I was going to argue but he was already in the vehicle and firing up the engine.

"Take it slowly," I said. "We only need to shift it a little bit to pull the saw out."

I watched the front wheels spin on the Suzuki and the tree wobbled a little. I pulled at the saw but it was still solidly embedded in the trunk. I tapped on the window of the car and he wound it down.

"You haven't got it in all-wheel-drive mode," I said. "The wheels are spinning."

He looked down at the gear controls. "Ah, yes. Hang on." He shifted the gear stick. "I think that's got it. I'll try again."

I stood back as the engine revved loudly. "Try to take it..." A huge crack came from behind me and I turned to see the tree shuddering then start to fall. "...slowly."

Bob had his head out of the window and was looking back towards the tree. I noticed the look on his face shift from puzzlement to shock when he realised that the tree was starting to topple and heading in his direction.

The engine picked up more noise and all four wheels dug into the ground kicking the vehicle forwards. I realised with a moment of dread what he was about to attempt. He was trying to outrun a falling tree. A falling tree which was tied firmly to the vehicle in which he was trying to escape.

"Bob!" I yelled ineffectually over the screaming engine and cracking wood.

The Suzuki picked up speed, as did the tree which arced through the air and landed with a soft crunching thud on the roof. For a moment Bob continued forwards but the tangle of branches now cascading over the windscreen obviously conveyed to him the futility of his continued escape attempt. He stopped the car and got out.

"Well, that shifted it," he said. "Chain saw free?"

I glanced back at the mangled tree stump and noticed the saw lying on the ground next to it. "Yup," I said.

We dragged the tree clear of the car to survey the damage. It could have been much worse as fortunately it was only the top of the tree which landed on the roof and that was mostly thinner branches. There was however still a noticeable dent in the roof and quite a few more scratches than had previously been there.

"Next time we should use a longer rope," said Bob.

"Next time? We're not doing that again. I'm guessing there must be a way to cut down a tree without it falling on your car. Just need to work that out before we try again, that's all."

"José Felipe won't be happy," he said.

"We'll have to get it fixed for him." I checked my watch. "We've only got this saw for today anyway and we promised Fernando a pile of logs in exchange."

We spent the rest of the daylight hours cutting up the fallen tree and loading the logs in the back of the Suzuki. By the time we'd unloaded them again in Fernando's lockup, it was quite dark. I replaced the chain saw and locked the door.

We returned to the Casa de Pastores and I looked up how to cut down trees on my laptop while we waited for dinner. Comparing my efforts with the recommended methods it looked like I'd been lucky to come back with all my limbs. And oddly enough, none of the recommended methods involved tying the tree to one's car and trying to outrun it as it falls.

José Felipe brought our meals and I confessed about the damage to the roof of the Suzuki. He seemed okay about it, especially when I offered to pay for the repairs.

"You must take it to my cousin, José Martin; he is the best mechanic in Las Alpujarras."

My phone call to Julie the following morning wasn't quite as happy. As I stabbed at the number I realised I already had a cigarette in my hand.

"I thought we agreed you didn't *need* a car?" she said. "So how did you break a car you weren't supposed to have?"

I explained about the stuck chain saw and that only seemed to make things worse. "Chain saw? I don't remember a chain saw on your inventory list? In fact, I distinctly remember the absence of chain saws, 4x4s or any other form of mechanical assistance."

"I was being creative," I said.

"You're not supposed to be being creative; you're supposed to be using your survival skills."

"I'm going to need some cash to pay for the repairs. Shall I pull some out on the card?"

Silence for a moment then, "I suppose you'll have to. But please, no more cars or chain saws, this is a very limited budget. Our budgets have been cut and we're struggling to keep our houses open, let alone feed your habit for destroying cars. And I'll need the receipts."

I wondered how I was going to persuade anybody here to come up with receipts for anything. "Okay," I said.

"Oh, and your new Camp Colleague is arriving on Friday."

"Is he any good at cutting down trees?"

Julie ignored me and ended the call.

"Nick Brewer's coming on Friday and that only gives us two days to make it look like we've been doing something other than destroying cars," I said.

"The Para man?"

"Yes. We need to try and at least build something. Even if it's only a toilet shed."

"Really? I'm knackered after today. I was hoping for a day off. I'm not built for this," Bob said.

"Day off? All we managed to achieve today was to cut a pile of logs for somebody else."

＊

That evening I eschewed Spanish television with its noisy game shows and endless adverts in favour of pottering around the internet in search of local background. I discovered a distinct lack of local information. There were numerous promotional sites for horse trekking or skiing but strangely lacking were the local businesses or facilities. The village of Virriatos was not even mentioned and a search for local restaurants or hotels yielded no returns at all. I repeated the search for other towns or villages nearby and apart from the recognised tourist destinations, the results were similar. This whole region lacked any significant internet presence and that which did exist, was mostly driven by foreign owned businesses or multinationals. Even searching for local history yielded sparse results and mostly centred on either the Moorish Christian wars of the fifteenth century or the Spanish Civil War. I'd never realised quite how bloody the Spanish Civil War had been and it seemed particularly bad in this area, though for the life of me I couldn't see anything even vaguely of any strategic importance there. Needless to say, thousands were slaughtered in some of the most brutal skirmishes of the war.

I decided that the Civil War was probably not good website material and spent the rest of the evening trying to breach the DOJ's firewall in the hope of wiping out my recently acquired criminal record. But their security was too resistant to my casual attempt, although I did manage to set up a temporary redirect so that visitors to their site would be sent to a video of dancing cows I'd found on YouTube.

We faced the field the following morning with a distinct lack of enthusiasm. Gouged tyre tracks, scattered branches and a selection of trees with random axe marks gave evidence to the previous day's activity. The lack of any form of construction mocked us as we stared at the chaos.

"Okay," I said. "I think we should dig the hole for the toilets and kitchen waste. We'll give tree cutting a break for today."

We took a spade each and attacked the ground I'd previously marked with paint. I'd chosen locations of the toilets and kitchen carefully so that the natural shade of the trees would give extra protection. It didn't take long before I realised the problem with that decision. Big trees that provided welcome natural shade also came with big roots. After an hour of digging what amounted to a series of potholes around the trees we decided to move the location of the toilets and kitchen more out in the open. We painted more lines on the field then set to work. The digging proved slightly easier but we soon hit hard clay and the going became much harder. Another hour and we had only dug about a metre down but as digging was easier closer to the surface, we had gone wide rather than deep. We currently had what could best be described as a shallow ditch.

After a break for lunch, we resumed work and created a channel to run into our ditch which was intended to be a sort of run-off from the kitchen area. Due to the fact that the main hole wasn't very deep, by the time we'd allowed a decent slope for the run-off, it meant the kitchen area would only be about two metres from the toilets.

"We could always build a wall between them," said Bob, staring at the hole.

"We could, but we haven't had much luck building anything so far."

"Perhaps we should leave this for the moment and have another go at a shelter. We can come back to it later."

I stared at the trees. Whilst I wasn't enthusiastic about tackling more tree cutting, we were actually supposed to be living here and not hiding out in the Casa de Pastores hotel. Nick Brewer was going to be expecting some sort of evidence of our residence.

"We should make a living shelter and food area," I said finally. "We're going to be living here as soon as Nick arrives so we'd best build something."

We set to work once more with axe and saw. This time

however, we tempered our optimism and focussed on smaller branches. By sunset we'd actually made reasonable progress and had a sort of lashed together brushwood igloo. We stood back to survey our handiwork.

"It's a start," I said. "Might not be completely waterproof but I don't think they get that much rain here."

"Can we both fit in there do you think?" Bob asked.

"With a squeeze. But tomorrow we could build another one, now we've got the hang of it."

After we'd finished I drove down to the cash machine in Trevelez and drew out three hundred euros, the maximum I was allowed in one day, and set off to find José Martin, José Felipe's mechanic cousin. His workshop was at the bottom of a steep cobbled lane at the southern edge of the village. An ancient breakdown truck sat outside a large building which had probably once been a hay barn. The surprisingly spacious interior gave home to a large and diverse collection of partially dismembered vehicles. In amongst the jumble I noticed an old battlefield ambulance, a rotovator, several white vans with assorted dents and a battered JCB digger. Several large wooden benches were covered in rusting lumps of machinery and an ancient lift held aloft what looked like an Aston Martin.

An oil smudged face appeared from under the Aston Martin.

"José Martin?" I enquired.

"Si," said the man.

I explained I'd been sent by his cousin José Felipe and that I had his Suzuki outside which needed a bit of attention.

"Ah, yes," he said. "I was told what happened. A tree? I have lots of cars hitting trees." He waved his hand around the workshop. "But trees hitting cars? That makes for a different day." He laughed.

It seemed our little calamity was the talk of the village. He told me he could fix it within a couple of days and offered me the field ambulance as a loan car until it was fixed. At first I declined but he insisted that it worked perfectly and I figured that we still needed some sort of transport, no matter what Julie thought, so I took the vehicle. At its heart, the vehicle was a Landrover Defender and I guessed it was probably about thirty years old. The gearbox was interesting and the steering heavy but once I'd got the hang of it, it wasn't too bad to drive. I manoeuvred the vehicle up the narrow streets then parked it outside the Casa de Pastores.

Dinner was a huge mixed paella and I picked out the meat to put on Bob's plate. We drank copious amounts of wine and afterwards I headed upstairs, showered and collapsed into bed. Sleep came quickly and the morning quicker still.

~ *C h a p t e r   S i x* ~

We stared at the meadow, trying to understand what had happened. Our little shelter had been completely destroyed. Bits of it lay scattered around the area like somebody had put a large explosive charge underneath it. Only the absence of charring finally convinced me that had not been the cause but it still looked like a deliberate act of sabotage. At least when the wind had taken our first shelter that had been understandable. We'd built the wrong construction in the wrong place. But this wanton trashing of all our hard work just made no sense. We'd not noticed anybody in the village who looked like they might find this sort of behaviour their idea of a fun night out. Nor had we any indications that we'd upset any of the locals enough to cause them to do this out of spite.

We gathered up the scattered branches and tried to reassemble the shelter but it wouldn't go back together the way it had before. We set about with axe and saw to make more building materials, the old ambulance coming into its own carting branches around the field. We set about building shelter number three on top of the ruins of number two and by lunchtime we had a passable shelter once more.

"I think we're beginning to get the hang of this," I said. "It's even a bit bigger than the last one."

"Still don't fancy living in that for six months," said Bob.

"We can get better. Once the others are here we can chop more wood and build bigger shelters. Now we know what we're doing it's just a matter of scale."

We headed back to the hotel for lunch and when José Felipe brought the beers I broached the subject of the trashed shelter.

"Can you think why anybody would do such a thing?" I asked.

"Nobody here would do that," he said. "Why would they? Waste of effort."

We drank our beers, shared the tapas and watched the day starting to drift by.

"We really should be getting back to work," I said. "Our Camp Colleague is coming tomorrow and we've only got one shelter and no toilets yet. If we don't make it look like we've got some sort of handle on this they're likely to shut this project down."

"That's not too bad," Bob said. "The hostel's okay."

"You ran away," I said. "You think you're going back there like the Prodigal Son? It'll be the nick for both of us if we screw this up."

José Felipe appeared with two more beers just as I'd mustered the strength to head back to work. He planted the beers on the table. "I know who wrecked your shelter," he said.

"Who?" I asked.

"I talked to others and asked them, who would do such a thing? And then of course we understand."

"Go on."

"Jabalí," he said.

"Who's Jabalí?"

"Jabalí. He lives in the woods."

"Sorry, I'm still not understanding. Who lives in the woods?"

"Jabalí." He held his forefingers each side of his mouth and gave a snorting sound. "Very dangerous but tastes good with potatoes and garlic."

I suddenly realised he was talking about a wild pig, or boar. I remembered reading about those.

"Wild boar?" I said. "They would do that?"

"Of course. They destroy gardens and chicken houses. Worse than foxes. You must build more strongly." He disappeared back inside.

I pondered what he'd said. It had taken everything we had to build the previous shelter and the latest one wasn't going to be any stronger. If a wild boar could just turn up in the night and trash all our efforts so easily we might as well call this a day now and go back to a nice easy prison cell.

"We need foundations," said Bob. "Big logs deep in the ground then build from there. Like Robinson Crusoe. He built a big log wall to keep the wild animals out, we can do that."

"Robinson Crusoe? Apart from the fact that was just a story, I'll bet his island was nice easy earth anyway. We'd need a digger to get deep enough for any foundations out there."

"Where on earth would we find a digger up here?"

***

"It's not ready yet," José Martin said.

I glanced around his workshop until my eyes found the JCB digger I'd noticed on my previous visit. "I know," I said. "Do you hire that thing out?" I pointed at the digger.

"To you? I think that would be very stupid of me. I have seen what you can do with cars; I do not wish to see what you could do to my baby."

"Can I hire the digger with a driver?"

"Yes, I can drive for you. What do you want?"

I explained about the toilet drains and foundations.

"Easy, two hundred euros for the afternoon."

"How much is the Suzuki going to cost?" I had a feeling the money I'd drawn on the card wasn't going to come anywhere close. I also had no idea how we were going to pay the bill at the Casa de Pastores.

He picked two cans of beer from a bucket of water and handed one to me. "You pay in cash?"

"Of course."

"Three hundred euros."

"Five hundred in total then?" I found it fascinating how everything always came in such round, tidy numbers.

"Yes, I can do the digging now."

Five hundred euros, although good value, was way out of our league. I had an idea.

"How about I pay you in customers?" I suggested.

He took a thoughtful pull on his beer then, "How does that work?"

"I have noticed many crashes here in the Alpujarras," I said.

"Ah, yes. The Spanish are loco when they drive. Good business for the breakdown companies."

"And you don't get any of it. Why?"

"It is the insurance companies. They only give the franchise to big companies, shiny trucks and modern workshops which look like hospitals." He waved his arm around the chaos in his workshop. "Also, I think there is much money involved. Some of the companies like a… shall we say, a fee?"

"What if I could get you on the lists? And not just *on* the lists but as number one, the first breakdown chosen?"

"How is this going to happen?" José Martín tossed his

empty beer can into an old oil drum. "Look at my place, and my truck."

"Leave that to me," I said.

An hour later, José Martin's digger was making short work of toilet drain holes and foundation trenches.

"How are we going to pay for this?" Bob asked as we watched the digger work.

"All taken care of."

"How's that then?"

"Just a little bit of simple hacking. In fact, that gives me another idea. I'll take the ambulance back to the bar. You hang on here and keep an eye on things. José Martin can give you a lift back to the village."

***

I found José Felipe in the kitchen dismembering some unfortunate creature.

"Ah, Michael," he greeted me. "We have Jabalí for dinner. Paco had a good day hunting, now we have fresh meat and you have one less problem with your shelter."

I studied the lumps of dead boar scattered over every available surface. "I think I'll stick with pizza."

"You must try some. I will prepare my mother's special Chilindron for you." He kissed his fingers. "You will never forget it."

I tried to keep my expression neutral. "I'm sure I won't but I'm a vegetarian. I do not eat meat."

"Yes, I understand," he said. "But Jabalí is not just meat. It is the life-force of the Alpujarras, the spirit which links us to our ancestors. To share Jabalí with good wine and good company is to understand Spain."

"Still no. I might take you up on the wine though. Tell me, José Felipe, have you ever heard of The Travel Spy?"

"No, what is this?"

"It's a massive internet website where travellers leave reviews of places, like hotels, restaurants, resorts and so on. Everybody uses it."

"Except José Felipe." He laughed and cut through a shoulder joint.

"Really," I said. "If you get a handful of five-star reviews there you'll need one of those every night." I nodded towards the table top massacre.

He turned and looked at me, the hand holding the cleaver raised. I watched the blood trickle down his wrist. "Nobody uses the internet here," he said. "Why would we need the internet? We have the womenfolk, they know everything." He laughed.

"I'm not talking about here; I'm talking about making Casa de Pastores famous. World famous. People travelling from England and all over Europe, even America, to feast on your mother's Jabalí Chilindron."

He froze for a moment, then, "America, you say?"

"Yes. Possibly. For sure."

"We had an American here once. He was fat, like our friend here." He waved his cleaver towards the Jabalí. "His manners were much the same too, but his money was good. How are you going to bring Americans here?"

"As I said, The Travel Spy website is used by everybody. I can give you a slight commercial advantage there." I noticed José Felipe's puzzled expression. "Um… I can create some magic for you. You will be the place that everybody has to visit when they come to the Alpujarras. They will talk about the Casa de Pastores in the best Manhattan clubs and your dishes will be discussed in the society pages of the New York Times."

His eyes narrowed. "Why would you do this for me?"

"Well, to be honest, and I need you to understand the rarity of that statement, to be honest, I can't pay my room bill."

~ *C h a p t e r   S e v e n* ~

My phone ringing dragged me from sleep. I glanced at my watch, just gone seven. That would make it six in England and as nobody had my number here that meant somebody in England must be keen. I stabbed the ignore button and pulled the quilt over my head. The phone persisted, the thin quilt offering no sonic impediment to the sounds of November Rain, my current ring tone. I reached out from under the bedclothes and brought the phone in. Julie. At six o'clock? Either this was really urgent or she'd been up partying all night and misdialled me for the taxi. That would be it, I hit ignore again. Thirty seconds later Slash started running his notes once more. I succumbed and answered with a sleep filled grunt.

"Michael?" Julie's voice.

"Hmm."

"Oh, good. We have a slight problem."

"Hmm."

"It's Nick Brewer, he's arriving in Malaga this morning and I can't get a hire car for him."

I shuffled into sitting position. "Unexpected period of high demand due to the school holiday holidays?"

"Yes, how did you know?"

"Apparently it happens every year here about this time. What do you want me to do?"

"Can you hire a car your end and pick him up?"

"There's nowhere up here." I pulled the curtains open in the hope of a bit of daylight unclogging my brain. The sun exploded in my eyeballs and I hastily closed the curtains again.

"There must be somewhere. Just put it on the card, I'll clear it."

Ahh, the magic words. "I could ask José Martin, he's got a garage here, I think he hires cars."

"Good."

"I'll have to draw cash though. He doesn't take cards."

"Well, that's a bit irregular but I suppose we have no choice. Make sure you get a receipt. And please –"

"I know, budget cuts, keep it cheap. No problem. What time's his flight?"

"Lands at ten twenty, your time."

I looked at my watch; this was going to be tight. "Okay. Tell him to wait just outside the main entrance." I didn't want a repeat of the fiasco with Bob. "What's he look like?"

"I haven't the faintest idea. Use your initiative. Parachute Regiment, I'm sure he'll stand out amongst the sunburned beer bellies and screaming babies." The phone clicked dead in Julie's normal abrupt manner.

I took a quick shower, found some clean clothes and knocked on Bob's door.

He opened at the first knock; clearly he was an earlier riser than me.

"I've got to go and pick up this Nick Brewer chap from the airport," I said. "Can you just make sure the field looks like we've been doing something at least vaguely survivalish?"

"No worries. I'll start a campfire. They always look homely."

I didn't have time to try to dissuade him. "Just try not to burn Spain down," I said and headed off to find the ambulance.

I went via Trevélez so I could stop by the cash machine. Julie had been good to her word and upped the limit so I was able to pull out five hundred euros. I needed to remember to mickey up some sort of receipt later.

The difficulties of driving a thirty year old field ambulance down the twisty roads were more than outweighed by the fact everybody seemed to give me a wide berth. Especially the little white vans, it seemed that this time, I had the bigger, badder machine.

The airport car park had clearly not been designed for field ambulances and at several points I needed more than one go to manoeuvre round the tight ramp turns, much to the annoyance of the trail of following cars. On one riser ramp, the ambulance stalled and only restarted after three attempts when a cloud of black smoke belched from the exhaust and completely engulfed my followers. I eventually found a vacant space and managed to squeeze in between a Porsche and a BMW. I found the Arrivals hall just on ten thirty and allowing for passport control and baggage collection, that meant I probably had ten or fifteen minutes clear. I sat at the bar opposite the exit doors, lit a cigarette and set about rectifying the caffeine deficit caused by the disruption to my morning. The steady stream of people flooding through the doors gave little clue as to where they'd come from, but the British did tend to stand out with their pale complexions and union flag T-shirts. After twenty minutes and three coffees, I was on the point of giving up and phoning Julie for Nick's number when I spotted a familiar face coming through the doors. A young woman with short, sun-bleached hair and well-toned build stopped just outside the door to scan the area. She was the woman I'd met at Gatwick. Ex-forces, hadn't she been on her way to work for a private security contractor in Gibraltar? What was she doing here?

I stood up to make sure I wasn't mistaken. She spotted me, waved and headed over.

"Hi," she said. "I thought it was you. Small world."

"Seems that way. I thought you were off to Gibraltar? Blacklance Security wasn't it? What happened?"

She gave me a quizzical look. "Who are you here to meet?" she asked.

That was a very random question. "Oh, just some guy who's supposed to be helping with the project I'm on."

"What name do you have?" she asked.

I was slightly bemused by her questions. "He's a sergeant from the Paras. Nick Brewer. Why do you ask?"

"Ah." She dropped her rucksack on the floor. "I think there may be a bit of confusion." She held her hand out. "I'm Sergeant Brewer, late of Her Majesty's Parachute Regiment."

I took her hand and held it, not quite sure what to do. "But… you're a woman?"

"I can see there's no pulling the wool over your eyes." She shook my hand.

"No, I mean. What?"

"My name's Nikki. But people often call me Nick. Sometimes Knick-Knack and even Knickerless, but usually only once."

I felt my mouth working but no words appeared. I tried again. "You're my new Camp Colleague?"

"If that's what you want to call me. Or you could just call me Nikki if you prefer. We going to stay here or have you arranged transport?"

"Oh, right. I've got an ambulance."

"I suppose that shows forethought. Expecting casualties?"

"You've not driven through Órgiva before, have you?"

It took fifteen minutes to locate the ambulance. I'd carefully remembered the position but then totally forgotten on which floor I'd parked.

Nikki studied the ambulance. "Good grief, I didn't know any of these were still running."

"Hmm, running is such an optimistic word."

The engine started on the second bang and filled the enclosed area with a thick black cloud. I lit a cigarette and waited until the exhaust fumes had cleared enough to see where we were going. I shuffled the vehicle out of the tight space and searched for the exit signs.

"Long time since I've sat in an ambulance with a smoker," she said.

"Sorry." I took the hint and screwed the cigarette out in the ashtray whilst heaving the ambulance round the tight exit ramps and out into the sunlight.

"So, what happened with Blacklance Security?" I asked, once I'd settled in to the drive.

"That's who I'm working for. They took the contract with the Department of Justice to provide supervision for this project and I got the job."

"Lucky you."

"It wasn't quite what I had in mind." She pulled her boots off and stretched her feet out on the dashboard. "That's better. I was hoping to be assigned as CQP for some film star, or at least a wealthy businessman, but it seems as I was the only one with a vagina, I get the babysitting jobs."

"Well, at least you're not likely to get shot doing this." I wrestled the gearbox into third to overtake a bus.

"How about you?" she asked. "You told me how you ended up as the EWO in an SAS unit but why the army in the first place? You don't…" She hesitated. "You don't really strike me as a natural. If you know what I mean?"

"We had a crap career master at school. He was also our history teacher, totally obsessed with World War Two movies. His idea of a history lesson was to put on a DVD of the Great Escape while he buggered off outside for a fag. As far as he was concerned, all boys were going in the army and all girls were to be secretaries." I dropped a gear to gain a more acceleration in passing the bus and blew thick black smoke over a moped rider.

"And you just went along with that?"

"I didn't feel I had much choice after he dismissed my first choice of career."

"What was that?" Nikki fiddled with the air vents in a fight against the building heat inside the vehicle.

"I thought I was all set to be the Video Game Specialist on the International Space Station. I've always had a natural aptitude for languages and loved computer games so I thought I'd be a natural."

"Video game specialist?"

"Hey, I thought it was a thing. I was sure they'd need somebody to steer the ISS through an asteroid field. When he told me there was no such job I was at a bit of a loss and just went along with his idea of joining up."

"I've always thought asking a fifteen-year-old to make career decisions was a crazy system." Nikki gave up her fight with the air vents and undid a couple of buttons on her shirt. Altogether way too distracting when trying to keep an ancient ambulance going in a straight line past a trail of traffic. "Most teenagers' idea of forward thinking only extends as far as whether to order pineapple or anchovies on their pizza. Doesn't this thing have air-con?"

"Sorry, it's a last minute replacement. We had a hire car, a Fiat, but it caught fire so we rented the Suzuki truck from the local hotelier."

"This isn't a Suzuki," she said. "I'm not much with cars but I am fairly sure this isn't a Suzuki."

"No, Bob dropped a tree on that one."

"Bob?"

I explained about Bob and his penchant for impersonating random people.

"I'm not sure I should be here," she said. "I'm a soldier, I don't really do care in the community. What about the rest of them?"

"Just Bob at the moment. The others arrive on Monday and I haven't got a clue about them. All I know is there's five in total and they're all what they term, low level recidivists."

"And we're supposed to look after them for six months?"

"That's about it. I get my discharge, Judge Carrington gets his gong and we all go home."

"What's the site like?"

"Um, at the moment it's a field. I'm supposed to be teaching them how to build shelters and stuff. Which reminds me, I need to Google compost toilets. Bob and me are living in the local hotel."

"Is that really within the spirit?"

"Probably not. But I think they've got another room if you want one."

***

We arrived back in time for a late lunchtime drink and tapas. José Felipe welcomed Nikki with a glass of the local red wine and a plate of jamon.

"It's a good system," I explained. "We drink, they feed us. This meat is a local speciality, apparently. The Alpujarran equivalent of ambrosia."

She sampled the meat tentatively. "Not bad. You not eating?"

"No, I don't eat meat."

"Isn't that going to prove tricky when teaching survival skills?" she asked.

"I was rather hoping you could take charge of that side of things." I gave her my best charming smile.

"Oh you did, huh? I thought I was just here in a supervisory role?"

"It can be our little secret."

"Along with the hotel room?"

"It's all about ticking boxes anyway. Nobody actually cares what we do up here."

Bob appeared from the stairs at the end of the bar. I introduced them.

"This is Sergeant Brewer of the Paras, our new Camp Colleague and security."

Bob stared at her for a moment. "But she's a woman."

"Yes," I said. "We figured that one out at the airport."

"But she can't be a woman. We haven't got anywhere to put women."

"We haven't got anywhere to put anybody. Did you finish the holes with José Martin?"

Bob continued to stare at Nikki. "What? Yes, holes. All done."

"Holes?" asked Nikki. She took a step away from Bob. "Why do you need holes?"

"Ah, our first shelter blew down –"

"And the second," interrupted Bob.

"Yes and the second. So we thought we'd dig some holes to plant the timbers in to make it a bit more secure."

"Makes sense," said Nikki.

We ordered more beers which José Felipe brought to our table and a few moments later his wife, Conchita, brought a dish of paella. I picked around the fish and meat.

After lunch we piled into the ambulance and headed up to the meadow. I stopped the vehicle at the edge of the clearing trying to take in the scene before us. A series of holes and trenches spread across the meadow in all directions, interspersed with piles of earth and several uprooted trees.

"What the hell happened here?" I asked.

"Well, José Martin was doing so well that I got him to dig a few extra just in case. Seemed a shame not to."

"But we only needed a drain for the toilets and a small foundation trench so the shelter doesn't blow down again. This looks ready for Barratt's to move in and start work on a housing estate…"

"Okay, I might have overdone it," Bob said. "But it was cool watching him. I even had a go myself. You see that hole there?" He pointed at a huge circular hole in the centre of the meadow. "I did that one."

"Good," I said. "And what about the trees?"

"Oh, those? That was José Martin's idea. He thought it would save us time and trouble chopping them down. Though to be honest, I think he was a bit worried we'd drop another one on his ambulance."

"But we'll never use this lot. There's enough here to build a small frontier town."

"On the up side," said Bob. "We'll be alright for firewood for a while."

"I see what you mean about holes," said Nikki. "Where are you planning on putting up the sleeping shelter?"

I stared around the mayhem then pointed to a particularly large hole in the centre of the meadow. "I thought about there."

"Out in the open?" Nikki asked. "That means a much more substantial construction. You also don't have the use of any readymade uprights like trees. It saves a lot of work if you build against existing trees."

"We were going to do that," I said. "But the ground was too hard to dig. To be honest, I'm not much good at building shelters. My job never really started until there was a thirteen amp socket and a decent Wi-Fi connection. I was no use to the British Army sat under a stone in the middle of the Iraq desert."

"I can see that. And where are the toilets?"

"There," I said, pointing at a nearby hole which I didn't want to move too close to as I couldn't see the bottom. "Next to the kitchen area."

"Next to the kitchen area?" Nikki seemed puzzled. "Why would you do that?"

"Saves holes," I said. "One drain for the two, half the digging."

"And twice the dysentery."

"Dysentery?" I eased closer to the hole but still couldn't see the bottom.

"Yes, very popular in the Middle Ages with those communities who didn't like digging."

I looked around the field. There certainly wasn't a shortage of holes. "We could use that one for the toilets," I suggested, pointing at a random hole. "It's not like we're stuck for choice."

"Oh, I thought that would be our firewood store," said Bob.

"A ten foot deep hole in wet mud for a firewood store?" I said. "And when it rains I suppose we call it our firewood pond?"

"I hadn't thought of that."

"And what the hell were you planning for that one?" I pointed at the huge circular hole right in the middle of the meadow. "The one you dug, what's that for?"

"I thought that could be the Community House. We could have meetings there."

"And where were you planning on putting the cinema?"

"You say the others are coming on Monday?" asked Nikki.

I looked at her. "Yes, why?"

"Because there's nothing here other than holes. Nowhere to sleep, nowhere to cook, no toilets."

"I thought I'd get them to do that," I said. "Part of their training."

"But you need the basics. They can't just turn up here and be expected to build their shelters the moment they arrive. This is supposed to be a D.O.J. project not Botany Bay. Didn't anybody plan this?"

"I think they were leaving it all to me," I said. "They seemed to think I knew what I was doing. To be fair, I did try telling them I didn't."

Nikki stared around the chaos. "We have two days to create something here. If we don't, the first little oik to arrive is going to complain to his probation officer that living in a hole contravenes his human rights to a semi-detached house in Woking and we'll all be on the first bus home. And I don't plan on screwing up my contract with Blacklance over this fiasco. There's not so many openings for ex-forces these days and I need this job."

"I could ask Fernando for help," I suggested.

"Who's he?" asked Nikki.

"The local contact. He's holding our initial kit in his lockup, there's also a load of other stuff he said we could borrow. Might be worth another look."

I rang Fernando and he agreed to meet us at his lockup at five in the afternoon. At five thirty he turned up.

Nikki stared at the pile of clutter in the garage. "Well, I suppose if we want to paint the field white then we're good to go, other than that, I don't see much of any use here."

"There's some tarpaulin and cable ties over there." I nodded to a cardboard box.

"I stand corrected," she said. "We can build a bivouac and paint it white. No saws or axes or anything else of any use?"

"Oh yes. But they're all in the back of the Suzuki, in José Martin's workshop." I studied her disparaging look. "I'll give him a ring."

José Martin answered at the second attempt.

"Hola, José, it's Michael, are you in your workshop?"

"No, I have a breakdown to collect and take to Granada."

"Oh, when are you back here?"

"I do not know. Maybe tomorrow. Very busy, lots of insurance breakdowns suddenly. Thank you, my friend." The line went dead.

"Well?" Nikki asked.

"Slight problem," I said. "I sort of boosted his business and now he's too busy to get back here and unlock the workshop."

"My cousin Paco can help," said Fernando. "He is a builder."

"Okay," I said. "A builder should have some useful tools we can borrow."

We headed back to the Casa de Pastores to await Paco. The moment we arrived, Bob disappeared into the kitchen and I briefly wondered what he was up to but then Paco arrived and I forgot all about Bob.

Paco was a large man with a weathered face and a pony tail which pulled together what was left of his white hair.

"Can you ask him if he has some tools we can borrow for a few days until we can get ours unlocked?" asked Nikki.

I translated and Paco replied that he didn't lend out tools but he'd be happy to do some work for us. He promised to make us a good price as we were friends with Fernando.

"Did the Department of Justice give you a budget?" I asked Nikki. "Only I've already overspent mine."

"Not really," she said. "Just enough for food. Nothing else was supposed to be needed. They certainly didn't expect me to be employing builders."

"Employing is such a defining term. Mutual collaboration is much friendlier."

We ordered food and beers and I chatted with Paco about his business. Nikki's expression veered between suspicion and warning as she managed to pick up enough of the conversation to realise I was negotiating something but not quite enough to know what. By the time the food arrived, Paco and I had reached a conclusion and we shook hands across the table.

"What are you up to?" Nikki demanded.

I tore off a piece of bread and dunked it into my bean stew. "Paco's offered to give us a hand putting up some basic shelters," I said.

"Now why would he do that?" Her eyes narrowed.

"Apparently, José Martin told him about the little tweaks I did to give his breakdown business a bit of a lift." I took a spoonful of stew. "You should try this, it's delicious."

"No thanks, I've got some ribs coming. What tweaks?"

"Oh, it was just a minor tweak to the insurance company database that lists the breakdown companies and their catchment areas. They had it all wrong for this area. All sorted now."

"All sorted? The insurance company's database?"

"Yes, Paco wants me to do something similar for his business. Do you happen to know if insurance companies all use the same building firms for emergency repairs?"

"No, I haven't the faintest idea. What are you planning?"

"Just trying to support local businesses."

"By hacking insurance company websites?"

A huge plate of ribs and fries appeared on the table in front of Nikki. I looked up and Bob grinned at me.

"What are you doing?" I asked.

"Helping out in the kitchen," he said. "I've made some bread and butter pudding. They've never heard of that here, who'd have thought? Do you want some?"

"No thanks, I'll stick to my bean stew."

"Suit yourself." He headed back to the kitchen.

"What's he up to?" asked Nikki.

"I'm not sure but he's being enthusiastic and in the short time I've known him, enthusiasm in Bob is always something to be slightly afraid of."

After we'd eaten, I sorted out a room for Nikki and when she'd unpacked and showered, we sat outside with a couple of enormous gins, watching the stars appear one by one in the black velvet above us.

"I wish I could pick up languages," Nikki said. "How many do you speak?"

"Spanish, Arabic, Russian, some Chinese, and I can get by in Hindi."

"That's an eclectic mix." She took a sip of the gin. "Oh, that's strong."

"They're the languages of the hacking community," I said. "It pays to learn a bit when dealing with fellow hackers. One can't very well use Google Translate when you're trying to understand somebody's code for hacking the Pentagon. Tends to set off a few alarms." I tried the gin, Nikki was right, it was very strong.

"You hacked into the Pentagon?"

"Everybody does it; it's a sort of rite of passage for new hackers."

"So what's the most difficult one? The Kremlin? The Bank of England?"

"No, they're all quite easy to somebody who knows what they're doing. The difficult one is the Chipping Sodbury Bowls Club membership register. For some reason nobody's ever been able to get into that. It's regarded as the Holy Grail. There's a prize of 10,000 dollars been put up by a Zimbabwean hacker for the first person to crack it."

"Wow," Nikki said. "That's worth having a go at, isn't it?"

"Not really." I supped at my gin, it was really very smooth, and getting smoother. "They're Zimbabwean dollars, so that makes the prize worth about twenty quid."

We sat in silence for a while, letting the gin work its magic and watching the constellations gradually sprinkle the sky until the Milky Way smeared itself across the night like a carpet of diamonds.

"I suppose there're worse places to be stuck for six months," Nikki said. Her eyes danced around the glowing canopy. Her elbow rested on the table and she held the gin glass against her cheek. I wasn't sure if she was enjoying the coolness of the glass or if she was using it to prop her head up with.

"Depends who we're going to be stuck with," I said.

"Might be the Lavender Hill Mob." She giggled, hiccoughed and spilt gin down her white cotton T-shirt. The wet patches turned translucent. That wasn't fair.

"Knowing my luck, it'll be Fletcher and Groughty."

We chatted until the chill air forced us inside and I went to my room to work on my laptop. Creating a simple website for Paco took no more than an hour once I'd gathered a pile of images of happy builders and immaculately tidy building sites. Okay, it probably wasn't an entirely accurate image of Paco's crew but it would do the job. By the time I'd planted a hundred or so backlinks around and several glowing reviews on various sites, I was fairly confident it would have the desired effect. But just to be sure, I added a page of images of an immaculate Golf Resort on one of the Costas. I'd done a search on the firm who had actually built it and they were long gone, owing the banks several million, so they were unlikely to complain at the purloining of their images.

~ *Chapter Eight* ~

We arrived in the meadow just after sunrise. Bob hadn't joined us even though I'd knocked his door twice, once just before breakfast and again when we were about to leave. We didn't wait as Paco had wanted an early start so he could do the bulk of the heavy work before the heat of the day. José Martin's digger was back on site, this time flattening areas which Bob had so recently dug up. Three other men were already busy with saws and hammers working on the felled trees.

"Are you sure this is within the guidelines for the project?" Nikki watched the activity laid out across the field. "Only, I was under the impression you were supposed to be building a couple of survival shelters not a new twin town for Milton Keynes."

"Survival shelters are for the inmates… clients… what am I supposed to call them?"

"I don't know; do I look like a social worker?"

I eyed her up and down. Faded and scuffed jeans, a skinny white T-shirt which clung to every muscle and a pair of no-nonsense leather walking boots, no, definitely not a social worker. "Scallywags then," I said. "They can do the survival shelters; they're the ones here to be put through the mincer, not me. I need a good night's sleep."

"You're not one for irony, are you?"

"Irony is how a tank tastes."

A flatbed truck meandered its way across the field and dropped several lengths of plastic piping near one of the trenches. A couple of men manoeuvred the pipes into the trench and the digger pushed piles of earth back on top of them.

Paco drove up in his van and stopped next to one of the half constructed shacks. He called me over.

"I have some toilets and basins," he said. "We took them from a house we were demolishing. I can put them here for you. It is better than a hole in the ground and they were just taking space in my yard."

I helped him unload the porcelain then spent the rest of the morning holding bits of wood in strategic positions while his men sawed, hammered and bolted stuff into place. By lunchtime we had in place the framework for two constructions and a functioning drainage system.

Paco and his crew headed off for siesta and we made our way back to the Casa de Pastores for lunch.

We ordered beers and settled outside to watch the world pass by. Or whatever strange section of humanity represented the world in this place.

"So you said Blacklance never gave you any clue as to who they're sending here on Monday?" I asked. "They must know, surely?"

"No," Nikki took a long pull on her beer that cleared half the glass. "It was all a bit last minute; they were only contracted a few days ago. It will be fun, a surprise."

"A surprise? I don't do well with surprises. In fact, I'm worse with surprises than I am with having my sleep disturbed."

"Not a good combination for a member of an elite frontline fighting unit."

"I did try explaining that to my C.O. when they assigned me but nobody was listening."

Nikki paused thoughtfully for a moment, then, "Did you ever see action?"

"No, I was mostly stuck in a tent staring at a screen." I took a bite of the tapas I hadn't even noticed arrive. "I *heard* a lot of action though. Tents are not very good at keeping out the sounds of gunfire and RPGs."

She punched my arm, playfully I was sure, but it really hurt. "Idiot," she said.

I looked at the plate of food we'd been presented with. Tapas were always an adventure and were one of the few exceptions to my No Surprises Rule. I looked at the plate in front of us. It looked like a selection of small spring rolls but they contained a type of mild cheese and jalapeno peppers. Quite unusual. "These are good," I said.

"Do they always bring food with drinks?" Nikki asked.

"Just in this region. The rest of Spain you have to pay, here it comes free with your drinks."

"Seems like a good system." Nikki slipped one of the spring rolls into her mouth. "I could get used to it."

I ordered another pair of beers and Conchita brought them a moment later. "Did you like the rollitos?" she asked.

"Very good," I said.

"Bob is excellent. You did not tell me he was a famous chef."

"Bob?" For such a short name for some reason I found it very hard to articulate. "Bob?" I repeated.

"Yes, you did not know? He is showing me how to make Scottish Eggs."

I looked at Nikki. She shrugged and bit the end off another spring roll. "Don't ask me. I only just got here."

I looked back at Conchita. "We are talking about the Bob who came with me?"

"Yes." She laughed and gathered the empty glasses. "You are a crazy man."

I stood and pointed to the kitchen. "Do you mind if I have a word with him? Bob?"

"Of course, it's nothing."

I headed into the kitchen where I found Bob carefully squashing sausage meat around some hard boiled eggs.

He looked up when he saw me. "Oh, hi, Michael. Sorry I couldn't get to the field today. I've been helping here a bit."

"I see," I said. "Why?"

"Because Conchita taught me how to make Alpujarran bean stew yesterday."

"Of course. Silly me, I should have realised. What the hell are you talking about?"

"Bean stew. You had some yesterday, you liked it. Remember?" He rolled a completed Scotch egg in flour and dropped it on a baking sheet.

"I remember eating bean stew but I wasn't aware of the contractual obligations surrounding it. Care to explain? Only I had this idea you were supposed to be helping me build survival shelters."

"Conchita showed me her bean stew and I showed her my jalapeno crispy cheese rolls and bread and butter pudding. She really liked that. And now, I'm showing her how to make Scotch eggs. I assumed that as Paco was building the shelters that you didn't need me anyway." He brushed his hands together and they disappeared in a cloud of flour. "I'd have just got in the way."

"I didn't even know you could cook," I said.

"I did most of the cooking when I was helping in the Newstart House. Gordon Ramsay taught me everything."

"Gordon Ramsay? The TV chef?"

He dug his hand in the bowl of sausage meat and started work on another egg. "Well, not so much in person. If you see what I mean? I did watch all his programmes though and when Ibrahim Asani down in the Good Luck Kebab Shop mistook me for him one night I didn't want to disappoint him, so I worked nights there for a while."

"As Gordon Ramsay? In a kebab shop?"

"Yes. Went down a treat with the locals, especially at chucking out time from the nearby techno dance club. It was probably because I'm very good at swearing. Mind you, that lot were usually so pissed I don't think they could have spotted the difference between Ibrahim and Nigella Lawson."

"And now you're telling Conchita that you're Gordon Ramsay?"

"What? No, of course not. That would be silly."

"So where did Conchita get the idea that you were a famous chef?"

"Oh, that would probably be because I told her I was Robert Carstairs from the Michelin starred restaurant, Bob's Pie Shop."

"Bob's Pie Shop?"

"She caught me on the hop; it was the best I could come up with on the spur of the moment. Not bad though, huh?"

I left him to his sausage meat and went to the bar to pay for our drinks.

José Felipe refused my payment. "You are going to make Casa de Pastores famous," he said. "And now we have the best chef in all of Spain, you are welcome here as family."

I found Nikki still at the table outside. "Well?" she said. "Did you get to the bottom of it?"

"Um, yes, sort of. Bob is now a world famous chef moonlighting here from his Michelin starred restaurant, Bob's Pie Shop. That's when he's not being Gordon Ramsay working in the local kebab shop, of course."

"That's okay then. Just as long as he's not doing anything odd."

"We've got free drinks so I'm not saying anything."

We made our way back to the field to find Paco and his crew putting slatted roofs on the two constructions. "You like?" he asked as we approached.

"Yes, I wasn't expecting this. I was just hoping for a simple log construction but this is amazing."

"It's more easy." He patted the sheets of second-hand plywood he'd used for the walls. "I had all this stuff in my yard going bad. It's better to use it for something than see it wasted. And it is faster than cutting trees." He laughed.

We spent the afternoon helping Paco and his men build what seemed to be turning out to be a small village. As the sun started to drop behind the trees and their long shadows draped across the field, we stood back to survey the result. The two main constructions had been built from odd sheets of used ply with a few young fir trunks for added support. A bit of a strange mix, especially as the plywood sheets had clearly been salvaged from a school or something and were scrawled with graffiti and tags. Sheets of tarpaulin had been secured across the roofs to make them watertight and their random nature added to the general feeling of colourful chaos. A separate kitchen had been built of mostly of what looked like scrap scaffolding planks, complete with drips and splashes of paint of various colours. A similar, but slightly smaller, construction lay a little apart from the others and contained the reclaimed sanitary fittings, now fully functional.

"Well, that's a bit more civilised than I was expecting," said Nikki. "Perhaps it won't be such an ordeal after all."

"I still prefer the Casa de Pastores," I said. "They have hot showers and air conditioning."

"You're planning on staying there? You can't do that. You're supposed to be teaching these people self-sufficiency."

"I am. It's all just levels in the same game. At one level you learn how to catch locusts and make omelettes from wild penguin eggs and at the other end, you learn how to hack websites and grateful locals shower you with truffles and ice cream. Who the hell cares anyway? For me, it's just a way of avoiding a prison sentence and for you…" I looked at Nikki. "I guess it's probably better than getting shot at again."

"Hmm, you might have a point, being shot at was certainly one of my least favourite parts of army life. But we'll still need to build something which looks like a survival shelter for the photographs."

"What photographs?" I hadn't reckoned on photographs.

"You don't think they're going to let you sit up here for six months without wanting some sort of reports as to what you're doing? This is taxpayer's money after all and there'll be paperwork to be done."

"Hadn't thought of that. We'll get the Scallywags to do that then. That can be their first lesson."

"As long as we get some good pictures before one of these wild pigs comes round and knocks it down again," Nikki said.

"It's a bit like the story of the Three Little Pigs," I said. "Except in reverse. It's the pigs knocking the houses down." I pondered that for a moment. "I suppose that makes me the wolf."

Nikki looked me up and down. "You? The wolf? The only thing remotely wolfish about you is your ability to scavenge a free meal."

"I'm quite good at growling."

We did a tour of the site. The constructions were still a bit haphazard but certainly a lot better than anything I could have built. Thanks to the tarpaulins, they should be reasonably waterproof and the mishmash of salvaged timber and newly felled logs gave a peculiar strength to the buildings even if they did look like a glorified, kid's den.

"There aren't any doors," Nikki said, staring at the gaps in the walls that gave access.

"I guess they didn't have any," I said. "It would have been much more complicated anyway."

"We should have something, even if just for a little privacy in the toilet shed."

I stared at the gaps. Doors would have proved a challenge that was for sure. Due to the random nature of the constructions, nothing was straight. Trying to hang any sort of door would have proved impossible.

"We could rig up a sort of flexible screen-curtainy thing," I suggested. "That can't be difficult."

"Screeny-curtainy thing?" Nikki repeated.

"Yes, we can make it out of…" I stared around the field but couldn't see anything which looked like a curtain or a screen. "Leafy branches," I said lamely after a few moments.

She stared at me as if trying to ascertain if I was being serious. "I'll tell you what; we'll ask Fernando if he has some old painting dustsheets."

"Well, yes, I'd already thought of that," I lied. "I was trying to be more authentic."

"Authentic? As in Brazilian Shanty Town authentic?"

We continued to wander the site as Paco and his men cleared up their equipment. It was all very rustic but it would keep the weather out, give somewhere to cook and if we could rig up a bucket and hose, it would offer some sort of showering facility.

"Do we know what they're bringing with them?" Nikki asked.

"What do you mean?"

"Like sleeping bags and cooking equipment."

"I really don't know," I said.

"Who actually organised this?"

"Well, the idea was dreamt up by an ageing judge, although I'm not sure there's any other type, with a bit of help from the house manager and then overseen, modified and generally buggered about with by a committee from the Department of Justice."

"That fills me with confidence," Nikki said. "So there's every chance they're all going to turn up here with nothing more useful than a bottle of suntan lotion and a beach towel."

"I wouldn't count on the suntan lotion."

~ *Chapter Nine* ~

I spent most of Sunday morning setting up a website for the Casa de Pastores, complete with a review section full of glowing reviews and a page of local interest, sections of which I'd simply lifted from the Junta de Andalucía's webpage. It only took me around half an hour to hack the website of Travel Spy and plant a few glowing reviews about the hotel and its multi awarded Michelin chef, Bob. KwikJet's website, however, proved a little more difficult to access. I gathered a list of the senior executives from their corporate site and emailed them all with an important message from their CEO, complete with a little virus courtesy of the techies in GCHQ. Within half an hour, I had a backdoor. Ten minutes later and Casa de Pastores was the KwikJet recommended partner for visitors to the Alpujarras.

I wanted to pad out the website with a bit of local history but could find nothing of the area other than a few anecdotes about the wars between the Moors and Christians which seemed cut and pasted from every tourist site across Spain. Not much material here for tourist bait so I had to embellish a little.

With a good morning's work accomplished, I headed downstairs for lunch. Nikki and Bob were already there.

"Thought you'd overslept," Nikki said.

"Just doing my bit for the local tourist trade," I said.

"I don't think I want to know. I'm supposed to be keeping an eye on you lot."

José Felipe brought me a beer without asking. A both comforting, and at the same time, somewhat disturbing sign.

"You go to fiesta today?" he asked.

"Fiesta?" I said.

"There is a fiesta in San Tadeo, the village over there." He pointed to the mountain rising across the valley. "It is their saint's day. They have good fireworks and a giant paella."

"I'm not good with fireworks," I said.

"That is a pity. It's one of the best fiestas in Las Alpujarras." He gathered some empty glasses and headed back inside.

"I've received an email from the Department of Justice," said Nikki. "We've finally got a list of participants." She looked at me. "Scallywags." She grinned.

"Murderers, gangsters, international jewel thieves? What have we got?"

She scrolled through a screen on her smartphone. "Sean Brennan, he's an art forger, Donny Howard, a car thief, Jason Langstaff one-time high flying banker, Ryan Edwards a dopehead and Robert Cyrankiewicz, an identity thief." She looked at Bob. "I guess that means you."

Bob looked affronted. "I don't steal identities. I just inhabit them for a while. I never steal anything."

"Oh what fun," I said. "A forger and a car thief, okay, that's about what I expected. A dopehead I can ignore, but a banker? Really?"

"Do you want me to ask if they'll swap him out for a Taiwanese pole dancer?"

"Would they do that?" Bob asked.

"No," said Nikki. "You've got to live with a banker for the next six months and that's it."

"How are they getting here?" I said. "They're not all going to get in the back of the ambulance, that's for sure."

"They're being brought here by a Blacklance secure transport vehicle. It's picking them up from the airport and due to get here around midday tomorrow."

"There goes the neighbourhood." I supped my beer and picked at the cheese slices Conchita had brought out. "You not cooking today, Bob?"

"No customers. I was going to do a nice shepherd's pie, this being the house of the shepherds and all. Thought that could be my signature dish."

"How long do you think you're going to be able to keep passing off basic British dishes as haute cuisine?" Nikki asked. "You'll run out soon."

"I already have," he said "The shepherd's pie is just about it. Unless I do kebabs. Do you think I can get away with a doner kebab?"

"I shouldn't think so," I said. "Even up here they probably know what a doner kebab is. So that was your total repertoire? Jalapeno and cheese spring rolls, bread and butter pudding and shepherd's pie? That's it?"

"And Scotch eggs," he said. "Don't forget my Scotch eggs. My mother was very proud of her recipe for those."

"What's so special about her recipe?" Nikki asked.

"I don't know," said Bob. "She never told me."

José Felipe appeared with replacements for the empty glasses and I took the opportunity to try to gain some background for his website. "Do you know much about the history of the area?" I asked him. "I want to include a bit on the website but I couldn't find anything."

He thought for a moment. "There are tales of a great shepherd who came this way," he said finally.

"That's it?" I said. "A shepherd? I was hoping for a bit more than that."

"But he was a *great* shepherd," said José Felipe.

"I think I'll just invent something," I said.

"How about a crashed spaceship being buried here?" suggested Bob. "It worked for Roswell, they get millions of tourists and they have a bar with pictures of aliens and everything."

"Okay, in the absence of any grown-up suggestions, I'm just going to scrape together a bit of nonsense about some queen or other stopping here one day and leave it at that. It's only padding anyway."

***

After lunch I finished the last bits on the website and took a walk out to the project site. The ramshackle buildings rose starkly against the fir trees which flanked the meadow. I headed towards the open end, where the ground dropped away into the valley. The Mediterranean sat in the V between the mountains, a slightly darker blue than the sky above, but only just. The coast of North Africa hovered in the ethereal area between sea and sky, tantalisingly offering glimpses before disappearing in the haze again. The views were truly stunning from up here.

I studied the area where the ground started to drop away. A gentle slope at first and then steeper with terraces providing large level areas before the next drop. I followed the slope down to the first terrace. A grassy area about a hundred metres wide by about twenty deep before the next drop. The grass had been cut short, probably by countless goats or sheep and was surprisingly green. In one area though, the grass looked thinner. I went to check it out. A rough circle, an area of about ten metres in diameter, sat in the middle of this lower meadow. I looked more closely and noticed the circle was actually quite pronounced and almost a perfect circle. I scuffed my foot at the grass to see if I could find any reason for the sparseness of the grass here. My boot scuffed stone. No, it was flatter, almost paved. I kicked at the surface and cleared bits of grass and dirt to reveal what looked like patio stones, flat enough on the surface to be either manmade or carefully selected and each laid tight to the next. I straightened and surveyed the area. A large circle of flat stones as if it had once been a courtyard or something but why here?

I heard the shot and I dropped to a crouch even as my head turned, searching for the source. A puff of white smoke appeared on the opposite side of the valley. Too much to be a sniper or even a shotgun. Then another. This time because I was looking in the right direction, I saw the flash and the puff before I heard the crack. Another three flashes in quick succession and the puffs of smoke merged into one even as the triple crack hit my ears. Fireworks. José Felipe had said something about a fiesta over the valley, somewhere called San Tadeo? I straightened up and studied the area but it fell to silence once more. I found I had a cigarette in my hand so I lit it.

Once the nicotine had spread its comforting glow, I followed the outline of the circle to see if I could work out what it was for but it gave up no clues.

I headed back up the first slope to the edge of the wood and settled on the ground with my back against a tree and gazed out through the valley and to the sea beyond. The air was still and pleasantly warm, laden with the scent of pine and rosemary. I supposed that if I had to be stuck somewhere remote for six months then this wasn't too bad. I'd seen worse places. Much worse. An eagle came into view and wheeled across the sky before rising again out of reach of my eyes. The warmth seeped into my body, bringing a fleeting sense of a peace I half remembered or perhaps I'd just half imagined.

The gunfire ripped into my senses. Rapid fire, automatic weapons. I pushed back into the trees and peered out. Nothing. I froze. If I moved I could give my position away. More shots, this time individual but interspersed with heavier fire. Mortars? Risking a move, I slipped deeper into the woods and pressed myself into the base of a large fir. I put my hands to my head to shut out the sounds but some of them were inside with me. Eyes closed, arms pulled tight over my head, I tried to control my heart which was threatening to beat its way through my ribcage. I stayed still. Very still. The tighter I pulled my arms around my head the more the gunfire faded but the more noise my heart made, thumping, driving and forcing blood and adrenaline around my system. Don't move. They don't know where I am. Wait. Wait.

I didn't know how long I'd stayed motionless but I knew I was cold. The gunfire had stopped and the air was silent. I felt damp. My clothes clung to me like I'd been caught in a summer shower. I touched the ground but it was dry. A rustling sound snagged my attention and I turned my head to look. The creature stared back at me. We were about three metres from each other, no more. It was a large animal with coarse rust coloured hair and deep eyes that locked with mine. The unnaturally long snout twitched at the air as if trying to understand what this strange creature was that sat crunched into the roots of the trees.

We stared at each other, the Jabalí and me. I felt no sense of threat from the creature, only a mutual curiosity. Certainly it looked capable of causing huge damage and not just to primitive survival shelters. The short tusks, almost flat against the snout, looked dangerous enough but the real threat was the sheer muscular power this creature looked capable of generating.

We watched each other for a while longer then the boar appeared to lose interest. It gave one last snuffle and ran through the trees at a remarkable pace for something so large. I fumbled a cigarette from the pack and managed to persuade the lighter to stay still for long enough to catch. The nicotine flooded my veins, forcing the remains of the adrenaline out. The calm drifted through me with each breath of soothing smoke I drew. I waited a moment to gather my thoughts then when I felt my legs might be capable of taking my weight, I headed back to the Casa de Pastores just as the sun readied to give up the sky to night.

***

"We wondered where you'd got to," Nikki greeted as I came down the stairs into the bar area.

"I've been out reccying the area," I said. I didn't mention the large gin, the nap or the fifteen minute shower.

"Are you alright?" Nikki asked as I sat down at the table. "You look a bit washed out."

"I'm fine," I said. "Just been a tense few weeks and now it's make-or-break time I guess."

"Hmm," Nikki said. "Well, if you ever want to talk you know where I am. At least for the next six months."

"Did you see the fireworks?" asked Bob. "Sounded like World War Three had taken off."

"Yes, I saw them across the valley." The sound still rang in my ears. "Mostly thunderflashes by the look of it. Not very exciting."

"See anything interesting on your travels?" Nikki asked.

"You can see Africa," I said. "Just about. And I found a strange stone circle."

"What like Stonehenge?" asked Bob.

"No," I said. "Like a circular patio area. Big. Very odd. I'll ask José Felipe later to see if he knows what it is."

"Might be an alien landing area," Bob said.

"We're not doing Roswell."

"But –"

"No."

~ *Chapter Ten* ~

Monday morning brought with it a slight sense of panic. I had somehow managed to not think about the reality of being responsible for a group of miscreants for six months. I'd never been much good with responsibility. I'd managed to avoid having children, or even a dog, and my time in the army had been a continuous saga of shirked duties and ducked obligations. I'd never even had a relationship which had lasted for six months so I didn't really rate my chances of this working out well. We toured the site one last time while waiting for our scallywags to arrive.

"Well, they have far more here than they're supposed to have," I said.

"I expect they'll be overjoyed then," Nikki said. "The graffiti's a nice touch too; it'll save them the bother."

"Are we going to have to live here?" Bob poked his head around the paint splattered dustsheet that currently served as a toilet door. "Only it's going to be a bit cramped with seven of us."

"I have to stay in the hotel," I said. "It's the Command Centre." I caught Nikki's acerbic glance. "I need to stay connected, in case of emergencies. Really, it says so in the rules."

"Well, in that case I have to stay there as well," Nikki said.

"I'm supposed to stay close to the Chief Scoundrel. That's what it says in *my* rule book."

"That means Bob has to be our Man on Site. You up to that Bob?"

There was no reply from behind the curtain. I tried again, "Bob? You okay being our Onsite Head Supervising Officer? Bob?"

A crashing noise from behind the curtain hinted at problems. "Bob?" I called again. "You alright?"

Finally, "I think I've blocked the toilet," he said from behind the curtain.

"How can you block the toilet?" I asked. "It's just a ten foot hole in the ground."

"I was using the bucket to tip earth down, you know, the flush system thing we're supposed to do after we've done, you know, and it fell in."

"Well, it's not the end of the world, we can find another bucket."

"And my shoe."

"Your shoe?" I listened to some scraping and scrabbling noises coming from behind the curtain.

"I think I might need a bit of help," he said after a while.

I pushed through the curtain and it took me a moment to understand what I was seeing. Only the top half of Bob was showing above ground level. He struggled to push himself up from the hole but each time he wriggled, a bit more earth gave way from the edge of the hole and he slipped deeper.

"Stay still," I said. "You're just making matters worse."

"What the hell…" Nikki appeared through the curtain. "How did you do that?"

"I dropped the bucket." Bob twisted to look at Nikki and dropped another inch into the hole.

"Stop moving." I grabbed him under his arms and pulled but he didn't move.

"You were trying to go down after the bucket?" Nikki said.

"No." Bob wriggled and slipped again. "Just trying to get my shoe."

"Of course, your shoe." I pulled again at his shoulders. "If you keep wriggling you're going to end up down the bottom."

"Get me out!"

"Nikki," I said. "Can you dig away the edges while I try to pull?"

"How did you lose your shoe?" Nikki gently scraped at the earth around Bob's midriff.

"I was trying to hook the bucket out with my foot when it came off. The shoe, not my foot. But I couldn't reach."

I braced my feet on the opposite side of the hole and pushed as hard as I could. More earth gave way under my feet and for a moment I thought I was going to be joining Bob in the hole but after a quick repositioning, I secured enough purchase to pull him up. We both collapsed backwards.

"Why on earth did you think you could reach to the bottom of a ten foot hole with your leg?" I said once I'd got my breath back. "How tall are you? Five eight?"

"Five foot eight-and-a-half actually," he said. "And I have spatial awareness issues, actually. I can't judge distances and stuff. That's why they wouldn't let me be an airline pilot."

"A pilot? Really?" Nikki said.

"Well, that and all the exams. I mean, what's the point in all that maths anyway? It's not like they have to add up how many miles they go or anything, I expect they've got computers for that."

I looked into the hole, there was no sign of the bucket or Bob's shoe, only a pile of fresh earth.

"Looks like we're down to one toilet until somebody can dig it out again," said Nikki. "Not the end of the world."

"As long as they stay off the Vindaloo," I said.

With still a little time to kill before our scallywags arrived, we headed down to the end of the meadow where Nikki wanted to see the stone circle.

"Looks like an alien landing pad." Bob hobbled up and down as he insisted on still wearing his remaining shoe. "I saw pictures on the internet of the one at Roswell. Looks just like this."

"Looks more like somebody's patio." Nikki crouched and ran her fingers across the stone paving.

"But why here?" I said. "It's a bit of a random place for a patio. There's no house nearby."

"Good view though. You were right, that's the Atlas Mountains over there." Nikki shielded her eyes against the brilliant blue of the sky.

We wandered around a bit more and I spotted a hump in the grass I'd not noticed before. I wanted to have a closer look but time was slipping so we made our way back to the Casa de Pastores.

We sat outside in the sun, enjoying our last peaceful lunchtime drink before the arrival of our scallywags. As it happened, the minibus was late and didn't turn up until nearly three.

"You know this place isn't on any maps?" the driver said as he climbed out of his vehicle. "You Mick Purdey?"

"Michael," I corrected. "I assume this lot are mine?" I nodded to the group of faces staring through the windows of the minibus.

"You're bleeding welcome to 'em," he said. "Done nothing but whinge and moan since Malaga. Too hot, seats uncomfortable, no on-board entertainment consoles. You got your work cut out here, mate." He looked across at Nikki. "Oh, hi, Nick; didn't know you'd copped this gig. Who'd you upset?"

"Apparently the lack of a penis renders me unsuitable for close protection duties so until they need somebody to make the tea I'm stuck here."

"Best place if you ask me. Everybody else's been drafted in to cover a sudden visit by Trump to Dubai. That can't go wrong."

"Oi," a voice called from the bus. "Can we get out now? I'm busting for a piss."

The driver poked his head back in the door. "There's paperwork to do first. If you can't hold on to it for a few minutes I'll come in there and tie a knot in it for you." He handed Nikki a clipboard. "Just sign here and I'll offload 'em and get on my way. Be glad to get back to a war zone after listening to this lot for the last four hours."

The driver refused all offers of refreshment and drove off leaving four slightly confused men standing by the side of the road.

"What time's dinner?" asked a stocky man with a shaven head.

"When you catch it," said Nikki and headed back to the table to finish her beer.

"She serious?" asked the man.

"You should probably count on it," I said. "You are…?"

"Donny," he said.

I looked at the clipboard. "Ah yes, Donny Howard. Taking a motorised conveyance without authority, I guess that's legal speak for Car Thief?"

"You ain't supposed to know that. I thought all that was privileged what-d'ya-call-it?"

"You signed away all your privileged what-d'ya-call-its when you agreed to this fiasco," said a tall man with a haircut that probably cost more than all the clothes I owned. "We all did."

I looked at the man. "Jason Langstaff?"

"Of course," he said. "I assume you're Michael Purdey, the Robin Hood of the SAS and scourge of the wealthy politicians?"

"And your host for the next six months." I turned to the next man, a wiry individual with straggly hair tangled across his shoulders. "Ryan?"

"Everybody calls me Digger," he said.

"Nobody calls you Digger," said Jason.

"And you must be Sean?" I said to the fourth man.

He grunted, shrugged then, "Who's that?" He nodded to Nikki.

"That's Sergeant Brewer, your supervisor."

"But she's a woman?" His accent told of his Dublin heritage.

"Really? I did notice something odd about her but could never work it out," I said. "Do you think I should tell her?"

"Whatever."

"Okay, gentlemen," I said. "If you'd like to follow me, it's just a little hike to the campsite where your thousand star accommodation awaits."

"Thousand star?" asked Donny.

"Yes, from the comfort of your own personal sleeping space you will be able to see at least a thousand stars. No extra cost." I picked up the rucksack of basic supplies and headed off towards the meadow. The others followed after a moment's confusion. Potential rebellion number one over.

The normal twenty minute walk took neared thirty due to

grumbles about sore feet, heavy bags or, 'Nobody told us we had to do a marathon'.

"Here you are." I waved my arm around the field. "Home."

"What's with the piles of scrap wood?" asked Jason.

"They're shelters for you," I said. "I know you're not supposed to have them but we thought it would be better than field shelters."

"I was told there'd be log cabins," said Donny. "Like they have at CenterParcs."

"No, the deal was that I would show you how to build your own field shelter from available wood. But I thought I'd help you and create this instead. All ready for you to move into."

"It's shit."

"Then pick a spot over there somewhere." I pointed at a far corner of the field. "And build your log cabin. Any other complaints?"

"What time's dinner?"

I hoisted my rucksack to the floor. "I've got some sausages and burgers and stuff here, so while you guys are getting settled, we'll get a fire going and start cooking."

"Well, let me know when you're ready to sing Kumbaya, I'm going to find a bar." Jason turned to go.

"Nobody goes anywhere," said Nikki. "You have to stay here. Sorry."

"You can't do that," said Donny. "We've got rights."

Nikki turned to him. "Really? Are you sure?"

Donny looked confused. "What d'ya mean?"

"You all signed a contract and the deal is that you all stay here or you all go back to serve your sentences. Personally, I don't care which it is. If one of you wants to go back, you all go back and that's fine by me, I still get paid." Nikki headed to the fire area and started arranging the firewood.

"Well, I still need a drink," Jason said. "Anybody coming?"

"You can't," said Sean. "I can't go back inside. We've got to stick together."

"He's right, man," said Ryan. "It's cool, just six months then you can go back to counting your hedge funds."

I opened the rucksack and took out a plastic bag. "We all need a drink, here." I pulled cans of San Miguel from the bag and handed them round. It seemed to head off the revolt, at least for the moment.

I left the scallywags sat on the grass and went to help Nikki and Bob with the fire. It probably didn't need three of us to build a campfire but I thought it best to leave the others to it for a while. I gathered a few bits of wood and tossed them on the pile Nikki had arranged. My fire building skills were probably up there with my rabbit catching abilities and I didn't want to take any risks so I took the petrol can we had left over from our chain sawing adventures and doused the kindling. Just to be sure. A botched camp fire barbecue was a good way of losing this lot again.

I collected the sausages, burgers and other random chunks of dead animal and spread them out on the rack Nikki had set up above the fire.

"You should have lit the fire first," Bob said. "It's better to put the meat on a hot fire."

Nikki arrived with a bundle of dry kindling and arranged it at the base of the fire. I took my lighter, lit a cigarette then set light to the kindling.

"Better stand back," I said as I straightened up. "I added a little bit of unleaded to give it a good start."

"Shit," said Nikki. She moved backwards as the flames flickered around the base of the fire.

"What's up?" I asked.

"I added some too. I didn't want to risk a failure to ignite in front of that lot."

We took another step backwards and watched, with a growing sense of trepidation, as Bob continued to back further away from the fire.

"You too?" I asked him.

Bob nodded and we all moved back a bit further.

"Maybe it evaporated," I said, watching the little flames licking at the base of the fire stack. "You never know, it might –"

The whoomph sound was not quite up to the standard of a Taliban IED but not far off. Even at the distance we'd put between ourselves and the explosion, the heat flash was intense and I could smell singed hair. I felt various objects hitting me and brushed at my clothes in case of burning wood. I felt something soft in my fingers and squinted through the retina flash at a piece of mangled sausage.

I heard a voice from the scallywags say, "Cool." Followed by somebody else, it sounded like Donny, shouting, "What time's dinner?" then a general disintegration into giggles.

As my eyes returned to normal, I looked around. Little bits of burning wood lay scattered around the area and the metal grill which had supported the meat was now embedded in the side of one of the shacks, right through a very artistic piece of graffiti depicting a set of highly exaggerated male genitalia.

I looked towards Nikki and Bob. They seemed okay although Bob had a piece of bacon on his shoulder.

"That could have gone better," I said.

***

Casa de Pastores came to the rescue with an impromptu grill

of various meats and spicy potatoes. We sat outside watching the sun smear the last of its glow across the sky and swapped stories about our various encounters with the criminal justice system. I picked pieces of jamon from my vegetarian omelette and allowed myself to relax a bit as, against the odds, the group actually seemed to be gelling.

"So, when Sir Richard poncy-face Claythorne coughed up fifty grand for Van Gogh's 'Beach at Scheveningen' I thought all my Christmases had come at once." Sean Brennan laughed and dipped a piece of chicken in a red sauce.

"But he must have known it was a fake?" Jason said. "I mean the real one must be worth millions."

"To be sure. But these toffs don't care. They want to keep them in a safe somewhere and pretend to their mates they've got the real thing. It's just a slightly more expensive version of the Gucci handbag you buy off the lad in the market. It's all about the bullshit."

"So what happened?" Jason asked.

"The real one turned up in Italy two weeks later and the old bastard wanted his money back."

"And you didn't want to give it back?"

"Couldn't. I lost the lot on a horse. Well, it was called Van Go-Go Gogh and was running the very next day. I mean, I had to, didn't I?"

Everybody laughed and more beers flowed until darkness started to take the sky and I suggested it was best if they sorted their sleeping arrangements out while they could still see. I drove the four scallywags up to the site in the ambulance, it was a bit of a squash but it was only a short drive. The beer and food had calmed the irritability of earlier and they seemed to accept their new lodgings. At least for now.

Bob disappeared to his room as soon as we returned to the

Casa de Pastores so Nikki and I sat outside having a nightcap and watching the stars gradually take over the sky.

"They seem to have calmed down," I said.

"For now," she said. "But don't let your guard down. We have to keep control."

"You're right; we need to keep them busy."

The explosions rattled across the hills in quick succession. I felt the spike in all my senses as my system readied for action but a quick grasp of where I was caught hold before I moved. *Calm. They're only fireworks.* I breathed deeply and took a nonchalant drink of my beer.

"You alright?" Nikki asked. Clearly I hadn't controlled myself as well as I'd thought.

"Bloody fireworks." I fought a cigarette free from the pack. "What is it with the Spanish and their damned bangs?"

I felt her hand cover mine. She took the pack from my struggling fingers and tapped a cigarette free.

"Thanks." I took the cigarette and touched it to the flame she held for me. "Just a bit on edge. That's all."

"I'm not surprised," she said. "It's been a stressful few days getting this all set up."

I studied her face, looking for sarcasm, but she seemed genuine. "Yes, I guess."

She touched my arm and I managed to supress my natural flinch response at the sudden contact. "What've you got planned for them tomorrow?" she asked.

"I thought we'd knock up a couple of field shelters for some photos. You know, keep them happy back home. Make it look like we know what we're doing."

"Good plan. How about catching something to cook as well?"

"You mean a pizza trap?"

"Well, I suppose, although I was thinking more along the lines of trying to shoot down a couple of kebabs but I don't know if they nest in this area." The laugh started in her eyes and spread across her face, bringing a lightness I'd not seen in her before.

"I'll look it up on the internet. There's bound to be a video."

Her hand slid from my forearm to my hand. She gave it a fleeting squeeze before breaking contact and picking up her beer. She raised her glass. "Well, here's to the next six months."

I raised my beer in salute. "To keeping out of trouble and out of jail."

The evening chill started to settle so we finished our drinks.

"It'll be alright," she said as we stood to go back inside. Her eyes danced across my face. "Really."

I purposefully chose to misunderstand. "Depends on the weather."

She gave me the sideways look which said, 'You're not fooling me,' then said, "see you in the morning."

I returned to my room at the Casa de Pastores and searched the internet for ways to trap a wild boar. I figured if I could at least catch one, Bob might be able to cook it and we'd look more like we knew what we were doing. Finder-Spyder failed to find anything about trapping live Andalusian wild boar but came up with lots of ways to trap a rabbit. Becoming rapidly irritated by endless 'Sponsored Results' featuring holidays in Malaga or instructions on how to trap Xylonic Boar Mutants in Game of Warlords I decided the principles of rabbit trapping and boar trapping were probably broadly similar. It would just be a matter of scale. Couldn't be that difficult.

~ *Chapter Eleven* ~

Breakfast over the campfire proved slightly more successful than the previous night's explosive supper, although I had limited the options for disaster by sticking to a pot full of boiled eggs, a couple of baguettes and a marked absence of any fire accelerants.

We gathered around the fire eating and downing large quantities of coffee.

"We need to build some field shelters," I said.

"I thought we were living in these shacks," said Ryan.

"You are, but you're not really supposed to have them and I need to send regular sit-reps back to the UK."

"You want us to mock up some field shelters?"

"Sean can do that," suggested Donny. "He's good at fakes. What d'ya reckon, Sean? Got to be easier than the Mona Lisa?"

"I could probably paint one but I'm not sure about building one," Sean said.

"I watched Bear Grylls once," said Ryan. "He built a shelter out of a parachute and then made a hammock from a tent."

Jason studied Ryan for a moment then said, "Why didn't he just put up the tent as a shelter in the first place?"

"Well, then he wouldn't have had a hammock, would he," said Ryan.

"But he… Oh, never mind."

"I have a couple of tarpaulins," I said. "We just need to construct some 'A' frames and hang them over. It's only for the photos anyway."

"We could actually do it properly," said Nikki.

"What do you mean?" I asked.

"Well, it's not difficult. We have tarpaulins, we have rope, and we have trees."

"We tried that and we had Jabalí run rampage and destroy everything."

"A Jabalí?" Nikki queried.

"It's a sort of cross between a wild pig and a giant orc," said Bob.

"A giant orc?"

"Lord of the Rings," I said. "Big monsters."

"I know what an orc is, I was just curious as to how one happened to be running loose in Andalucía."

"Bob might be exaggerating… a bit, but they are big and destructive things."

"They also taste lovely with a nice garlic and herb dressing," added Bob.

"Bob's a famous chef," I explained. "He taught Gordon Ramsay to cook kebabs and now has his own Michelin starred restaurant."

"Of course, the one where he cooks orc pie for Gandalf. Now, if we can curtail this little flight from reality, we'll rig up the shelter over there in those trees," she pointed to the edge of the woods. "They're solid and straight and well-spaced. Come on."

We stripped tree branches, tied ropes where instructed and pulled tarpaulins taut. Within fifteen minutes we had an array of survival shelters which looked as if they might actually work.

I stood back to admire our handiwork. The tarpaulins were stretched taut on guy lines tensioned between the trees and provided good shelter underneath. The fact they were not connected to the ground made them more resistant to the attentions of rampaging boar.

"Where'd you learn to do that?" I grinned at Nikki.

"Basic training. But I suppose you were playing Pacman at the time?"

"Second Life, actually." I used my smartphone to take lots of pictures of happy projecteers standing by survival shelters. I'd upload those to the blog later - that should keep the Powers happy for a while.

"We don't actually have to sleep under those, do we?" Bob looked concerned.

"Not unless you want to," I said.

My phone rang and the screen told me it was José Martin. "Hola, José," I said.

"The Suzuki is ready for you now. Will you collect it? I need the space."

I arranged to collect it straight after lunch and returned to the group to find them busy planning an exploration of the area.

"You're supposed to stay here." I waved my arms around the field. "It's the deal."

"Nobody will know," said Jason. "They're 2,000 miles away. Who's to say anything?"

I looked at Nikki. "Don't involve me," she said. "I really don't care. As long as none of you die, that would look bad on my CV."

"Well, I suppose as long as we are just reccying our surroundings that should be alright. But we have to stay together." I looked around the group.

"Of course."

"No problem."

"Where would we go?"

"To be sure."

We headed into the woods to the east of the field and followed what looked like a goat track. In the few days we'd had here before the coming of the main group, I'd not really thought about exploring. We'd been too concerned with setting things up. The path drifted through the fir trees then dropped out onto the southern edge into another huge meadow. I calculated this was roughly level with the bottom of our meadow, around where the strange paved circle lay. This position also offered superb views across the Mediterranean with the meadow sloping away gradually until it disappeared below our line of sight.

"What's that over there?" asked Ryan.

I followed his pointing arm to see a ruin of some sort just at the point where the ground sloped away. It looked to be close to where I'd found the circular paving.

"Looks like an old stable or something." I strained at the edges of my distance vision and wondered why I'd not noticed this the previous day.

"Cool, let's go look." He set off across the field before I could argue.

I turned to Nikki for support but she just shrugged and followed the rest. I followed them down the meadow until we came to the remains of a building. Old stone walls meandered across the grassy slope, tracing the outlines of what may have once been rooms or sheds. I realised that this was in a slight dip and not readily apparent from the strange patio.

"Wow, this is awesome," said Ryan. "I'll bet they had conquistadores here or something. Hey, they could've done the inquisition right here that would be so cool."

"It looks like an old farm," I said. I studied the ruins. The walls were very thick, some parts a metre or more but that was probably nothing unusual for stone buildings. The tallest wall stood around two metres high but that was just a corner section, most of the walls were little more than grass covered bumps in the ground.

"Yeah, if a farm had castle walls and a drawbridge."

I looked around the area. "A drawbridge?"

Ryan paused and scanned the site. "There," he said finally. "Look that dip there with the remains of the bridge."

I followed his pointing finger. "It's an old ditch with a log in it."

"Well, of course it is *now*. But back then, a hundred years ago or whatever, back then it was a drawbridge. You can see that."

"I'm not sure I can."

Ryan had no intention of being diverted in his reality drift. "It's a mega place for a castle," he said. "You can see why they put it here. They could defend against the hordes of... invaders from... from..."

"Mordor?" I suggested.

"Yeah, they'd never take this place."

"He's got a point," said Nikki. "It's a great defensive position. You can see all the approaches and even the sea."

"It's only a defensive position if one has something one actually wishes to defend," I said.

"Huh?" Ryan looked at me as if I'd just suggested Father Christmas wasn't real.

"There's nothing here." I waved my arms expansively. "I know most of my military strategic information came from noises outside my tent but I always got the idea that the first requirement of a defensive position is that there generally has to be something worth defending." I looked around the field. "Other than rabbits."

"And dope plants," said Ryan.

"What?" I scanned the area he seemed interested in. It looked like a patch of scrubland with some random wildflowers and weeds. Much like the rest of the field.

"There," he pointed to a large scattering of leafy plants just below one of the ruined walls.

"Are you sure?" I squinted at the plants.

"Of course I'm sure," he protested. "That's why I'm here. I used to have a couple of hundred of those things in my loft in Chingford. That was before the Old Bill decided they wanted them for themselves." His face broke into a huge grin as he studied the plants. "Sort of karmic really, ain't it?"

"We can't leave them here," Jason said. "We get caught with those anywhere near us and we're all back inside. The idiot local police are bound to think we arranged this."

"What do you suggest?" I asked. "They're not ours. We can't just mow them down."

"We've got to destroy them," said Jason. "Set fire to them."

"Good idea," said Ryan. "We could do it a bit at a time, wrapped up in little bits of paper." His eyes scanned the plants. "Might take a while."

"I think we should just forget we ever saw them," I said. "Somebody planted those and they're not going to be too pleased if we mess up their crop. It's all a bit Duelling Banjos up here as it is."

"Chill, man," said Ryan. "Those are straggles. Nobody's farming them. They've been here a long time, may've been cropped once upon a time but these ain't been touched for years."

"Didn't you tell me there'd been a sort of hippy encampment up here at one point?" asked Nikki.

"That's what the breakdown driver told me. Apparently they all went higher up to a Buddhist retreat somewhere up there." I nodded towards the rambling peak of the Mulhacen which stared, always impassively, over our shoulders.

"Then they won't mind if we take a little harvest." Ryan pinched off a couple of leaves and ran them under his nose. "Not bad. Not quite up to my Chingford Delight but not bad for wild growth." He dropped the leaves in his shirt pocket. "I'll give you my professional verdict later." He patted his pocket then resumed his explorations of the ruins.

On closer inspection, the ruins extended further than had first appeared but still resembled nothing more than a tumbledown house with a few sheds.

Sean sat on one of the lower walls and stared out across the falling hills to the sea in the distance.

I settled next to him to take in the view. "Quite stunning, huh?" I said.

"I was just thinking I'd quite like to try painting this," he said.

"That would be good." I stared out across the view. I could see how an artist would find inspiration in something like this and at his heart, I guessed Sean was actually a passionate artist. Maybe there was something in this crazy idea after all. If somebody like Sean, an inveterate conman, could find a new beginning from this fiasco then perhaps it would be worth it.

"I was wondering if I could truly capture the dark soul of these mountains. They're very big."

"Why don't you give it a go?" I said. If we could just get one person to come out of this a reformed character, we might actually pull this off. I could go home with the slate cleaned and old Carrington can have his gong. Happy days.

"I'd have to add some angelic hosts or what do you think? Maybe a tortured face with an arm reaching from the dark clouds? Does that seem more like the job to you?" He turned to look at me as if expecting me to understand what the hell he was talking about.

I looked at the landscape and thought for a moment. "That's not quite how I see it. That seems a bit… heavy?"

Sean patted my shoulder. "That's the show then," he said. "Heavy is good."

"Really?"

"To be sure. El Greco wasn't exactly known for his subtlety."

"El Greco?"

"The artist fella. He was big in these parts around four hundred years ago. Do you know, they were never sure they'd found all his work? Makes you think, doesn't it?"

"Um, yes?"

"What if one of his long lost masterpieces turned up? That'd be a big day wouldn't it, right?"

"I guess."

"That'll be the plan then." Sean stood and patted me on the shoulder. "You're a good kid. You have a sound vision." He wandered off back up through the ruins to join the others.

I sat for a moment and tried replaying the conversation. But no matter which way I twisted it, I couldn't escape the feeling that the art world was shortly going to be presented with a long lost El Greco. If I knew who he was I should probably be worried.

I picked my way back through the ruins and found Nikki hunched in a corner formed by the remains of two vine covered walls.

She looked up as I approached. "Hey, I saw you gave up trying to talk sense into Ryan," she said.

"Yes, I think he's planning a market garden. What you doing?"

She brushed dirt from a lump of rock and handed it to me. "What do you reckon that is?"

"A lump of rock?"

"Philistine, look more closely."

I pushed at the dirt embedded on the rock to reveal some markings. "A lump of rock with some scratches on?"

"It's writing," she said. "Don't know what it says though. You speak Spanish."

I studied the rock, cleaned it on my sleeve then studied it again. "It's not Spanish," I said. "Not quite, probably Latin. I don't do Latin, it's a dead language." The rock was about ten centimetres long, rugged on both ends and slightly rounded on one side. Whatever it was, it had clearly once been part of something bigger. "Probably just says Part A." I handed it back to her.

"Hmm, you're probably right." She dropped the rock back in the corner and straightened. "We need to get back. Haven't you got to take the ambulance back?"

"Oh, hell. I forgot."

**

José Martin greeted me as I slid through the huge double doors of his workshop.

"Hola, Michael."

"Hola, José. You have the Suzuki ready?"

"Yes, all ready, it's out the back. They keys are inside."

"How much do I owe you?"

"Is nothing. You and your magic have brought me much work. More than I can manage, Maria is very happy and a happy Maria makes José Martin a very contented man."

"Are you sure, José?"

"You have paid your account now take José Felipe's car and try not to break it again. Do you want to buy the ambulance? I can make a good price for you."

"No, thank you."

"I have a nice camper van." He insisted on taking me outside to show me his nice camper van.

The huge vehicle dominated the collection of half repaired cars and vans that crowded round his workshop.

"It's certainly big," I said.

The camper van looked more like a chalet bungalow on six wheels. The bodywork showed signs of many repairs with badly matched paint emphasising, rather than concealing, the myriad of dents and fills. The tyres had a dusting of greenery to them that betrayed many years of stagnation and the plastic trims were showing the damage caused by too many Andalusian summers. An old satellite dish hung at a crazy angle from the roof and a collection of wires draped from various points of ingress to the inside.

"Where did you get that? It's a monster," I said.

"One of the old hippy communes down by the river," he said. "The police asked me to collect it as it had been abandoned for many years. They have nowhere to put it so they say I can have it to sell."

"Well, I appreciate the offer but I'm quite comfortable in the Casa de Pastores."

"But with this you can travel the world in comfort and luxury. Look, he has a place to keep a table and chairs." He opened a hinged panel on the side of the vehicle to expose a small compartment containing a picnic table and two foldaway chairs. The hinged panel fell from its hinges and clattered to the floor at José's feet. "I will fix that for you," he added.

"No, you won't. I don't want it."

"I will keep it for you until you've decided."

I took the Suzuki and drove carefully back to the hotel and parked it outside. The others were gathered around a large table under the shade of a huge San Miguel umbrella.

"He did a good job." Nikki studied the roof. "Where did the tree land? I can't see where the dent was at all."

"It caved in a huge dip all over here." I ran my fingers across the centre of the roof. I couldn't detect any sign of the damage.

"Are you supposed to give it back to him now?" She indicated José Felipe who was approaching with a tray of beers. "I thought we weren't supposed to have a vehicle?"

"José," I said. "José Martin has finished the repairs to the Suzuki. Do you need it back?"

"No, I have no need of it at this time. You keep it for now. Just don't break it again or I will make you buy it."

"Okay, I promise."

"You're not supposed to have a car," Donny complained. "They told us that. They said no modern stuff. Like Hamish."

"Hamish?"

"Yeah, you know; the guys with the beards and pony carts. They're not allowed iPhones and stuff."

"You mean Amish," I said.

"Yeah, him too. Anyway, how come you get a car and we don't?"

"Because… I don't know…" I thought for a moment and still failed to come up with a reasonable explanation. "Because I've got one and you haven't. How's that?"

"That's not fair."

"Life isn't fair. If it was, I'd be supping Margaritas on a beach somewhere while that supercilious, inbred, Benefits Minister, Stephen Look-How-Rich-I-am Lethbridge, has to sleep in a field and squat over a hole in the ground each morning."

"But you're not exactly –" Nikki started before I cut her off.

"Don't undermine my sense of self pity. You know what I mean." I turned my gaze to Donny. "And don't you go getting any ideas about nicking one either."

"I don't nick cars." Donny looked offended.

I studied him to see if he was trying to wind me up. "Then why are you here? Only the piece of paper I have says you were facing a two year stretch for car thieving."

"That's just how they call it," Donny said. "Makes me sound like some cokehead who nicks your auntie's Fiat just to do a few donuts round the Southbeck Estate before totalling it up against tree. Tossers. I'm a Facilitator of 'igh-end motors for the discerning client."

"Huh?" I said.

"He steals posh cars to order," Nikki translated.

"I like to think of it as redistribution of assets for enhanced usage," he said.

"Enhanced usage?" I set my empty beer glass down and tried to catch José's eye.

"Yeah. These rich bankers…" He looked at Jason. "Present company excluded, of course, Jase..."

Jason raised his glass and nodded. "Accepted. And it's Jason."

"Yeah. Well," Donny continued. "These wanker-banker people they get their bonuses and you know what they do with them?" He looked around the table.

"Please tell," said Jason.

"I'll tell you what they do with them. They go and buy themselves a limited edition Lamborghini for 250k then cover it in bubble wrap and hide it in an air-conditioned garage where nobody will ever see it. That's what they do." He emptied his glass as he saw José approach and waved it towards him. "That ain't no way to treat a motor like that. I mean, they're designed to be driven, not hidden away like your dad's porn collection."

"So you steal it?" I asked. "How does that help?"

"Because when a punter contracts somebody like me to break one of these beauties free, he only pays a fraction of the value. See?"

"No." I took my replacement glass and nodded my thanks to José.

Donny shook his head in frustration. "Look, you pay quarter of a mil for a motor and you don't want to be parking it outside Tesco's while the missus does her weekly, do you? But if you only pay ten percent of that, well, you don't mind risking a few dinks and dents. Ipso facto, the Lamborghini gets used for what it's meant for. Banker gets his insurance money, my client gets to drive a nice motor and the guy what built it, he gets the satisfaction of knowing somebody's actually getting some fun from it and not just using it as an ornament to impress the totty."

A tapas of squid rings arrived and I pushed the plate away from my end of the table.

I looked at Nikki. "We need to be thinking about getting back to the meadow. I want to set up a boar trap for the photos before we lose the light. You lot want a lift or are you walking?"

We all somehow managed to squash into the Suzuki and we trundled up the hill and across the track to the meadow.

"Boar trap?" Nikki asked as we plopped out of the vehicle like a circus clown convention.

"Yes, I looked up how to make one on the internet."

"We're going to make a boar trap following directions from the internet? This can't go wrong."

"Well, in truth, it's just a sort of upscaled rabbit trap but the principles must be the same. It's only for the photos anyway."

The site we selected for our boar trap was just at the edge of the woods and chosen more for its photogenic properties than any evidence of boar. In the absence of wire for the noose arrangement we used a length of old rope I'd borrowed from Fernando's lockup. I reasoned it would show up better on the photos. A couple of hastily fashioned stakes to hold the rope in place and with the end of the rope firmly attached to a nearby tree, we had the trap ready to go within an hour.

"What about bait?" asked Nikki.

"Bait?" I repeated. "Ah, yes. Forgot about bait. It suggested carrots on the internet."

"But that was for rabbits. Unless you're planning on catching a two hundred pound rabbit in this thing, I don't think carrots are going to work."

"What do boars eat anyway?" I looked round the group. "Anybody?"

"Apples," said Bob.

I thought about apples for a moment. "Are you sure? Only that seems an odd choice for Andalusian wildlife, I don't even think apples are native here. Why do you say apples?"

"Because when I saw José first cook a boar, it still had an apple in its mouth when he put it in the oven. Poor little bugger never had a chance to eat it."

"How about some pork sausages?" suggested Ryan. "We've

got some we never got round to cooking last night, on account of the exploding campfire and all that."

"That seems slightly cannibalistic," I said. "Feeding pork sausages to a wild pig. Haven't we got anything else?"

"There's some bacon," offered Ryan.

"What are you worried about?" asked Nikki. "It's not as if we're actually trying to catch one, it's all just for show."

Against my slightly battered vegetarian principles, we laid the trap with the remains of the exploded sausages and took lots of photographs. When we'd done, Donny fired up the campfire and we set about lightening the load on the beer supplies. Bob skewered chunks of lamb onto some wooden skewers he'd fashioned and handed them round. I declined the meat but we had a good supply of vegetables so I found some cobs of sweetcorn and peppers which should survive being skewered and grilled. As the sky gradually darkened, we tucked into our improvised supper but an hour later there was still a significant quantity of meat and vegetables left. It had been a long time since I'd bought food for more than one, especially meat, so my judgement as to quantities was somewhat flawed. As we had no refrigeration in the field, I guessed the meat would be past its best by the next day so we packed it in a carrier bag and left it just outside one of the sheds. We didn't want it inside attracting crawlies and wrigglers. The beer however, I had badly misjudged and by eight o'clock, we were on our last few cans. I caught the flash of a cigarette lighter and smelt the sweet fumes of cannabis smoke.

I glanced over at Ryan. "What are you doing? Where did you get that?"

Ryan drew deeply on the joint. "So many questions. It's a joint and rather a good one. I'll be sharing it shortly, or thereabouts. It would be a shame not to, as it's rather good. But I think I said that already. Er... sorry, what was the other question?"

"Where did you get it?"

"Ah, yes. I remember now. Ummm..." He raised his arm in an oddly foppish manner and scanned the darkening field. "About..." His arm found its target and he pointed off into the distance. "Over there. I think."

"That's not your first of the day, is it?"

"No, but it *is* my duty, which I take with great... erm... seriousness... osity... to sample the product of our little smallholding over yonder ways." He pointed again. "Which I did, at great self sacrifice to myself, and I found it to be good." He took another deep breath then passed the joint to Bob.

"The plants growing by that old ruin?" I asked. "I thought you only took a single leaf? For professional evaluation, you said."

"Ah, he comes on the wind and like a whisper in the very breath of the trees he snatches the... the... has anybody got any Marmite sandwiches? I really have a need for a Marmite sandwich."

"I can do Marmite sandwiches," said Bob, through a cloud of grey smoke. "I have three Michelin stars."

"That's very cool." Ryan stared up at the sky as if trying to find Bob's Michelin stars. "I got a star for the twenty-five yard breast stroke."

"How come you've got Michelin stars?" Jason asked. "They're only awarded to the world's top restaurants."

"It's for my culinary..." He took another draw on the joint and looked at it in a slightly puzzled way as if wondering where it had come from. "My... culinary exquisiteness in my premier destination restaurant, Bob's Burger Bar."

"Bob's Pie Shop," I corrected.

"Are you sure?"

"Quite sure, I built the website for it, remember?"

"Ah, there we go then. Bob's Pie Shop."

"But that's fraud," said Jason. "You can't just go awarding yourself Michelin stars. That undermines the whole ethos."

We all stared at Jason for a moment then finally Donny said, "Fraud? Ain't you 'ere for fiddling with the LIBOR rates and nearly bringing down Webley's Bank?"

"Whilst I accept the apparent irony of the situation, it's not quite the same," Jason said. "Firstly, I was set up by the board of Webley's –"

Derisive laughter rippled round the group.

"Like the way the Old Bill planted all that grass in the back of my car while I weren't looking?" said Ryan.

"You must have been not looking for a very long time," said Nikki. "Your court papers show there was ten kilos of the stuff."

"See, they've got it in for me. Anyway, there was supposed to be twelve kilos," Ryan said. "Thieving gits."

"But I really was set up," Jason protested. "I was just a mere functionary, acting on policies decided at board level. It's a conspiracy that goes to the top of government."

"Like the moon landings," said Bob. "That's another conspiracy. So we'd never know about the alien base on the moon."

I studied Bob for a moment then somebody else rolled a second joint and I excused myself from the group. It looked like becoming an all-night session and I had no desire to get that stoned. Not in front of other people anyway.

"I'll see you all in the morning," I said. "We need to build a bit more stuff for the photos."

"I'll come back with you," said Nikki.

We drove slowly back to the hotel, carefully avoiding potholes, boulders and goblins.

"Shouldn't you be stopping them doing stuff like that?" I asked Nikki as I negotiated a hairpin bend in the track.

"What? Smoking pot? That's not my problem, I'm just here in a watchful capacity, making sure they don't go AWOL. Nobody said anything about keeping them on the straight and narrow. Isn't it your job to be the upstanding example of goodliness?"

"I'm not quite sure what my job is anymore." I pulled the car up outside the Casa de Pastores. "I can't teach them much about survival and I don't think they'd listen even if I could."

We sat at an outside table to enjoy a last drink before bed. The full moon cast its light with such brilliance that I could even read the lunchtime menu board. 'Bob's Special Fried Egg Kebabs and Baked Beans'. I toyed with that mental image for a moment.

The searchlight raked the area and I was caught full in its beam as it passed over me. I froze, waiting for the shots. They never came. I was sitting outside the Casa de Pastores not in a ditch outside Mosul. It was just a passing car. Get a grip.

I felt Nikki's hand on mine. "You alright?" she asked.

"Yes, why?" Instinctively, I jerked my hand free and fought a cigarette from its pack. "Why do you ask?"

"It's okay to talk, you know." She took my hand again, this time I let her.

My free hand snapped the lighter and brought it to the cigarette with perfect stability. "About what?"

"I don't know; anything you like." She took a sip from the beer José had just set down for her. "The best film you ever saw? Who was your first girlfriend? What happened to you in Iraq?"

I laid the cigarette in the ashtray and sank half the beer. "Groundhog Day, Jennifer Ansil and nothing."

"Nothing?"

"Nothing at all. Mostly sitting in the back of a truck in the desert staring at a computer screen."

Her hand felt warm against the cooling evening. I realised my eyes had been locked on the table and I looked up. Nikki smiled as I caught her gaze and her hand gave a slight squeeze. I felt my breathing shorten and my thoughts bounced, refusing any focus I tried to bring. I pulled my hand free and stood.

"I need to write up the blog." I finished the beer and replaced the empty glass on the table. "They'll only start stressing back in England if I miss a day."

Nikki finished her beer in as swift a movement as I had ever seen from even the hardest drinking troopers. "I'll give you a hand."

"How's your typing speed?" I asked.

"About three words a minute but I am very good at making up crap."

***

I set my laptop on the pine dressing table, plugged in my phone and transferred the day's pictures.

Nikki sat on the bed. "How come you get a king-sized bed and I get an ancient metal framed divan?"

"I thought Paras were supposed to be hard," I said. "Besides, it's my genius keeping us here in the first place."

I tried to log on to the blog website but the connection timed out. I did a speed test and the results indicated it would be faster to tie a roll of film to a donkey's tail and have it dropped by Boot's for developing on the way to Bristol.

"Internet's turned to sludge," I said. "Must be something big on the Expat streaming channels. Probably the finals of Celebrity Pogo Stick Challenge or something. I'll do it later."

"Probably just as well," she said. "Dope and beer are not really the best creative ingredients for a report to the Department of Justice." She stood to go. "I'll catch you in the morning."

I suddenly realised I wanted her to stay a while longer. I stood and said, "We could always watch TV until the internet clears up a bit. I've got a bottle of gin somewhere." I glanced around the gentle chaos of my room.

She tipped her head slightly as if puzzled. Her eyes held mine momentarily. "You should get some rest," she said. "You've had a lot on your plate these last few days. Besides, you can always catch Celebrity Pogo Stick on iPlayer tomorrow." She touched my shoulder briefly before slipping through the door.

I took a shower, found the bottle of gin in my sock drawer and tried the internet once more. Not good but accessible.

Day Seven

Today we set up some field shelters. The pictures show our group by one of the shelters. The team felt really positive about the experience of living out among the trees and stars. In the afternoon we explored our area a little and came across some ruins which may once have been a fortification of some kind. Sean is thinking about taking up landscape painting and we laid a trap to see if we can catch one of the wild boars which inhabit the area. You can see in the pictures that is a version of the standard snare trap. Easy to construct and highly versatile.

~ *C h a p t e r   T w e l v e* ~

Wednesday brought blue skies, the promise of more heat and Bob's Big Breakfast. Nikki and I emerged blinking into the bright light like a pair of moles. The rest of the group sat at a large table and were enthusiastically tackling the piles of bacon, eggs, sausages, hash browns and other random breakfast items.

We sat down and I poured coffee for us both and helped myself to some eggs, mushrooms and hash browns.

The group were looking somewhat subdued and I guessed it was due in no small part to the effects of the previous night's impromptu party.

"Sleep well?" I asked nobody in particular.

A few mumbles greeted my enquiry then Donny said, "Not easy to sleep when you've got a troll tied up outside, bellowing its lungs out all night."

"Huh?" I looked up from my breakfast.

"It's not a troll," Ryan said. "I've seen trolls before. This is more like Cerberus. Only with one head. And not quite so dog-like."

"So, nothing at all like Cerberus," said Jason.

I refilled my coffee cup. "Sorry, I seem to be missing something. What's going on?"

"It's your trap," said Sean. "You've gone and caught yourself some sort of creature in it."

"Creature? What sort of creature?"

"How would I know? It was dark," said Sean. "What kind of eejit goes poking around in the dark for wild animals? Not me, that's for sure, my mammy never brought up no eejits. It made a right hullabaloo all night though, that much I know."

I took a moment to process this information. "The trap? You mean it actually caught something?"

"It's probably a boar," said Bob from around a forkful of beans.

"Probably a boar?" I queried. "Nobody bothered to check?"

"It's your trap," said Donny. "I ain't going nowhere near it." He speared a sausage from the central dish and dropped it on his plate. "Evil things, trolls. They should fly me home 'cause I'm sure it's against my human rights or something. Having to put up with trolls, nobody said nothing about no trolls."

Nikki looked at me. "Sounds like you've caught yourself a wild boar," she said.

"In my rabbit trap." I drained my coffee cup. "I think I need to investigate. Anybody coming?"

Bob grabbed a sausage and bit the end off as he stood. "I'll come. Saves walking."

Nikki joined us and we drove up to the field.

Everything appeared calm and normal as we approached. I drove slowly round the shacks until we had a good view of the tree line where we'd laid the trap. Still no sign of movement, much less a rampaging troll. I eased the Suzuki closer, turned one-eighty and reversed gently back. If I needed to get away quickly I'd rather be going forwards. I stopped about twenty metres from the tree line and scanned the area before getting out.

We walked quietly forwards until I could see the place

where we'd laid the trap. A huge creature lay on the ground at the bottom of a tree. It was certainly more boar-like than troll-like, but only just. It seemed to be asleep. The ground surrounding the tree had been churned up in a near perfect circle, so I guessed the thing was still attached to the rope and the scuffed grass marked the limits of its range.

I took another step forwards and a twig cracked under my foot. My Basic Training instructor would have been so proud. The creature lifted its head and snuffled at the air. I froze. I wondered briefly if this was the same creature with whom I'd had my evening encounter the other night but then I figured they all looked the same.

The boar sprang into life with a speed I'd only ever seen in cats before. One second it seemed to be in a state of semi-dozing stupor, the next, I had a hundred kilos of ferocity straining and snarling at the end of its rope, inches from my face. The forward momentum it was developing lifted its forelegs off the ground as it strained at the rope's limit. We were virtually eye to eye. I stepped back with a start and stumbled in a pothole. I felt arms grab me.

"Quick," said Nikki. "I don't know how long that rope will hold."

I scrambled to my feet and we ran back towards the car. The beast had not followed so Nikki and I resisted the temptation to dive into the car after Bob. It wouldn't have been possible anyway, I realised, as he'd locked the doors behind him.

"Why's it not coming?" I asked.

"I think the rope is still holding," Nikki said. "I don't know why, it wasn't very thick."

We watched as the animal strained a semi-circle at the limit of the rope then settled under the tree once more with a loud exhalation which sounded rather like a sulky huff.

"What now?" Nikki asked.

"I don't know," I confessed. "We should let it go but firstly, how do we get close enough to cut the rope? And secondly, how do we stop it chasing us once it's loose?"

"Or we could kill it and take it back to José for a barbecue," Bob suggested through a gap in the window.

"Off you go then," I said. "We'll watch from here."

"I wasn't saying me. I was just suggesting. You know, thought experiments. You guys are the survival experts."

I glared at him and contemplated explaining once again my complete lack of foraging and hunting skills but instead I shook my head and made my way cautiously back to the boar.

This time it greeted my approach with a sort of bored nonchalance, barely opening one eye to glance in my direction.

"Looks like it's calmed down a bit," Nikki said. "Can we get close enough to cut the rope?"

"It's just a ploy. We get close and it will pounce."

Nikki smiled. "So, you've gone from knowing sod-all about these things to being a porcine expert in five minutes flat?"

"I had a Guinea Pig once. That was an evil little bugger, nipped my nose when I tried to stroke it. This is just a supersized version."

"I'll mind my nose then," said Nikki. "What if one of us keeps its attention while the other sneaks behind and cuts the rope?"

"That's probably not going to end well for whichever one of us is in front," I said. "As soon as it's free it's going to eat whatever is standing in front of it."

"This is a boar, you know. It's not Godzilla."

"You didn't see what it did to our first camp."

I studied the boar and surroundings. What we needed was something to tempt it to run away from us. I had an idea and motioned for Bob to come and join us. He took a bit of persuading to exit the relative security of the Suzuki but eventually he came over to us.

"Do we have any more of that bacon?" I asked him.

"There's some in the kitchen shack." He ran off to find it, relieved at the chance to put distance between him and the animal.

As he returned, the boar lifted its head and snuffled at the air in Bob's direction.

"What are you up to?" Nikki shuffled back a little from the boar's sudden interest in the proceedings.

"Here's the plan," I said. "I go behind, you keep the boar interested here and then Bob waves the meat. Once it's focused on Bob, you run round the back here and I cut the rope. The thing will then chase Bob, he throws the meat and jumps in the car and brings it back to us while the boar is finding the meat."

"Sounds insane," she said.

"I know. Let's get on with it before this breaks free and eats us anyway."

The plan went well until the point at which the boar decided it wasn't going to wait for me to cut the rope. Nikki did her coaxing until Bob had its attention then just before I made my move, the boar lunged towards Bob and the rope broke at the tree.

Bob squealed and ran towards the car clutching the bacon. The boar thundered across the ground towards him.

I yelled at Bob to throw the meat and get in the car.

He stopped briefly to look at me and then at the boar which was rapidly closing on him.

"Bob!" I yelled. "Throw meat. Get in car!"

He stared at me momentarily, threw the meat in through the

open rear door of the Suzuki and continued running across the field to who knows where.

"Or that's another option," I said as Nikki slid up to my side to watch the drama.

The boar gave barely a glance at Bob. With the scent of the now pungent smelling bacon driving its senses, it leapt straight into the back of the Suzuki which creaked and rocked under the sudden invasion of a hundred kilos of furious animal.

"I don't remember that being quite how you planned it," Nikki said.

"Told you I was no good at planning. We'd better do something before it eats the bacon and starts looking for something more substantial."

I motioned for Nikki to go round the front of the vehicle to draw its attention while I ran up behind and slammed the back door. For a moment the boar seemed bemused then after an explosive attack on the door and rear seats, it settled down to chew on the bacon.

Bob appeared as if out of the ground and looked at the Suzuki. "That worked out well," he said.

"You think?" I said. "I was rather hoping it would be the other way round. You know, us in the car and the boar outside."

"Oh, you should have said."

"How are we going to get it out?" asked Nikki. "It can't stay there."

"José Felipe's going to be pissed," I said.

"What's happening?" a voice called.

I turned to see the others approaching.

"Just been doing a bit of boar trapping." I pointed at the vehicle. "It's in there; you guys can take it from here."

They studied the now docile boar which filled the back of the little 4X4.

"No, you're on your own with that one," said Donny. "I prefer my bacon between two slices of bread with a good dollop of ketchup."

"You can't leave it in there," said Ryan. "It's cruel, apart from anything."

I peered through the car window. The boar seemed contented after its meal and didn't even bother to lift its head as I observed it.

"I'm going to try to drive it somewhere remote and let it go," I said. "I don't think it can get over the back seats. I hope."

"I'll come with you," said Nikki.

"No, that's probably not wise. It's easier for one person to get out of the car in an emergency than two."

I entered the Suzuki as gently as I could but the boar didn't stir and seemed content in its post-breakfast snooze. The quicker I could do this the better.

As I bounced the vehicle over the field I heard a grumbly snort from the back but I just carried on. If the boar took to explosive activity I was just going to hit the brakes and dive out but until that point, I'd keep going.

Once I'd hit what passed for maintained road in the Alpujarras, the going became smoother and the noises stopped. I drove about ten kilometres along the twisty mountainous tracks until I found a gravel cut into a pine forest and pulled over. The boar stirred but didn't seem in a particularly violent mood. I slipped out of the car and walked round to the back door before I realised I didn't have a plan for this part of the operation. I stared at the door then looked at my passenger. If I just opened the door, the boar might just climb out and run away, on the other hand, it might decide to eat me. As long as I positioned myself behind the door when I swung it open, I should have enough time to jump back into the front before the thing could turn around and come after me. In theory. I wasn't totally convinced.

I reached for the door handle at arm's length and eased the catch open. The beast didn't move. Okay, so far, so good. I contorted my body so my feet were shuffling closer to the driver's open door as my outstretched fingers tugged at the rear door handle. It swung open and I dived into the front seat, slamming the door behind me.

I waited for the explosion of a hundred kilos of enraged fury but it never came. The boar seemed unconcerned with the open door and continued to snooze in the back. That wasn't quite what I'd anticipated. I had mentally played through several possible scenarios, including wrestling with the creature in a frenzied attack but I hadn't figured on the thing refusing to get out of the car. I shouted, I banged the doors and I sounded the horn but the boar seemed singularly unimpressed and continued to doze. In fact, it was only when I did my best Basil Fawlty impersonation and beat the back door with a branch that it even bothered to open one eye. Although even then, it only looked briefly up at me before settling back down.

I tried driving up a steep hill with the back door open in the hope it might fall out and I reversed quickly into an emergency stop but still nothing. I sounded the horn, revved the engine and span circles as quickly as the little vehicle allowed, all to no avail. Eventually, I gave up and headed back with the creature still firmly ensconced in the back.

Nikki gazed into the back of the car when I pulled up. "Did you forget to put the boar out?" she asked, with a mischievous smile dancing on her face.

"Ha ha," I said.

Bob sidled up and started when the boar raised its head to

stare back at him. "I thought you were taking it up to the woods?" he queried.

"I did," I said. "And we had so much fun that we're thinking about going again tomorrow."

"Huh?"

"It wouldn't get out of the car," I said.

"It'll come out when it's hungry," Nikki said. "Don't worry."

"Well that's not likely to happen for some time as we've just given it probably the best meal it's had in months." I tapped the window to see if I could rouse any interest from my passenger.

"What ya doin'?" Donny asked as he arrived by the car.

"It won't get out." I pointed at the boar.

"Bummer. Happened to me once."

I stared at him.

"I nicked a Porsche Cayenne with a baby in the back once," he explained. "Didn't realise it was there till I stopped at South Mimms for petrol. I thought the squealing noise 'ad just been dusty brakes."

"What did you do with it?" Nikki asked.

"Sold it to a Russian property speculator."

"You sold the baby?" Bob looked horrified.

"What? No! The Cayenne I sold, not the baby. Dropped that off at the late night chemist's shop in Hemel Hempstead. I'm not a monster."

"You're all heart, you are," said Nikki.

"Have you tried poking it with a stick?" suggested Bob.

I looked at him to see if he was being serious. He appeared to be so I picked up a twig from the ground and handed it to him. "Here, have fun. I'm going for a drink." I looked at Nikki. "Fancy a pre-lunch cocktail?"

"She checked her watch. "Bit early, isn't it?"

"Only if one is planning on staying sober for the rest of the day."

***

We wandered slowly from the meadow and down the track. A touch too slowly, almost as if Nikki was purposefully prolonging my journey to the bar.

I pondered the morning's antics as we walked and decided that I actually felt an odd kind of empathy with the boar, despite the aggravation it had put me through. It was the king of this domain and I guessed it had no natural predators here. Just man. And now it was sat in the back of the little 4X4, completely out of its familiar environment, not quite sure how it had got there but absolutely determined not to be moved. I remembered feeling something similar in Iraq. The claustrophobic and hellishly hot trucks in which I spent most of my time there. Strangely isolated from the chaos outside but knowing that if the shit hit the fan, then my only protection was a quarter inch of steel plate. My breathing tightened.

"You seem a bit on edge today?" Nikki's question caught me on the hop.

"What? Oh, no. Just wondering what we do with the boar."

Nikki said something in reply but I didn't hear her words. The sound of the gunfire demanded my full attention. Two shots in rapid succession. Double-tap, the technique favoured by the Regiment in close environs.

"Get down," I yelled as I rolled into a small cut by the side of the track. My ears strained, listening for clues to the location of the shooters.

I felt a hand touch my shoulder. I squashed lower. "Stay

down," I yelled. "Can you see them? Where are they? Bastards."

Two more shots, with a greater interval between them this time. That was wrong. The timing was wrong and the sound was wrong. Those weren't MP5 rounds. Who was out there?

The hand on my shoulder moved. Stroking. I tried to ignore it and strained at the restricted view I had from my position. Just trees, they could be anywhere.

"Michael? Michael?" Nikki's voice. "It's okay. It's just shotguns, double barrelled by the sound of it. Probably farmers or hunters."

My eyes danced, refusing to focus on anything. The trees seemed to fill my field of vision. I held my hands over my eyes hoping that a moment of darkness would reset them.

Nikki's hand seemed to spread across my back and I heard her speaking but her words muddled with the sound of gunfire, faint shouts from my comrades and swished with white noise. I drew my hands away from my face and the field came into view. A large meadow, lined with fir trees some distance away.

"You okay?" Nikki's hand squeezed at my upper arm and I turned to look up at her.

"Yes," I said. "I thought it was… I must have tripped."

"Yes. You need to watch where you're going," she said.

"You heard the gunfire?" I asked. "It was real, right?"

"Of course I did. I'm not deaf! Hunters out with shotguns more than like. I think I heard dogs as well. You okay? Not sprained anything?"

"No." I straightened up and fought my pockets for my cigarette packet. I stared back the way we'd come. "Hunters, huh?"

I dragged a cigarette out of the pack and fumbled for my lighter. Nikki stayed silent and just watched me. The lighter took a couple of goes to ignite then for some reason I couldn't get the cigarette and lighter to connect with each other. Nikki's hand covered mine and steadied it until my cigarette caught. I drew deeply and waited for her to say something. She didn't. She simply kept looking at me like I'd just thrown up over her cat.

"They sound like they're up at the camp," I said, dispelling the awkward silence. "Think we should check?"

"I thought you were on a beer mission?"

I glanced in the direction of the bar then back towards the camp. "I don't suppose they're near the camp," I reasoned. "Even here they wouldn't shoot where there's people about."

"So, we're still on for the beer then?"

"Guess so."

* * *

José Felipe had the beers ready as soon as we sat down. He must have seen us coming.

"Feeling better?" Nikki asked as she watched me demolish the beer.

"What? Oh, it's the heat I guess. Still getting used to it."

"Of course. And on a totally separate subject, did you have a full discharge medical when you left?"

I picked the glass up and studied it. "Yes, well sort of. We came to an understanding."

"An understanding?"

I finished the beer and scanned the bar area for José Felipe. "That they'd stop dicking around inside my head and I wouldn't trash their office. Where's José got to? It can't be siesta time already."

"That was a very adult response." She waved her hand and

annoyingly, José Felipe immediately appeared. He left a plate of various cheeses on bread and took my glass for a refill.

"I wasn't feeling very grown up at the time," I said. "It was just after the fiasco at Masad and they were looking for a sacrificial lamb."

"And you figured they were looking at you?" She studied a piece of cheese and dipped it in a drop of olive oil before popping it in her mouth.

"I wasn't going to give them the chance. I was the outsider, the obvious choice." José Felipe placed another beer in front of me and I put my hands around it, feeling the chill of the glass penetrate my hands. "They just wanted to stick me with a nice tidy psychiatric label, close the file and then they could all carry on as usual." I took a very measured sip of the beer and returned the glass to the table. I ensured it was positioned equidistant between two of the wooden slats which made up the table. For some reason that seemed terribly important.

Nikki watched me and settled back in her seat. "You do realise that Blacklance Security is headed up by some quite senior ex-service personnel, including a captain from your regiment?"

I wasn't sure what she was driving at. Most of these private security contractors were ex-services. "So?" I said and dragged another cigarette from the packet.

"So, when I knew who was running this, I asked him to have a look into your background."

"I see." I lit the cigarette with no trouble this time and pulled the smoke deep into my lungs. "And what did you find out? That I'm a certified nutjob who conned his way into the Regiment for a five quid bet and ended up getting half his unit blown up?"

"You think that's what your file says?"

"Why else would they want me labelled, bagged and tucked away in some secure unit out on Dartmoor?"

"You don't know that's what they were planning on doing."

I pushed the beer away and stood. "I should get back; Donny's probably sold the Suzuki by now."

Nikki reached across and took my forearm. Her grip was surprisingly strong. "Finish your beer first."

I hesitated and looked to the mountains for help. They remained as sane and stable as ever. I slumped back in my seat. "I should never have been there. If I hadn't wormed my way in over some stupid bet Jimmy Langdon wouldn't be riding a wheelchair right now and Bodger Blackstone would still have both arms." I emptied the beer glass. "This stuff isn't working today. Fancy a gin?"

"No thanks. I'll stick with beer. It's still a bit early for me."

I attracted José's attention and pointed at the gin bottles arranged behind the bar. He took the message.

"You do know that the Regiment knew who you were and what you were doing right from the start, don't you?" Nikki said.

Her words came from nowhere, like a sniper's bullet. "Of course they didn't. Otherwise they have locked me up from the off."

"Sorry, we are talking about the same SAS here, aren't we? The elite fighting regiment run by some of the best strategists in the business and with access to the world's top military intelligence sources? That SAS?"

I fidgeted with the empty glass. "What are you saying?"

"I'm saying that they knew exactly who you were, what you were up to and what you could do. And that they wanted your particular skills. I'm saying that your expertise in hacking the guidance systems of ISIS drones while in flight saved countless lives." She picked up the glass in front of her, drank it down and placed it back on the table exactly on the damp ring it had just left. She leaned forwards. "That's what I'm saying."

My brain rattled through snippets and details that had niggled for years. Those little bits that had never quite made sense. "That's ridiculous. Where did you get that idea?"

She ignored my question and continued with her prepared piece. "You need to stop beating yourself up over one drone that got through. Nobody was ever going to stop them all. Not even you. Just be thankful you at least caused that one to come down short and it wasn't a direct hit."

José Felipe placed a gin and tonic in front of me and another beer in front of Nikki. I stared at the glasses, trying to process the information she'd given me.

I drew a breath to speak but Nikki cut across me.

"I know it's shit that your mates got injured. Believe me, I know about that one. But they're alive and that's down to you." She pushed at my gin glass. "Now, drink your gin and let's go see if Bob's managed to persuade your pig to get out of the 4X4."

Her smile disarmed my readied argument.

***

Bob came over to see us when we arrived back in the field.

"No luck getting it out then?" I said when he came within earshot. I nodded towards the Suzuki where the boar lay fast asleep in the back.

"I tried to tempt it with a bag of oranges," Bob said. "But it just ate them all and went to sleep."

"I think we're probably feeding it too well," said Nikki. "It's never going to leave if you keep giving it sausages and fresh fruit."

"We'll just have to leave it there," I said. "It will get out at some point. It has to." I looked at Bob. "No more food. We're going to have to starve it out."

"Where are the others?" Nikki asked.

"Ah, you noticed." Bob gave a little shuffle with his feet, betraying his desire to be somewhere else. "Jason went… um…" Bob looked around the field as if hoping to spot Jason. "Um… I don't know. I think he said he needed a car."

"He's not allowed a car," I said. "That breaches the conditions. He'll get us closed down. What about the others? Where did they go?"

"They didn't go for a car."

"Well? Where *did* they go?"

Bob shuffled a bit more. "They went with Ryan."

Nikki turned to face Bob. "So, where did Ryan go, Bob?"

Bob looked around the field once more then pointed in the direction of the village. "That way."

Nikki moved closer to Bob until they were facing each other no more than inches apart. "Why?"

"I don't –" Bob started.

Nikki gave a low growl which oddly, resembled a noise I'd once heard as a child when a huge dog had taken my hotdog at a local fair and I'd attempted to retrieve it.

Bob flinched backwards. "He might have had a plastic bag with him..." His eyes scanned Nikki's face for signs of softening. None came. "I think he'd been doing something down there." Bob pointed down the field to where the dope plants grew. "I think. He didn't tell me. If he'd told me, I'd have stopped him. But he didn't."

I looked at Nikki. "He's gone off to sell some of the hash plants."

"You don't know that," she said.

"Seriously? His one skill in life is growing dope plants and we left him alone to mind them. Not only will they shut us down but they'll stick another lot of charges on us all for conspiracy to supply or something. Nobody's going to believe I was stupid enough to leave a dope dealer in charge of a dope field. They'll probably think it was all my idea."

Nikki touched my arm. "Calm down. We'll go find him before he has chance to sell them. Nobody will know."

"How long ago did they go?" I asked Bob.

He looked at his watch. "About an hour. More or less."

"We can take the 4X4," Nikki said. "They can't have got very far. Not on foot."

I stared at the 4X4. "Slight problem with that plan." I nodded towards the back of the vehicle.

"Ah, yes," Nikki said. "Forgot about him." She tapped at the window to see if the boar would move. Nothing.

"You can take him with you," suggested Bob. "He's fast asleep anyway. Probably gone into hibernation by now. Like squirrels. They go into hibernation after a big meal; David Attenborough did a thing on it. Or was that meerkats?"

"We don't have much choice," said Nikki. "He's got to try to find a buyer so the less time he has to do that the better."

"You're suggesting we take the boar into the village?" I said.

"It sat in the back perfectly happy when you took it to the forest," she said. "It might like an afternoon out in town."

"I can't believe we're doing this," I said. "Come on."

Nikki and I climbed into the front but Bob declined to join us on the basis the back seat was just a bit too close to our unwanted passenger. He did have a point so I didn't push it.

The boar gave a grunt when I started the engine but beyond that minor protest, he seemed to stay asleep for the journey down the hill.

We drove past the Casa de Pastores and on towards the village. Cars jammed the main road and side streets and streams of people picked their way between them.

"What's going on?" asked Nikki.

"Market day, at a guess," I said. "Didn't think about that. Most of the villages have one though."

I drove back up the road until I found a parking spot on a bit of waste ground. The boar was still asleep so I wound down a bit of window and carefully locked the vehicle. As I checked that I'd locked the door, it did occur to me that even Donny wouldn't be crazy enough to try steal a car with a wild boar lodged in the back.

We threaded our way through the crowds, scanning the sea of heads for any sign of our missing felons. The market was a real mixed bag of stalls. Everything from the expected fruit and vegetables, through various dried meats and fish to all manner of arts and crafts. For such a small village, the market was quite an ambitious affair which clearly not only attracted the locals but a huge contingent of visitors and tourists. The prices of the fresh produce seemed ridiculously cheap but the touristy stalls with their leather dream catchers and macramé hats were clearly taking advantage. Several stalls specialised in second-hand tools and equipment and it was at one of these that I spotted Donny. I slid up beside him and said, "And what are you up to?"

He started and turned towards us. "Oh, hello. Thought we'd find you here." He picked up a boxed screwdriver set and asked the man behind the stall, "What d'yer want for this, chief?"

"Diez euros," the man replied.

Donny looked at me. "What'd he say?"

"He said you have no need of a screwdriver set," I said.

Donny turned back towards the stallholder and waved a five euro note at him. "I'll give you one of these for it, mate."

The man looked at the note, shrugged and took it from Donny's hand then turned his attention to an elderly, weather-beaten man who was showing interest in an ancient electric drill.

"What are you doing here?" I asked as we turned away from the stall and into the crowd.

"Just thought I'd pick up a few bits and pieces we might need. You know, if the car breaks down sort of thing. Don't wanna be clocking up bills every time a wiper blade goes a bit wonky."

"I've got a deal with José Martin in the event of a wiper blade going wonky. Where are the others?"

"Last time I saw them they was haggling with some dude on the antiques stall down there." He waved his hand towards a thicket of stalls about twenty metres further down.

"We'll see you back at the camp," I said.

"Yeah, laters. Need an electrical circuit tester. You ain't seen any of those in your travels 'ave you?"

"No, and you won't be needing one of those either."

We weaved and nudged our way deeper into the market until I eventually caught sight of the unmistakable semi dreadlocks, semi tangled mess that was the back of Ryan's head. I sidled in alongside him to see what he was doing. He held a piece of old masonry in his hand and was trying to negotiate with the man behind the antiques stall. I tried to see what was so special about the piece he was holding but it just looked like an old brick. A vaguely familiar old brick.

"What on earth do you want that for?" I asked.

Ryan started. "Oh, hey, man. Just the person I want. This guy can't understand English."

"Who'd have thought," I said. "Why do you want an old brick?"

"Huh? I don't. I'm trying to sell it but this guy keeps jabbering and I don't understand a word he's on about. I think he's trying it on."

I took the brick from Ryan and examined it. It wasn't quite the same as the one I'd seen up at the ruin, but close. It was about the size of an ordinary house brick but clearly much older and was probably granite but my knowledge of geology was limited. Going by the fractured edges, it was once part of something much larger. Carved into the face I could make out some lettering which looked a bit like Sulpicius Galba, (Gaiba?) or something. It was almost certainly Latin.

"Is this from the wrecked building in our field?" I asked.

"Of course," Ryan said. "Sean said it was really old so I figured it was probably worth something. I know how much old stuff can fetch, you ever watched Celebrity Antiques?"

"I try not to."

"So where is Sean?" Nikki asked.

I scanned the area. I'd thought he'd be with Ryan but there was no sign of him.

"He was over there with the guy selling the paintings," Ryan said. "He was supposed to be helping me with this but he wandered off. Toad, he knows I know nothing about old stuff."

"So this is what you were carrying in the bag?" I hefted the brick in my hand.

Ryan looked puzzled. "Yes, why? What did you think I was carrying?"

"Oh, nothing. Just wondered. You're not supposed to be selling bits of somebody else's house, you know. I'm sure there's a rule about that in the paperwork we signed."

"Nobody's lived there for... a hundred years at least, I'll

bet. It's all fallen down. Help me deal with this guy, will you?"

"I'm not helping you sell an old brick. It's not yours to sell and we're supposed to be living off the land, not dismantling old houses and selling them a bit at a time."

Ryan looked towards Nikki for support. "What's with him all of a sudden?"

"He's got a point, Michael," said Nikki. "It's not really much different to your deals with the bar or the garage, is it?"

I looked at the brick I was holding and tried to think of a reason as to why this situation was different but failed.

I caught the stall holder's attention. "Genuine Roman carving," I said. "Will you give me fifty euros for it?"

We haggled to and fro a bit and settled halfway at fifteen euros. Ryan looked pleased with the result and stuffed the money in his shirt pocket.

"Let's go see what Sean's up to," I said to Nikki.

We found him where Ryan had indicated. He was engaged in a reasonably fluent discussion with the man selling supposedly original oil paintings of the area. I hadn't realised that Sean spoke Spanish.

"What's he up to?" Nikki asked.

"The stall holder is trying to convince Sean that these are all original oil paintings by local art students."

"And are they?" Nikki asked.

"Sean doesn't think so. He's telling the man that he knows they come from Chinese student painting factories for around five euros a piece."

"Why? What's his game?"

"I'm not sure but… hang on… Ah, now he's telling the man he can supply a genuine lost El Greco."

"Oh, shit," breathed Nikki.

"My thoughts exactly."

"Look what I got," Ryan's voice interrupted from behind me.

I turned to see him looking at me through an old brass telescope. "I see no ships," he said.

"Where did you get that?" I asked.

"Off the guy who bought the bit of rock off us," he said. "Only fifteen euros. Bargain, huh?"

"Why?"

"It's a valuable antique, might even be the very one Nelson used at Waterloo."

"Nelson was at Trafalgar," Nikki said. "Waterloo was Napoleon."

"You sure?" Ryan queried.

"Quite sure. I did a battle re-enactment of the Battle of Waterloo and I'm fairly sure there weren't any ships involved. I think I'd have remembered."

Ryan looked disappointed. "Trafalgar, huh. Well, I knew it was in London somewhere," he said.

By the time I'd returned my attention to Sean, he'd finished his conversation with the art stall holder.

"What are you up to?" I asked him.

"Just fixing up a little bit of part-time work. You know, keeps the boredom monkeys from stealing my cheese."

"Part-time work? We're supposed to be living off the land, naturally."

Sean shrugged. "It's natural to me."

The sounds of loud screams and shouts grabbed my attention. I grabbed Nikki by the upper arm and nudged her between two stalls then stood between her and the crowd which had started to sweep down through the crowded market. Sean and Ryan disappeared as the wave of people gathered them up and washed down the road.

"What's going on?" Nikki asked from across my shoulder.

"I can't see. Something's causing a panic. Best stay here."

I felt her push forwards to gain a better view. Instinctively, I moved my arm to keep her back, out of harm's way but then remembered that she was probably far better equipped to deal with whatever was happening than I was.

I turned to see her giving a knowing grin in my direction. "Why, thank you, brave sir," she said.

"Okay, well, I've got the situation under control; you can take over from here." I swept my arm forwards giving her access to the chaos.

"I know," she said. "Always down to the Paras to clean up everybody else's mess."

The crowd gave a sudden surge then separated. An old lady in a black shawl pressed in against us and I moved aside to let her pass. I turned back to the panic in front of me just in time to see our boar hurtling through the newly created gap. People broke to the sides as it thundered through and then disappeared into the throng of people ahead.

Nikki turned to look at me. "I thought you had this under control?"

"I might have exaggerated. Do you think we should try and get it back?"

"No, I think we should go now before anybody associates that thing with us."

I scanned the heads of the crowd looking for Sean or Ryan but there was no sign of them. I figured they'd been swept along by the human tide. We pushed our way through the still chaotic crowd. That's the thing with crowds; they actually work much like water. When they are going in the same direction, all is fine but drop something unexpected into the flow and the swirls and flurries cause mayhem and uncertainty.

We had been forcing our way against the flow of the tide for several minutes when I realised the resistance had become weaker. The force against us was definitely subsiding. I stopped and looked around. Fortunately, I was taller than most of the crowd and I was able to watch the bobbing heads for some distance. In our immediate area, a lot of the heads had stopped and those that were moving, moved in a more random fashion than I would have expected from people trying to flee a specific danger. It didn't make sense.

"What's happening?" Nikki asked.

"Not sure," I said. "I think that now the beast has gone, everybody's slightly confused."

A new surge in the crowd hit me like being caught too close to a mortar strike.

"Hang on," I yelled across the rising noise. "They all seem to be heading this way now, I think it's coming back."

All around us, the yelling grew more frenzied and the pushing more violent. I caught hold of Nikki's hand and pulled her behind a pile of stacked fruit and veg crates. We watched as the surge flooded uphill now, spilling tributaries of humanity into various stalls as it went. Then our friend appeared for a second time. The crowd parted in a crescendo of noise as the boar burst through and thundered past us in a cloud of dust and spilled vegetables.

Only now, it was wearing what appeared to be a pink nightie.

"Was that...?" Nikki clearly didn't want to voice the obvious for fear she'd imagined it.

I put her mind at rest. "Yes," I said. "It seems to be wearing a nightie. A pink nightie."

"Oh good. I thought it was just me but that's alright then."

"Not an obvious choice but I think it suits him."

"Really?" queried Nikki. "I think I'd have gone for the black myself."

We followed the cleared path uphill. Stallholders had started repairing their displays with the sort of equanimity that said this was just an everyday occurrence and by the time we cleared the market at the top of town, one would never know anything had happened.

We found the little 4X4 more or less where we'd left it. More or less, because the back door was now some three metres from the rest of the vehicle. As was, for some inexplicable reason, the fluffy yellow seat cover from the driver's seat. I picked the door up and examined it. The plastic interior trim had been ripped off in several places and the door handle was nowhere to be seen. I tried to work out if there was any way I could reattach it but the hinges were twisted and the bolts had been sheared.

"José Felipe's not going to be impressed," said Nikki.

"Do you think he'll notice?"

We set out back to the camp, keeping half an eye out for the others. There was no sign of Sean or Ryan but we did find Donny halfway up the hill out of the village. We stopped and he climbed in the back, casting an eye over the damage as he did so.

"Determined little beast, that one," he said. "We should have turned it into hotdogs when we had the chance."

We parked in the field near the main sleeping shack. Jason appeared from inside.

"Where did you get to?" I asked.

"There." He pointed at the shack.

"You weren't here when we came up earlier," I said. "Bob said you'd disappeared. And where is Bob?"

"Oh, I just went for a wander. Exploring, that's all. Not seen Bob though, he was gone before I came back."

I turned to Nikki. "This is like herding cats."

"We really should have some more photos," she said. "We've been here long enough and the chittie-pushers back home will expect to see something happening."

I looked around the field and shrugged. "We've got nothing to send them."

"They'll know something's up if we don't keep feeding them stuff." Nikki scanned the field. "It'll take a while though. It needs to look like we've actually put some effort in and should at least appear to be weatherproof."

"You have seen my track record with building stuff, haven't you?"

Nikki remained silent and continued to study the field.

"I've got an idea," said Jason.

I looked at him. "Have you ever built a wooden hut?"

"Well, yes, actually. But that was a flatpack playhouse log cabin for my sister's kid. Came from Homebase."

"Well, unless Homebase happen to deliver to the Alpujarras, I'm for calling that one Plan B."

"No," said Jason. "You see, it was a playhouse. Miniature, but just like a real one. Katie loved it. We had a clown make it appear at her second birthday party, you should have seen her face. Well, it terrified her actually. How was I supposed to know she was frightened of clowns?"

"Have you been at Ryan's stash while we were out?" I asked.

"Wait," Nikki said. "He's got a point."

I stared at her, trying to work out whether she was winding me up. "Really? Clowns? Playhouses? This is making sense to you?"

"Yes, a photograph doesn't know scale. We build a miniature shelter and photograph it close up. Nobody will know it's not full size."

I pondered this for a moment. "How big?"

"Doesn't matter," said Jason. "The smaller we make it, the bigger the branches look, so the more substantial it appears."

"We'd never get away with that," I said. "Would we?"

"I don't see why not," said Nikki. "Steven Spielberg does it all the time."

"Okay," I said. "You two start gathering some wood and I'll nip back and fetch the camera."

I headed back to the Casa de Pastores and retrieved my camera from my room. On my way back out through the bar, José Felipe stopped me.

"Have you seen Bob?" he asked. "He was going to show Conchita how to do a Dhaga Kebab. She has killed the chickens."

"I haven't, no," I shrugged as I dashed through the bar not wanting to become involved with Dhagas or dead chickens. "I'll remind him if I see him."

I jumped in the Suzuki just as Donny, Sean and Ryan appeared from around the corner.

"Hop in," I said. "I'll give you a lift up the hill."

They climbed in and surveyed the damage.

"I see the Hogfather's done a little pimping." Donny pushed a torn side panel back into place but it fell straight out again. "Nice detailing."

"Hogfather?" I wrestled the gears and started up the hill. "Oh, I see, Hogfather. Yes, I think he's done enough sightseeing."

By the time we arrived back at the field, Jason and Nikki had already started to build a miniature wooden shack. It sat on the edge of the tree line and stood around half a metre high. Four stakes marked the corners and the one completed wall consisted of several rows of horizontal, stripped twigs, tied with string to the uprights.

"Is that it?" I asked.

"Well, it's not finished yet but yes, that's the basis." Nikki stood back and stared at the construction. "Looking good, huh?"

"No, not really. Even if we photograph it close up, we'll still see the trees in the background and unless we can convince everybody we've camped next to a giant sequoia forest, it's not going to work."

"No, hang on," said Sean. "It'll work, look." He picked up a fir branch and stuck it in the ground behind the miniature cabin. "See, it's all about perspective. If we put a row of these behind it, they'll look like fir trees."

I stood staring at the twigs and half built miniature wall and tried to visualise it big. It didn't work. All I could see was a pile of twigs. "It looks more like the beginnings of a bonfire," I said.

"Have some faith," said Ryan. "Sean's the man. If he can sell a new Van Gogh to a Spanish museum, he can make this look real."

I looked at Sean. "You sold a new Van Gogh to a Spanish museum?"

"No, not exactly," he said. "It was a Picasso."

"Oh, good. That's alright then, I don't know what I was worried about."

We set about gathering twigs while Nikki and Sean created the tiny cabin. Half an hour later we had a hobbit version of Uncle Tom's Cabin. I tried looking at it on the tiny screen on the camera and for the first time it began to take on the desired optical illusion. The line of fir twigs really did look like trees.

"What do you think?" Nikki asked as we stood back and surveyed our handiwork.

"I think it works," I said. "I'd never have thought it but it seems to look good on the screen. Look." I handed the camera around to murmurs of approval.

I took a series of photographs then Nikki and I returned to the Casa de Pastores for our evening meal.

A group of five occupied our usual table so we took the next one, slightly closer to the road.

One of the occupants of the other table called over to me. "Hey, Michael," Bob waved at me from the table. "Come and meet some friends of mine."

I looked at Nikki and did my best puzzled expression. She shook her head and shrugged. We moved over to Bob's table and everybody shuffled round a bit to make space.

"This is Nikki and Michael," Bob said towards the other four. "Nikki, Michael, this is Nate." He pointed to the first man to his left and I shook his hand.

"This is Madison," he said and continued round the group. "And Kyle and Faith."

I shook hands, smiled and repeated each name in turn. "Nice to meet you."

"Rupert here tells us that you're a military man," said Nate. "Respect to you, sir. My uncle on my mother's side served with the Marine Corp in 'Nam. Semper Fi." He looked at Madison.

"Rupert?" I looked at Bob. He furrowed his brow slightly and gave the smallest of nods.

"These guys are here on a walking holiday from Milwaukee," said Bob.

"That's a long way to walk," I said.

Kyle looked at me then after a brief pause, he said, "We didn't walk from Milwaukee."

"Oh."

"No," Bob said. "They're starting tomorrow. I'm going to be their guide."

"We were really lucky to find Rupert here," said Kyle. "Real lucky."

"Yes," said Faith. "A real life historian, and right here where we're staying. Who'd have thought?"

"Indeed, who would have?" I studied Bob but he studiously avoided making eye contact with me.

"He's a professor at Castle Cary University, did you know?" said Faith. "An English professor from a real life castle. All my Facebook friends are so jealous."

"I'm sure," I said.

"Rupert's taking us to see some old ruins tomorrow," said Nate.

"There are a lot round here," I said and felt Nikki kick my ankle.

"Well, we'll leave you in peace," said Nikki. "It seems you have a busy day tomorrow."

We moved back to our original table just as José Felipe brought our drinks.

"Rupert the historian," Nikki said.

"From the University of Castle Cary, no less."

"What's he up to?"

"Oh, I doubt he has a plan." The gin was cool. Laden with ice and the glass frosted. "He just can't help himself. There's probably a long complicated Latin name for it."

We sat in silence for a while just enjoying the cool evening air. The night times there come in fast, I'd noticed. A brief sunset then the blackest sky pierced with the sharpest of stars.

I felt Nikki's hand cover mine. "How are you feeling now?" she asked. "The chaos in the market didn't throw you?"

I thought for a moment. "No, oddly. I think I'm okay." I turned my hand and took hers. "I think this place might actually be doing me some good."

We finished our drinks and headed upstairs. We paused outside Nikki's room as she fiddled with the archaic lock. The door swung open in front of her but she didn't go through. Instead, she turned to face me and I felt her eyes searching mine. My arms already knew what it would feel like to hold her tight, to pull her close. I would feel the firm warmth of her body as we embraced. Instead I said nothing and just stood still as she placed the briefest of kisses on my lips and said, "Get some sleep. Proper sleep." She touched my upper arm briefly then she was gone, the door closing softly behind her.

~ *Chapter Thirteen* ~

By the time Nikki and I reached the field in the morning there was no sign of Bob or Ryan.

"They went off with a bunch of Yanks," said Donny. "Think Bob's lost the plot; he's started talking all posh, like he's doing the news on Radio Four or something."

"And Ryan?" I asked.

"Yeah, him too. Though we wasn't talking funny or nothing. Well, no more'n usual."

"I'm guessing Bob's taken them up to that tumbledown house," said Nikki.

"And Ryan? Why would he go?"

"I expect he wants to keep an eye on his smallholding."

The walk up to the ridge took about twenty minutes. Even in the distance as we approached I could see the four Americans and Bob kneeling on the ground. They appeared captivated by something in the grass. Ryan was hovering between the group and the cannabis plants.

Bob spotted us and motioned us to join them.

"Oh, hi," greeted Faith. "This place is so cool. You guys are so lucky to have all this history right here on your doorstep. We have to go all the way down to Washington if we want to see real ancient stuff."

"Professor Rupert's just been showing us the viewing

circle," said Kyle. "To think, Queen Isadora herself stood here."

I nudged Bob to one side. "Isadora?" I whispered.

"That was her, wasn't it? She was June Whitfield in Carry on Columbus?"

"I think you mean Isabella?"

"Oh yes. She's the one." He turned back to his group. "And on this very spot." He swept his arms around the stone circle. "Queen Isabella stood as she watched Christopher Columbus set out for the New World."

"I thought you said Queen Isadora?" queried Nate.

"Yes, I did. To the public she was known by her Royal name of Isabella but her closest friends called her Isadora. But you should never really use that name in Spain of course. They see it as a sign of disrespect."

The four Americans pottered around the circle, stopping every so often to examine a rock or to look out to sea, possibly in the hope of spotting Columbus on his travels.

I said quietly to Bob, "You're getting your Spanish history from Carry on Columbus?"

He shrugged. "I'm sure they did their research. Anyway they're made up with this. It's the highlight of their holiday; they'll be talking about it for years."

Kyle wandered across the old paved circle, holding his arms outstretched. "You can feel the history here."

"Is that England over there?" Madison shielded her eyes from the sun as she tried to focus on the shimmering shoreline across the brilliant blue of the sea.

Bob looked at me and raised his eyebrows. I came to his rescue. "That's North Africa," I said. "Morocco actually."

"I ain't never seen Africa," said Nate. "Except in the movies of course but that's not the real thing."

"My great, great, great… um… great, great aunt on my mother's side came from Spain." Kyle crouched on the ground and stroked his hands across the levelled stones. "She might have stood on this very spot."

"So what was Columbus doing round here?" asked Faith. "I thought he set out from the west coast?"

Bob looked at me once more and his eyebrows danced in a plea for help. For a moment, I thought about letting him flounder but he looked so much like a puppy that couldn't understand why he was in trouble for chewing one's slippers that I relented.

"They did a quick circuit here as a salute to the queen before finally leaving," I said.

"Yes, that was it," said Bob. "Like a fly-by." He waved his arm out to the Mediterranean in a circling movement then pointed east.

I coughed and Bob looked at me, his arm still pointing into the Mediterranean and towards Greece. We made eye contact and I gave a brief shake of my head.

Bob caught the message and swung his arm through a hundred and eighty degrees. "And then they set off this way. Towards the New World."

"That's amazing," said Nate.

"Yes, isn't it," I agreed.

After the Americans had spent the best part of an hour studying the Royal Viewing Circle and the remains of Castle Isabella we headed back towards the Casa de Pastores. As we skirted the edge of the field, I noticed a new feature had been installed. The huge camper van I'd recently seen behind José Martin's workshop now dominated the eastern edge of the site.

I pointed it out to Nikki. "What the…?" she said.

"You carry on back down to the bar with this lot; I'll try and find out what José Martin's up to. And don't leave Bob alone with those Americans or he'll have them believing the Inquisition took place in the wine cellar."

Jason greeted me as I neared the massive RV. "Oh, hi, Michael. What do you think?" He waved an arm towards the beast.

I stood for a moment, trying to take in what I was seeing. The thing was about twelve metres long and appeared to have once been a top of the range RV. Way back in the seventies at a guess.

"I think it's a slum on wheels. Why is it here?"

"I bought it off José's cousin, you know, the guy who runs the breakdown place?"

"You bought it? With money? What are you planning on doing with it? It's a bit big to take home on Kwikjet."

"It's to live in, look." Jason pulled at the door but it refused to move. "It's a bit stiff; I'll get that sorted with some WD40."

"How did you pay for it? You're not supposed to have any money." I poked my finger at some trim that looked in danger of coming away from the window. It came away from the window and fell at my feet. "We're supposed to be living off the land."

"Father gave me a little bung to tide me over, in case of emergencies."

"And buying a derelict apartment block on wheels was an emergency?"

"No, the emergency is not having to live in a shed with that lot for six months. Have you any idea how much gas they make between them?"

"You know this goes right against the rules and could end up getting us shut down?"

"Who's going to know?" Jason waved his arms around,

indicating the huge open space. "And I can always move it. We could all go down to Marbella for a few days. That might be fun."

I studied the vehicle. Moss and lichen grew from various places and the windows were so sun damaged it was impossible to see through. The original paintwork had probably once been cream but little of that remained visible under the random artistic expressions of the previous owners. I pushed my foot against the nearest tyre, it flexed under the pressure.

"These tyres are flat," I said. "How did you get it here?"

"Oh, José Martin brought it up her on his truck. He didn't charge me for that."

I looked around the field. "If you're planning on keeping this, I think you should put it over there." I indicated a break in the trees that made a small clearing. "It'll be out of the way in case anybody comes by. We can always blame it on the hippies."

Jason shrugged. "Okay."

Donny appeared from the sleeping shack. "I told him you'd be pissed," he said. "But if it stops him whinging about how I roll up my sleeping bag or not, I'd say it's worth it."

Jason turned to Donny. "If you rolled it properly we'd have more room to move about during the day. What with that, Ryan's plants drying out on every available surface and Sean's canvases hanging off the ceiling... is it any wonder I want a little privacy?"

"Why don't we move it now?" I suggested. "Will it start?"

"I don't know," said Jason.

"You didn't take it for a drive before buying?" Donny shook his head. "Didn't you even listen to the engine running?"

"No," said Jason. "José Martin said the battery needed charging. And anyway, I wouldn't have the first idea what I was listening for."

"Where's the keys?" Donny asked. "I'll give it a go."

Jason reached into his pocket and passed a bunch of keys to Donny. "I think it's the one with the blue insulating tape on it. Or that might be the gas locker. Or… I don't know."

Donny climbed on to the step and yanked at the driver's door. It swung open at the third attempt and came to rest at an angle at which doors rarely manage without actually falling off. He fiddled at the keys for a moment before finding the correct one then gave it a turn. Nothing. He tried a couple more times then gave up and fumbled under the dashboard for the bonnet release. I heard a click and the bonnet popped. Donny jumped down, found the bonnet catch and lifted it open.

"Well, I can see the problem," he said.

"What is it?" asked Jason. "Flat battery?"

"No, I think it's a bit more serious than that. Have a look." Donny moved to one side to let Jason peer into the engine compartment. "There, see the problem?"

Jason shook his. "I don't see anything."

"There you go," said Donny. "That's your problem."

"What? I don't understand." Jason removed his head from under the bonnet.

Donny sighed and shook his head. "You didn't see anything. That's why it won't start. You're supposed to be able to see an engine."

Jason poked his head back into the engine compartment. "Are you sure?"

"Fairly sure. They've been a standard feature in most vehicles for the past hundred years but I suppose this new development could have passed me by. After all, I only steal them, I don't fix them."

"Maybe it's in the back," suggested Jason. "Some vehicles have engines in the back… don't they?"

"Sometimes," Donny admitted. "But usually *not* the same ones which have huge empty spaces in the front. Although I suppose you could go check."

"But why would José Martin sell me an RV without an engine?"

Donny studied Jason up and down for a moment then said, "Because you're a fucking idiot." He dropped the keys into Jason's hand and headed back to the shack.

Jason looked at me and said. "I've got international breakdown cover under my American Express card. Do you think this is covered?"

"I'll have a word with José Martin," I said. "Why on earth didn't you ask for a test drive?"

"Because usually I order my cars from the main dealers based on the spec in the catalogue. I have never had to check to see if an engine is on the list of optional extras."

I stared at the RV for a moment. "I guess the trip to Marbella's off?"

I felt slightly sorry for Jason as I left him with his immobile home and headed down the hill to find the others.

I caught up with Nikki, Bob and Ryan at our usual table outside the Casa de Pastores.

"Where're the Americans?" I asked as I settled at the table.

"They're upstairs packing. They're heading back to the coast," said Bob. "They were only up here for an overnight stay."

"Let's hope they don't go checking any history books."

"Why? It was all true," said Bob. "Mostly. Well, Isadora might have stood there, who's to say she didn't?"

"Isabella," corrected Nikki.

The sun broke through the gaps in the overhead umbrellas

and I shifted my position to regain the shade. "Has anybody seen Sean?"

"He went off to talk to a man in town," said Ryan. "Something about El Greco. He had a rolled up piece of newspaper."

"Wasn't that the artist he was talking about the other day?" asked Nikki.

José Felipe brought some welcome cold beers and I supped deeply. "I'm not going to think about that."

Noisy chatter and the sound of suitcase wheels clattering over five hundred year old cobbles caught my attention. The group of Americans were exiting the bar and heading to their rental Seat just down from our table.

Madison parked her pink airline case by the kerb and came over to give Bob a huge hug. "It was so lovely meeting all you guys," she said. "Thank you for your time. Can I get a selfie?" Without waiting for Bob's assent she pushed her cheek against his and held her iPhone out. Her face snapped into a much practised pose just for the split second the shutter clicked. She glanced at the screen and smiled, obviously satisfied with the result. "Just one to show all the girls back at the hotel. You just know they're going to be so mad when they see this."

"Come on, honey," said Nate. "We've got to go. The flamenco starts at eight and it's a long way down this mountain."

Madison stuffed something into Bob's hand and they waved their goodbyes and headed for the car. I noticed Kyle clutching something and squinted against the bright sunlight which flashed from its surface. "Is that your telescope, Ryan?"

"What? That? Um… well he seemed really impressed with it and you know… I sort of thought… like, hey… what do I need a telescope for? And those guys don't get the old stuff like what we have… so…"

"So you sold it to him?" I finished for him.

"No. Well, yes. But only 'cus they're like, real cool dudes and they understand. You know what I mean?"

"Not really. I assume you made a profit?"

"No, well not really what it was worth. You know, a telescope like that, well, like if I'd put that up on eBay I'd have got double. At least."

"Probably more," offered Bob. "Queen Isadora's telescope? I'd say they got a bargain."

I stared at Bob. "Queen Isabella's telescope? You do realise that the telescope wasn't even invented at the time Columbus set out, don't you?" I looked from one to the other. "Both of you?"

"Well, *you* say," said Ryan. "But it might have been a secret one. You know, like the water powered car."

"Water powered car?"

"Yeah, everybody knows it's been invented but the big petrochem companies keep it hidden. It's a control thing and probably queen what's–her-name didn't want the people to see what was out there."

I shook my head and then noticed Bob's hand and the badly concealed wad of notes peeking out from his iron grip. "What did she give you?"

Bob slid his hand into his pocket. "Just a little token of gratitude. I didn't ask. They wanted to."

I looked at Nikki and she just grinned.

We finished our drinks then headed round to see José Martin.

"I have a bit of a problem with the rear door of the Suzuki," I said.

"Probably just needs adjusting, let me see."

I led him round the back of the vehicle to show him the door lying on the floor of the rear passenger area.

"It fell off," I said.

He looked at the hinges then ran his hand over the remains of the plastic trim. "Jabalí?"

I nodded.

"Why did you put a Jabalí in my car?"

"It got in looking for food. Can you fix it?"

"Of course, I am the best mechanic in the Alpujarras, of course I can fix it. But it will be expensive." He rubbed his thumb and forefinger together.

"I thought it might be."

"Do you want to borrow the ambulance again while I make the repairs?"

"Thanks, yes. I was going to talk to you about the big camper van," I said.

"Ah, too late, my friend." He patted my shoulder. "I have sold it now."

"Yes, I know. You sold it to a friend of mine and he's a bit upset. It hasn't got an engine."

"Did he want an engine? He didn't say. Not to worry, tell him I will find him one. My cousin has a breaker's yard, I will talk to him." He headed back into his workshop and we went to collect the ambulance.

"He's going to find an engine for that thing?" said Nikki.

"I'm guessing he can find one that will work. One of the engineers in our unit once put a Volvo truck engine into a squadron Jeep, went like a rocket. Bit difficult to control though. And you couldn't see where you were going as the engine sat too high."

We parked outside the Casa de Pastores and on the way

through the bar, my eyes lighted on a brace of rabbits on the counter.

"Are they for tonight's dinner?" I asked José Felipe.

"Tomorrow," he said. "They are best left to hang for a day. You want some stew?"

"No thanks," I said. "I don't eat meat."

"But this is not meat, it is rabbit."

"Still no. But I'd like to borrow them for a couple of hours."

José Felipe shrugged. "You are a strange man." He pushed the rabbits towards me. "You can borrow them but if you eat them you pay, yes?"

"Yes," I said and picked up the rabbits by the string which bound their legs.

"What on earth do you want with those?" Nikki asked.

"Photographs. We can set up a trap and place them in it. It'll look great."

We headed back to the site and found a suitable spot and set up the trap. I'd recalled the principles from our earlier boar trap which had been based on a rabbit trap. Pieces of string and springy twigs came together in an impressive contraption which would have delighted Robinson Crusoe. I placed the rabbits in the device and clicked off a dozen shots. They looked good on the screen so we gathered up the rabbits and headed back.

José Felipe studied the rabbits when I placed them back on the counter.

"I have some chorizo you can borrow as well if you like," he said.

"No thank you. I'm good."

We settled in for a quiet meal as there was no sign of the others.

"Perhaps they're getting the hang of living off the land," Nikki said with a touch of hopefulness in her voice.

"Don't believe it. They're up to something; I just haven't worked out what yet."

"Cynic."

Our meals arrived and I spent five minutes picking pieces of bacon out of my vegetarian Potatas Pobre. I felt a nudge against my leg and looked down. A set of huge brown eyes stared up at me. It was a stray dog I'd noticed there a few days before, about the size of a collie but with a glorious tangle of curly grey hair covering every inch of it. Every inch apart from the huge brown eyes. I dropped the bits of bacon in front of it and he ate hungrily.

"Got a new friend?" Nikki asked.

"I think he's twigged I'm a good target." I dropped a piece of bread which disappeared before it even touched the ground.

We took our time with the meal and enjoyed the cooling evening. José Felipe kept the drinks coming and I lost count, which is never a good thing.

Nikki raised her glass and said, "Well, we survived another day and we haven't lost anybody yet."

"We haven't seen Sean for a while." I looked at Nikki and watched the smile touch her eyes.

She relaxed back in the chair and pushed a hand through her hair. "I shouldn't worry about him. He's an art forger, there's not much scope up here for an art forger." The white of her shirt seemed to become starker as the skies darkened and the outside lights took over.

"I suppose," I said. "But I would like to at least complete this mission with a full complement. Coming that close to being locked up made me realise that I wouldn't survive."

She leaned forwards. I realised that with way the top

buttons of her shirt were open that the stark contrast between night sky and halogen lights exaggerated her slight curves and softened her slightly masculine figure.

She reached and touched my hand briefly. "It's not a mission, it's just a job. And that lot…" She waved loosely towards the direction of the camp. "They're going nowhere. They may not be the brightest crew you've ever been teamed with but they know this is far better than what's waiting for them if they screw up." Her eyes connected with mine and I felt something touch bits of me that had been closed for a very long time. "Relax, Michael. You're doing okay."

I held her eyes for longer than I knew I should but there was something captivating, ethereal and I needed to understand. It escaped as I tried to bring it into focus. Like the threads of a dream in the first waking moments, it vanished. I took the last cigarette from the pack and studied it for a moment before replacing it.

"You alright?" Nikki asked.

"I was just thinking that…" I felt her eyes searching mine as if she was probing my darkest, hidden places. "I just thought that maybe we should get away for a few hours tomorrow. You know; new space."

She gave me a querying look, then, "Okay. Where were you thinking?"

I hadn't thought. Not at all. "Pampeniera," I said with a degree of certainty which belied the random nature of my suggestion. As long as she doesn't ask why.

"Why there?" she asked.

I tried to recall where Pampeniera was and what it looked like. "Because it looked… um… pretty."

"Pretty?"

"Yes, pretty." The word even felt odd as I repeated it.

"What's with all the questions? It's like being back in the interrogation room during Selection."

"How would you know?" She gave a grin and tipped her head to one side. "You ducked that."

"I saw it on Bravo two Zero."

"Idiot! Okay, tomorrow we'll go to the pretty village of Pampeniera. I'll put on my best summer frock."

I lifted my glass in salute and watched her over the top of it for a moment. I returned her smile then emptied the glass. "Is that the one with the primroses on it?"

When the air finally turned to chill, we headed upstairs to our rooms. I wanted to send in my blog and upload the photographs before I got too tired.

"I'll give you a hand if you like," said Nikki. "I'm still too wide awake."

Like the gentleman I am, I let Nikki sit on the bed while I perched on the little wooden folding chair which wobbled with every breath. My laptop sat on the dressing table which served as a desk. I fired it up and Windows cheerfully announced it was going to improve my experience by doing an update. 3% completed and a stern warning not to turn off my computer.

"That always happens to me." Nikki stretched backwards on the bed.

"I usually use Linux but this thing belongs to the D.O.J. and I haven't got round to changing the operating system yet."

"Wasn't Linux the bird in Charlie Brown?" Nikki's eyes seemed fixated with the ceiling fan which circled lazily over her head.

I twisted round in the chair as carefully as I could without collapsing it. "You're thinking of Linus. And he was the young kid, not the bird. The bird was Woodstock."

"You sure?"

"Charlie Brown was a favourite of mine," I said. "He just keeps getting up again, no matter what."

"Mine was Homer Simpson." Her eyes seemed to be following the fan. "There was never a problem which couldn't be solved by another beer, a pizza and a can-do attitude." She shook her attention away from the fan and reached her arms forwards. "Give me a hand up. I'm feeling dizzy."

I took her hands and helped her into a sitting position. Our faces settled inches apart. She searched my face and I felt the warm grip of her hands.

"Too much sun?" I asked.

She shook her head. "I suspect it might be the gin."

"You have to watch the measures here." I twisted to look at my laptop. 12% and a little note from Windows telling me it was still enhancing my experience. I turned back to Nikki. "I don't think I'm going to be uploading anything tonight."

She smiled and said, "That's a shame." She tightened her grip on my hands and pulled herself closer.

I felt the warmth of her body and the light touch of her breath on my face. Her eyes drifted and seemed to lack focus. My body demanded physical contact and the yearning to wrap my arms around her was becoming overwhelming. Our lips touched. Light, fleeting, sensuous. I broke contact and moved backwards slightly, searching her face.

"I think we should call it a night," I said.

Nikki raised one eyebrow. "You sure?"

"Yes, I'm thinking I may have overdone the gin too."

"Never mind." She touched my arm. "We can always try for an upload tomorrow." She gave my arm a little squeeze and left the room.

I collapsed back on the bed and tried to clear my brain of the demons which were busy tearing apart what was left of my self-esteem. A little tune from my laptop demanded my attention and I turned just as Windows thanked me for my patience and announced it would now do a restart so it could continue with wasting my time.

~ *Chapter Fourteen* ~

I awoke with one of those strange feelings that something had shifted. After a quick shower, I headed downstairs to the bar and started work on the coffee. Strong, black and copious. Nikki appeared and helped herself to coffee and intercepted José Felipe to ask for a tostada.

"How are you feeling?" she asked as she sat down.

"I'm okay," I said. "Look, I'm sorry... It's –"

"I'm going to have to get José to order some PG Tips." Bob planted himself at our table and set about wringing as much juice as he could from the little teabag on a string. "Those Americans loved my proper English tea but they took my last."

"Can't you get used to coffee?" I asked. "It'd save a lot of trouble."

"Not for breakfast. That's far too sudden."

I poured myself another coffee. "Sometimes sudden is the only way to start a day. Nikki and I are heading out for the day, Bob. Can you keep half an eye on the others?"

"No problem. What're you up to?"

"Just getting away for a bit," said Nikki. She cast me a fleeting smile.

After breakfast we met outside and took the ambulance through the village on the way to Pampeniera. I caught a glimpse of somebody entering a shop. He held a folded artist's easel under his arm.

"Was that Sean?" I asked Nikki.

"I didn't notice. Where?"

"Just going into a shop with a load of painting stuff."

"Why would he be doing that?"

"I don't know," I said. "That's what worries me."

She stretched back in the seat and put her feet on the dashboard. "I shouldn't stress about it. He's probably just selling the Mona Lisa to the mayor."

Pampeniera wasn't as far away as I'd remembered it. We found somewhere to park and threaded ourselves into the already thronging tourists.

"This may have been a mistake," I said as a family of ten came to a sudden halt in front of us to examine a collection of hats on display outside one of the numerous tourist shops.

"I don't know," said Nikki. "It's nice to do something different. I'd forgotten what it was like to be a tourist."

We picked our way through the group only to become entangled in a guided group of Germans. For a while I was fascinated by listening in on the history of the Moors and the Catholic monarchs as they warred over the area but then a narrow alleyway caught my attention and suddenly, we were away from the crowds.

"What was that all about?" Nikki asked.

"Apparently this was one of the last areas to expel the Moors," I said.

"Was that it?"

"Pretty much. He talked an awful lot but didn't say very much. So yes, I guess the complete history here seems to be they threw the Moors out and then four hundred years later, along came the tourists."

"Hardly Rome."

"Still beats our village, Virriatos, where the only local history seems to be about a great shepherd who once passed through."

Once out of the tourist trail, it was surprisingly peaceful. We stood for a moment surveying the view. The village sat at the junction of a high valley and gave spectacular views down to the low valley below and on to the Mediterranean. The houses crowded behind us like a pile of children's bricks stacked with the care of a hyperactive two-year-old. While in front of us, the earth just dropped away into the valley below. We skirted the edge of the village for a while then went in search of some refreshment. The beers were expensive and the tapas sparse but it was good to relax away from the others for a while.

The tourist groups seemed never ending and it was fun for a while trying to spot the nationality of each group before their guide started their spiel.

"There's a lot of money passing through here," said Nikki.

I watched the groups as they milled about. What at first had seemed like haphazard meandering was in reality, a tightly controlled route through the village. The guides ensured that their groups stopped at very specific places for drinks, souvenirs and confectionary and quickly herded up those of their flocks who were tempted to drift. On closer observation, I noticed the guides were acquainted with the owners of each place they stopped on their seemingly random routes.

"It's all beautifully planned," I said. "You watch, these guys are getting pay-offs from the shop and bar owners."

We ordered more drinks and observed the choreography in action. As I watched, something started to niggle in that part of my brain which was attuned to look out for opportunities. That part which invariably led me into trouble but which, somehow, I could never resist.

Eventually, "These guys are missing a trick," I said.

Nikki stared at me as if I'd just suggested we should try naked folk dancing in the village square. Then she said, "Do you know how many kinds of dread I get when you say stuff like that?"

***

As evening settled over the Valle de Pastor, we took up our table at the Casa de Pastores. Sean had eventually turned up but had given little explanation for his absence beyond, 'having things to do'. I was about to have another go at trying to get him to open up when José Felipe appeared with a tray of beers.

He placed the tray on the table then leaned in to me. "Michael, I have to ask you a small favour."

"What's up, José?"

"I need your room for a few days. And the Señora's." José looked flustered.

"Oh, that's okay," I said, thinking it wasn't okay at all. Not in the slightest. It meant we would have to share the prefab with the others.

"It is only for a few days. I have a big booking. But you are not to worry. My cousin Juanita Antonia has a house where you can stay."

"Well, that's good news. Business picking up?"

"Yes, thanks to our friend Señor Robert here." He held out his hand towards Bob. "We have a full house." He smiled at Bob and patted him on the shoulder before heading back into the bar.

I glared at Bob. "Well?"

"Sorry, Michael. I didn't know that would happen. Honest."

"Didn't know what would happen?"

"The Americans. They loved their day out so much that they're coming back with the rest of their tour group."

I studied Bob for a moment. He fidgeted in his chair and nursed his beer with both hands. I pondered over this turn and the memory of the tourist processions we'd witnessed earlier down in Pampeniera. Sometimes the universe opens doors that are just too tempting to ignore.

"How many?" I asked.

Bob looked at me with a touch of puzzled surprise. "Five couples," he said then added, "that's ten people."

"Thank you, Bob. I was struggling with the maths."

"It's only for two nights." He eyed me carefully as if waiting for me to spring across the table at him. "And I'll split any tip I get with you."

I glanced around the group; they all seemed to be waiting for my reaction.

"I think we have an opportunity here," I said finally.

They continued to stare at me in silence. All apart from Nikki, who mumbled something I couldn't quite catch but sounded a bit like, 'Here we go'.

"We have a problem," I continued. "We, that is, none of us, can do this survival stuff –"

"Excuse me," Nikki said.

"Well, none of us apart from Nikki. We're not able to catch our food and we've yet to find out how to grow beer or pizzas, so anytime soon, very soon, we're going to run out of funds."

"It would probably help if you stopped trashing cars," Sean said with a big grin.

"That's not actually costing me anything other than a bit of internet bending but I take your point." I pulled the cigarette packet from my pocket, saw there was still only one cigarette left and dropped the pack back in my shirt pocket. "We've just about exhausted the emergency funds we were allocated and we can't ask for any more. We were sent here to learn how to survive on nothing so I'm suggesting we do just that."

"But you just said we can't do it?" Donny looked puzzled.

"I know. We can't do it the way they anticipated but we *can* do it our way. We all have various skills and I think it's time we worked together with what we have and stop trying to be the Swiss Family Robinson."

"You want me to nick some cars?" Donny asked.

"No, that's not what I'm saying," I said. "But between us, I'm sure we can work out how to generate a living here that doesn't involve hunting pigeons with a bow and arrow. For example, Bob's got these Americans coming up here and José's as happy as a dog with two sets of bollocks. Yesterday, we went down to Pampeniera and the place is awash with tourists looking for somewhere to spend their money. And what have they got to attract them there? Some pretty white chimneys, a few multicoloured rugs and a history book with one entry: the Moors and the Christians had a bit of a pop at each other five hundred years ago. That's it. These poor sods traipse all the way up the mountain looking for a bit of culture and history and they go home with a rug and a painted roof tile with a picture of a chimney on it."

"But there's even less up here," said Jason. "Are you suggesting we open up a gift shop or a tea room?"

"A tea room?" Ryan sneered. "Maybe a coffee house, like they have in Amsterdam. That'd go down a storm."

"Jason's right," said Sean. "There's even less to attract people up here. Where's the history?"

"We've got the ruin," I said. "It's certainly older than most of what they've got in Pampeniera."

"And the shepherd," suggested Bob.

"Who?" asked Nikki.

"The Great Shepherd," I said. "Apparently a Great Shepherd came this way once. That's why everything round here is called the shepherd this or that. Even the valley itself, El Valle del Pastor, the Valley of the Shepherd."

"That's it?" Nikki asked. "A tumble-down shed and a shepherd? That's what you've got to work with? We're doomed. I'll go pack my bag."

"He was a *Great* Shepherd," I said. "José Felipe assured me he was a Great Shepherd."

"Are you sure you don't want me to nick a few Porsches?" offered Donny. "I'm sure I could knock 'em out down in Marbella."

"Quite sure." I picked through vegetarian paella we'd been served in search of some vegetables. I found something which I thought was a piece of asparagus but it turned out to be a squid leg. I dropped it on the floor for the tangly haired mongrel that had just made a reappearance. "We're not going to do anything illegal," I continued. "Well, morally illegal anyway."

"By whose morals?" Nikki gave a provocative smile. "Charlie Manson's or Mother Teresa's?"

I gave her The Look then said, "Let's say somewhere in between." I returned her grin. "We're going to carry on taking photographs of dead rabbits and tree houses but meantime we work on ways of carving some sort of alternate income stream out of this place that doesn't involve nicking cars."

"I've got a little confession," said Sean.

"Do you want me to find you a little priest?" asked Donny

with the worst Irish accent since Sean Connery's Irish cop in The Untouchables.

Sean ignored the comment. "I got to chatting with this fella who owns the art shop in the village. He had what looked like a Van Gogh in the shop but I knew it couldn't be; there's no chance of any more of his stuff turning up. There's only two of his works unaccounted for and this wasn't either of those. Now, Rubens or Caravaggio, their stuff has been going missing for centuries. It could be anywhere. They turn up here, they disappear again there. And anyway, this one wasn't quite right. You see, Van Gogh always used to use a type of –"

"Are you coming to the point anytime soon, Sean?" interrupted Jason. "I'm just asking, because if this is going to turn into one of your homely folk tales would you mind terribly if I stopped listening?"

Sean smiled at Jason. "Why don't you go and see if you can bump-start your apartment block."

"You'll all be green when I get my Jacuzzi going in there." Jason emptied the last of the Rioja bottle into his glass. "You'll see."

"Anyway," Sean continued. "We got to talking about this and that, you know how it goes. I showed him my lost El Greco and he seemed impressed, asked me if I knew of any others the man himself might have mislaid. I wasn't going to say anything, but… well. First off, I only did it for the craic. But then…"

I thought for a moment. "What does he do with them?" I asked.

"He takes them down to the car boot sales in the Costas. He never puts any labels on them, never tells anybody they're nothing they ain't, just leaves them half hidden in amongst some old reproductions and other tat. Sooner or later some chancer comes along and thinks he'll take advantage of a stupid local."

I sat back, supped from my iced gin and listened as they talked. Ryan decided he would go to the market and buy some more telescopes. Donny thought he might see if José Martin could use a bit of help in cloning car keys should any of his customers lose one and Bob suggested that Professor Rupert Carstairs could publish a guide book for the area. For a late evening, alcohol tinged brainstorming session, most of the ideas were fanciful to say the least. But perhaps we might just make enough out of the mix to survive the next few months and get home before anybody notices.

After a while the conversation drifted into more normal topics such as why the Spanish have so much trouble making tea and whether or not dwarfs can grant wishes. I excused myself and slipped upstairs. I needed to pack some things if I was going to have to move house in the morning. I pulled my clothes from the wardrobe and drawers and laid them on the bed. Not much to show for half a life really. I'd always thought it a virtue that I had no ties, that I could fit everything I owned into a rucksack and be gone within twenty minutes. Now, looking at my possessions scattered across a pink blanket, it seemed somewhat pathetic. People my age were company directors or Rock Gods and there I was, a washed up squaddie with the only thing separating me from a stay at Her Majesty's, a bunch of scoundrels with the moral compass of a politician in election year.

A light tapping on the door lifted my darkening mood. That would be Nikki. I glanced at the chaos on the bed then hurriedly stuffed everything in the rucksack with a quick yell of, "Hang on!"

I swung the door open for Nikki. Except it wasn't.

Bob filled the frame of the Alpujarran pocket-sized doorway. "I brought you some cheese." He held out a plate of cheese and bread so I could see he was telling the truth.

"I don't remember ordering cheese," I said. "Although I may well have forgotten of course. I've been doing a fair bit of forgetting of late."

"No, you didn't order it. But I went to get some for you. I noticed you hadn't eaten much because of all the meat in the vegetarian paella." He moved his feet to and fro as if walking without actually going anywhere.

"Thank you," I said and held the door wider. "You'd better come in." I glanced briefly into the empty corridor as he brushed past me.

He walked in and stood in the centre of the room. "It's a nice room. Bigger than I thought."

"I'm sure your Americans will be very happy with it."

Bob wobbled the cheese plate as he moved from foot to foot. "I didn't mean that to happen. I didn't know they'd all come back."

"I know," I said. "You'd better put that plate down before you drop it." I waved a hand towards the dressing table.

Bob placed the plate down next to my laptop then sat on the edge of the bed. "I didn't want you to think I'd planned it, that's all."

The idea of Bob engaging in any sort of forward planning seemed faintly ludicrous. I took a piece of Manchego and dropped it on one of the pieces of bread then sat on the bed next to Bob. "Don't worry. As José said, it's just a couple of days." I bit on the bread and cheese. Manchego had always been one of my favourite cheeses.

"Cheese was all I could find easily in the kitchen," Bob said. "José's not very good with vegetarian stuff."

"Hmm, odd really, when one thinks that half of Europe's salads originate here." A movement by the open door caught my eye. I looked up to see Nikki hovering outside.

I stood quickly. "Oh, Nikki. Come on in. Bob was just… he brought me some cheese."

"I was only passing," she said. "I saw your door open, that's all."

"You can come," I repeated. "We have cheese."

"No, it's alright, you're busy and I have to pack. I'll catch you in the morning." She disappeared along the corridor.

My body deflated under me and I sat heavily onto the bed.

"I suppose I should have tried to find some olives," Bob said. "They always go nicely with cheese."

~ *C h a p t e r   F i f t e e n* ~

Juanita Antonia's house was a little terraced cottage in a side street just a short walk from the Casa de Pastores. Nikki and I had the place to ourselves as Juanita Antonia had recently moved to Granada for work. Two bedrooms and a small shower room took up the top floor while the ground floor was mostly open-plan with a small, but functional kitchen, adjoining a good sized living area. We drew lots for who got the back bedroom with the view to the mountains. I lost. The front bedroom faced onto the street with a tiny balcony, big enough for a plant pot or clothes airer but not both. I emptied my belongings into the drawers and wardrobe which swallowed them up with barely an impact on the available space. The room was a good size, significantly larger than the one I'd had at the Casa de Pastores; I guessed by the beam which straddled the ceiling that it had probably once been two rooms.

I headed downstairs and examined the kitchen while I waited for Nikki to unpack. She clearly had more stuff than me. The equipment in the kitchen was fairly basic and centred around a gas cooker supplied by a large orange gas bottle in the adjacent cupboard.

"Fancy a coffee?" Nikki walked over to the kitchen worktop and picked up a little metal espresso maker. "I've never tried making it in one of these before. Any idea how it works?"

I looked at the contraption which looked more like a miniature pressure cooker than anything which made coffee. "Where does it plug in?"

"It doesn't. I think you put coffee in this end," she pointed to the top section. "And water in the bottom then put it on the gas." She turned the pot around in her hands. "Or it might be the other way round."

"Looks more like something the Taliban might bury under a road," I said.

"Hmm, maybe we'll wait till we get to the bar." She put the device back on the worktop.

We locked up the little house and headed back to the Casa de Pastores.

We had to weave through a selection of badly parked hire cars, each of which seemed to be jostling for the closest point to the entrance, leaving little space between them. We shuffled our way past them and settled at an outside table. José Felipe brought coffee and tostadas without waiting to be asked.

"I see your guests have arrived." I nodded towards the cars.

"Yes," José said. "They stay two days. You can have your rooms back then."

"No hurry, José. Juanita Antonia's house is very nice."

A jabbering noise from inside grew louder and I turned to see a group of noisy tourists closed around Bob. The mini flash mob overflowed outside and suddenly our peaceful breakfast was overrun by a herd of Americans. I recognised a couple of them from the previous visit but I think I'd blanked their names.

I noticed Bob caught in the middle of the throng and called out to him. "Hey, Bo… Rupert." I caught myself just in time.

Bob heard my call and turned to look for me. "Oh, hi, Michael." He waved his hand high above the bobbling heads.

"This is my Experience Group up from…" He turned to the nearest American. "Where are you from?"

"Milwaukee, the home of the great Menomonee Lager. Only the best lager in the whole state."

"Mini mummy?" queried Bob.

"Menomonee, Milwaukee."

"Me no money?"

"Menomonee. Jeez, it's the biggest village in Wisconsin. You must have heard of it?"

I thought it might be time to rescue Bob. "I think Professor Carstairs meant, where are you from here in Spain?"

The American looked a bit puzzled for a moment then, "Ah, sure. Down the coast aways. Little place called Bahia Blanca. Nice place, like walking into a history book, they haven't even got a Starbucks yet. Can you believe that?"

"You must find that very challenging," I said.

"You betcha!" He looked around the group. "Hey, Nate, when're we going up to see Isolde's castle?"

"It's not Isolde," Nate called back over the heads of the others. "It's Isadora."

"You sure?"

"Yes, you're thinking of Christian and Isolde. Wagner did a song about them."

"So who the hell is Isadora?"

"She was the queen of Spain in Olden Times. Ask Professor Rupert, he'll tell you all about her."

Bob broke free of the melee and clapped his hands to get the group's attention. In his best BBC voice, "Thank you for your patience. Your rooms are now all awaiting so if one would like to make one's way to the reception foyer, the manager will check one in. We can reconvene again here in thirty minutes for the guided tour of Queen Isabella's Viewing Circle."

I heard the new American whisper to Nate, "Isabella? I thought you said Isadora?"

"It's her Royal Name. Professor Rupert told us all about it last time. It was a big secret at the time."

They headed into the bar and gathered around José Felipe who was beginning to look slightly intimidated as they vied for his attention.

Bob gave a long whooshing sound and collapsed into a chair like a punctured RIB.

"You're barmy," Jason said "You're never going to pull this off. Your memory's shit, you can't remember what load of bollocks you told them from one minute to the next and your accent is wandering from Buckingham Palace to Ramsay Street and back again via Dick van Dyke."

"Did you ever think about taking up motivational speaking, Jason?" asked Nikki.

"I'm not very good at accents," confessed Bob.

"Don't worry about it, Bob," I said. "They're unlikely to notice a regional accent variation. Just don't try too hard. Relax."

Ryan arrived from the direction of the village and dumped a bag on the table. "Nobody didn't have no telescopes."

I stared at the bag while trying to untangle the nest of double negatives. I gave up. "What's in the bag then?"

"Chocolate."

"You going to sell the Americans chocolate?"

"Huh? No, it's for me. I would've killed for some last night. Maybe I should grow some chocolate next to the dope plants. Wonder why nobody's thought of that before? It's a natural isn't it? Like cheese and chips." Ryan stretched himself out of his seat and headed for the track. "I need to do a little pruning."

The sound of approaching Americans spurred me to vacate the area.

"We'll see you up at the circle, Bob, Professor Rupert."

Nikki and I set a leisurely pace up the hill and by the time we arrived at the ruin, the sun already dominated the sky. I noticed Ryan in the distance, as he pottered up and down in the middle of his adopted crop, pausing every so often to clip a few heads into a bag.

We sat on the low wall and gazed at the sea line which broke land and sky.

"What do you reckon this place actually was?" Nikki asked.

I cast my eyes around. "Looks like a shepherd's lodge or something but maybe built on something older. That brick Ryan had was probably Roman. It certainly wasn't Spanish writing on it."

"So, what's your big plan? I'm guessing you weren't impressed by last night's suggestions."

"Oh, I don't know," I said. "Donny's idea about building a Spanish Galleon and having it sail up and down to add authenticity to Queen Isadora's viewing platform has some merit."

Nikki jabbed an elbow in my ribs. "To be fair, he did suggest using a miniature Airfix kit as the perspective would make it look real."

"Ah, yes. I forgot that bit."

"So?"

"So, I think we need a bit more history than Isabella waving bye-bye to Columbus or the Moors and Christians having a bit of a scrap in the general area."

"Like what?"

I waved my arm in a semicircle, indicating the immediate terrain. "Well, this area here for example, we know it's a ruin but of what? The language on Ryan's brick suggests Latin, so we could say the Romans had something here without too much of a stretch. And this circle," I pointed at the paved circle. "A gladiator's training ring perhaps?"

"It's a perfect lookout spot here," said Nikki, getting the feel of the direction in which I was going. "Maybe the Romans used a massive trebuchet to chuck rocks at incoming Moorish invaders?"

I gazed at the sea, some miles down the valley. "It would have to be one hell of a trebuchet but why not? Maybe the biggest one ever built?"

"And a battle, we need a big battle."

I pondered that as I gazed over the terrain in front of me. I could almost see the Romans and the Moors charging at each other across the landscape. "The Battle of Virriatos," I mused. "It's got a ring to it."

The noise of jabbering brought me back to the twenty-first century as Bob led his Americans over the ridge and down the slope to the ruin. As they drew closer, Bob's narrative came through the fug of general noise.

"And here is the viewing circle where the courtiers would put her throne so she could watch the boats sail out."

"I thought it was just one ship?" queried one of the new Americans, a tall gangly man with a Red Sox baseball cap.

Bob paused for a moment then, "Well, Christopher Columbus was only one ship, of course. But there were others. When the Armada went by for instance, she was here for three days there were that many ships."

"That'd sure be something to see," said Red Sox.

"Yes, they had a special Royal Tent just there." Bob waved his arm randomly but ended up pointing to where Ryan was gathering his harvest.

The group immediately turned and headed towards Ryan. He glanced up at the noise and stared wide-eyed at the oncoming charge of Americans as if it was Gettysburg all over again. He moved backwards slowly with arms outspread to protect his crop.

"Of course, the tent's not there now," Bob called after them as he realised the devastation his random historical event was about to cause. "There's nothing to see there anymore."

Ryan shuffled a few steps side to side and held his arms as wide as possible in an effort to make himself look big. "Woah!"

To his obvious surprise, the horde stopped dead. For a moment all was silent and then a faint female voice asked, "Is this where he said the Royal Tent was, honey?"

Bob caught up with the group and between attempts to breathe he said, "You have to be careful. This is the special Royal… um… Royal Plantation where they planted um… a special Royal plant in commemoration of… the Royal Tent." He bit his lip as the final reluctant words escaped and with them, the realisation of the nonsense he'd just uttered. He searched the collected faces looking for clues as to how they were going to respond. In the pause, the heat haze shimmered, flies buzzed and the only element missing from the frozen tableau was an Ennio Morricone film score.

A slightly pot-bellied man in a Nike T-shirt asked, "So, what was the plant?"

Bob's mouth moved but remained silent.

"It's a type of scented tobacco." I stepped in to help. "In commemoration of the tobacco brought back from America by Columbus."

"Is this it?" A gold bangled arm pointed at Ryan's garden.

Ryan shook his head furiously while Bob nodded his.

"What do you do with it?"

Ryan looked helpless in the onslaught of questions. He stared at me with eyes silently screaming, 'Help'.

Sometimes, when in a hole, the only thing to do is to keep digging to see if one can find a way out the other end. "It's used in a secret potpourri mixture which is still supplied to the Spanish Royal Family to this day. Now, if we look just down here," I pointed to the ruin. "We can see the remains of a Roman villa which was used as a defensive position against the Moors." That should divert them.

"What's it smell like?" asked Wrist Bangles.

"Can we have some to take home?" asked Nike T-shirt. "Grandma would be happy as a clam, she got potpourri all over the place."

Ryan's glare turned from 'Help' to 'I'm going to kill you if you don't get rid of these people'.

"It's very expensive," I said. "That's why it's only the Royal Family that can buy it. Now, in this big circle area down here –"

"How expensive?" Red Sox interrupted my feeble attempt at diversion.

The group closed on Ryan who eventually relented and let them smell the precious Royal Herb.

"Smells like my daughter's bedroom," said a woman whose linen jacket was a shade of pink surely created only to bring help to shipwreck survivors.

"Smells like hash to me," said Red Sox.

"I've been told it's quite similar," I said. "Okay, who would like to see the site of the Great Battle of Virriatos?" I needed to do something to divert them from Ryan's garden and the site of an ancient battle was the last bar in my battery. Fortunately, that seemed to do the trick and we led a strange procession back up the slope to our field.

I stopped the group in the middle of our field and Bob took charge with such an inspired description of rampaging Moors and disciplined Roman platoons that even I wondered fleetingly if it was all true. His accounts of the mayhem and blood were so graphic that I worried he might be overdoing it, but a quick look round showed his audience were enthralled and eating up every word.

I heard talking behind me and turned to see Ryan and Red Sox ambling up the slope towards us. Red Sox carried a small paper bag. I hadn't realised we'd left one behind. I left Bob to his oration and met the two stragglers as they approached.

"Everything alright?" I asked Ryan as they approached.

"Yeah, no worries," said Ryan. "Mitch here was telling me they got a castle in Las Vegas where knights do jousting fights while you have a steak dinner."

"It's not a real castle," said Mitch. "But I got to see King Arthur fight Lancelot. It was awesome."

"You should go listen to Bo… Professor Rupert, he's talking about the Battle of Virriatos which happened here."

"Right here?"

"On this very field."

"Wow!" Mitch scurried over to join the rest of his group.

"What's in the bag, Ryan?" I asked.

"What bag?"

"The one your new best mate was carrying."

"Oh, that bag."

"Yes, that bag. What was in it?"

"Just a little bit of Isadora's Potpourri."

"You know what's going to happen if he tries to take that on an aeroplane?"

"I mixed it with some of those yellow flower things, nobody will notice."

"Until somebody wants to know why a grown man is carrying a bag of buttercups."

Ryan just shrugged and headed across the field in the direction of the Casa de Pastores.

Bob finished his discourse on the Battle of Virriatos and took his group back down the track.

Nikki and I stood in the centre of the field.

"I think that could have gone better," I said after a while.

"I think we might need a better plan than just inviting a bunch of tourists up the mountain, feeding them bullshit for a couple of hours then sending them home with a bag of buttercups," said Nikki.

"I think I mentioned once before that I'm not terribly good at planning."

She raised her eyebrows and widened her eyes in an expression of mock shock. "Really? You do surprise me. And this from the man who thought destroying a politician's bank account was a good way of raising awareness to social injustice?"

"Okay, it wasn't one of my better ideas but in my defence…" I thought for a moment then, "No, actually I haven't got a defence. It was a crap idea from the off."

We ambled down the hill and joined the others at the Casa de Pastores for a lunchtime snack.

José had just set a plate of miniature tuna pies in front of us when Nate leaned in and wrapped his arm around Bob's shoulder.

Bob looked terrified but manged a forced grin. "Oh, hello, Nate."

"Good talk up there, buddy," Nate said. "Where's the gift shop round here? My friends want some postcards of the battles and maybe a souvenir teapot or two."

Bob looked around as if trying to find the gift shop.

"They've closed it down for refurbishment," I said. "It was up on the site of the battle, you probably noticed the construction going on? The multicoloured building?"

"Oh, that? I thought that was a hobo camp or something. Well, that's the way it falls I guess." He patted Bob on the shoulder. "Well, thanks again, Professor. Maybe give you a look up next time round." He headed back inside.

"A gift shop, huh?" Donny's eyes sparkled and a smile drifted into focus across his face. "How come we didn't think of that before?"

"Because we're trying to stay out of prison?" suggested Jason.

"No, not a gift shop." Donny's excitement was clearly growing as his eyes widened even more. "A Visitor Experience Centre." He held his hands out in front of him as if physically touching that which he was envisioning. "Like they've got in the Poldark Mine in Cornwall. There's this model of the village as it was in olden times where you can press buttons and the lights come on the little houses. It's really cool."

"We could make a model of the prison we're all going to be locked up in," said Jason.

"No," I said. "There's an idea here. We've just not been thinking big enough."

"Oh shit," I heard Nikki say but I ignored her and carried on. "If we're going to make this convincing, it needs something more up there than an old shack and Jason's un-mobile home."

"What do you suggest?" asked Nikki.

"A Visitor Centre maybe. Part gift shop, part displays of old stuff. We can scavenge the markets. And we need a few signs about, you know, this is the spot where Ikkiducias fell in the final battle."

"Ikkiducias?" queried Nikki.

"Don't be picky. I'll raid Wikipedia for some Roman names. And something big, we need something big people can be photographed next to."

"Like a tank," suggested Ryan. "I had my picture taken next to a tank once. It was in an Asda car park in Tooting. It had a parking ticket on it so it had probably been there more than two hours."

We all fell silent as each of us tried to work that through in our own way. Finally, I said, "Probably not a tank. They didn't really have so many of those in Roman days."

"How about a trebuchet," said Nikki. "After all, we've got the stone circle it stood on."

"We can't build a trebuchet," said Jason. "That's ridiculous."

"No." I picked at the olives which came as a garnish for the little tuna pies. "We don't need a whole one. It would never have survived. We just need some old wooden beams. Sean, you must know how to make things look old?"

"I've done it a few times with picture frames," said Sean. "Never anything as big as a trebuchet. But what the hell, it can't be that difficult."

And so the plans finally started to come together. I volunteered to get into Wikipedia, Travel Spy and the BBC History websites to open sections about Virriatos. Nikki agreed to write some historical stuff for a dedicated village website and the others said they'd get together to turn the shacks into something resembling a Visitor Centre. With the promise of more groups of tourists to come, José Felipe offered to support the shack rebuild with a supply of leftover paint and timber he'd accumulated over the years.

After lunch, we all headed back up to the field to better visualise our ideas.

"You need to do something with that thing, Jason." Ryan pointed at Jason's motorless home. "It's a bit of a rust heap."

"There's no rust on it," Jason said. "Well not much anyway."

"We could always push it down the hill a bit," suggested Bob. "You know, get it out of sight."

"You're not pushing that anywhere. It's my home for the next few months. And José Martin's on the lookout for a new engine for it, so once I get that fixed, I can move away."

We turned our attention to the random shacks which served as the camp. Structurally, they were quite sound, Paco's guys had done a good job and it wouldn't take too much to dress them up a bit. Painting mostly. I'd seen National Trust reception buildings in a worse condition.

"What do you think, Sean?" I asked. "Blue or yellow?"

Sean turned to stare at me. "You ask me that because I paint? You do know it's works of art I paint and not bus shelters?"

"As far as I know, you're the only person here who's actually held a paintbrush of *any* sort. By my reckoning, that makes you the resident expert."

Sean studied the sheds for a while then said, "Green and brown then. Blend them in with the surroundings. It's what Lord Balfont did on his estate."

"Lord Balfont?"

"The fella with all the racehorses, you must know of him. He bought a Van Gogh from me for his dining room. He had a bit of his estate open to tourists to pay for his coke habit. Painted the ticket office green and brown they did. So that's what I say, green and brown."

"Green and brown it is then."

***

That afternoon, Nikki and I headed into the village. Nikki set off to buy some food for the house; she'd decided it was time we started cooking for ourselves rather than being totally dependent on the Casa de Pastores for our meals. I didn't really see the need to change what seemed like a perfectly reasonable catering arrangement but as we were only going to be in the house for a few days it didn't really matter. I set out to explore some of the random shops that had little logic in their choice of stock and where it was possible to find socks, tins of tomatoes and bottles of embalming fluid all on the same shelf.

The first shop I entered presented a front of being a tourist trap but opened up inside to reveal itself as a hardware shop with a side helping of local produce. I scanned the dangling Jamon legs and the stacked and assorted jars of honey which vied for shelf space alongside a rather suspicious looking local wine. I picked up a bottle and examined the label which revealed little about the contents other than the fact it was a red wine. Out of curiosity and the fact it was only two euros, I decided to risk it.

The next shop looked a bit more hopeful and in amongst the socks, ten pairs for five euros, chain saw spare parts and eleven different varieties of bleach, I found some old farming tools. I chose a couple of ancient looking implements then my eyes lighted on an old knife. I turned it in my hands and rubbed at the grime encrusted blade. It was about twelve inches long and severely rust pitted but still held an edge. I couldn't date it but it looked old, I'd ask Sean, he might have a better idea. I bought the knife, along with an axe with a handle that was probably older than God, a ship's compass, several bottles which looked suitably antiquated and a mysterious contraption with a screw thread which drove a pair of ten centimetre arms open or closed. I guessed it was some sort of device for levering something apart – maybe a fruit peeler or a corn de-husker but I really had no idea.

Nikki was already back at the house by the time I returned with my treasures. The smell of cooking greeted me as I entered.

"Hi, honey, I'm home," I called.

"Yeah, yeah," she said. "Don't think this is going to be a habit. It's your turn tomorrow."

"Hope you like pizza."

She stirred a big pot on the cooker then tasted the spoon. "That'll do, see if you can find some bowls."

I dumped my purchases on the kitchen table and found a couple of bowls in the third cupboard. I placed them on the table and Nikki dolloped several ladleful's of a tomato and pasta mix onto each plate.

"I call it tomato pasta mix," she said. "It's a bit like pasta tomato mix but not quite so posh." She dug at some burnt-on pasta in the bottom of the pot. "You're on washing up by the way."

"I figured." I sat at the table and tasted the meal. It tasted of tomatoes and pasta. "Mmm, that's good."

"I'll try you on my other speciality next time. I call that one boiled potatoes and pasta."

"Can't wait."

She pushed the bottle of suspicious wine towards me. "You going to open this or is it just for decoration?"

I pulled the cork and poured a couple of glasses. I waited for a moment to see if the liquid burnt a hole through the glass. Okay, so far so good. I took a tentative sip and the liquid scored a trail across my tonsils and warmed my stomach in a way in which I was sure wine should never do. I watched in frozen anticipation as Nikki touched her glass to her mouth.

"What the hell is that?" Nikki's lips seemed to recoil from the glass.

"I'm not sure. I found it in a hardware shop."

She stared at me for a moment then, "Are you sure it's safe to drink?"

"Not entirely. But it does say 'Vino' on the label."

Nikki shrugged and took another sip. "Okay, it improves as it goes along."

We ate silently for a while, and then I said, "I bought you some presents." I pointed my spoon at the pile of random purchases on the table.

"I noticed. Aren't I the lucky one? Other men bring me flowers when I cook for them; you bring me a 1930's bayonet and a rusty speculum."

I studied the threaded contraption. "Ah, is that what it is? I thought it was an olive pipper or something."

"Trust me, it's a speculum. A woman never forgets what a speculum looks like."

I turned the screw on the speculum and it gave momentarily before seizing solid. "It looks very old. It might even be Roman. Do you think they had these in Roman times?"

"I wish you'd stop playing with that. It's giving me the jitters." Nikki took a large sip of the wine then tipped her head to one side and smiled. "I think I may have mis-underestimated this stuff. It's got a sneaky little punch under its suave and sophisticationary extorierior."

"Extorierior?"

"That's what I thought." Nikki suppressed a giggle.

I moved the bottle to the other side of the table but Nikki leaned across and dragged it back. "Not so fast, buddy. It's been a long week." She wobbled another refill into the glass. Mostly.

I finished my glass. She was right, it was powerful stuff. In fact, I wasn't even sure it was wine, maybe a home-made brandy?

"I think I'm going to have a siesta," Nikki announced and pushed herself into a standing position. "I've suddenly come over all… sleepy tired."

"Do you need a hand?" I asked.

She leaned gently on the table as her head swivelled in my direction. "I think that might be efficacious."

I helped her up the narrow, tortured staircase and into her room. She retained a fast grip on my hand as she flopped onto the bed. I lost my balance and ended up sitting next to her.

"You too, huh?" she said and shuffled her head onto the pillow. "Just give me a moment and I'll make us a nice cup of tea." She relaxed her hand but still held mine.

"I can do that," I said. "I was famous for it in my unit. Where are the tea bags?"

"Ah, I think there's a problem with the tea plan. Damn. I knew I'd forgotten something. More wine?"

"I think it's all gone," I lied.

"Oh. Are you okay?" Her eyes squinted in my direction. "I look as tired as you feel. I feel. I meant you look." She patted my thigh. "You should siesta as well." Her eyes drifted closed but her hand continued to stroke at my thigh.

I watched her as her breathing settled into a slower rhythm. Her muscular frame tested the white cotton of her shirt with each breath. I wondered if I should undo a couple of buttons but decided that could be misinterpreted. I needed another drink and I tried to ease her hand away so I could slide off the bed.

"No," she said. "You stay here. I was thinking…" Her hand explored more of my thigh. "We've done alright, haven't we? I mean; you and me."

"Well, none of them have died yet, if that's what you mean?"

She was still and silent for so long I thought she'd nodded off, then, "No. I meant you and me. You know…" She fell silent again and her breathing deepened. I tried again to ease myself free and this time her hand fell lifelessly onto the bed. I slipped free and went back downstairs.

I sniffed at the wine bottle, trying to guess at the contents but it made my eyes water slightly so I emptied the remains into my glass. No point in wasting it, whatever it was. I sank the glass then washed up and headed for the roof terrace with my laptop. Time for a little creativity on the tourist sites. I left a smattering of location reviews on Kwikjet's site with links to a newly created Virriatos Visitor Information Site. Several of the bigger hotels in nearby resorts had really lax security on their websites and it took only minutes before many of their visitors were singing the praises of the fantastic historic attraction just a short drive away. I sent several emails to some coach tour operators asking for timetables of their excursions to Virriatos. Little seeds.

The warm air and the wine worked at me until I lay the laptop aside and pushed back in the chair. Within moments, I was away in the land of warm fuzziness and drifting clouds.

~ *Chapter Sixteen* ~

We spent the best part of the following morning avoiding Bob's Americans. Although they were only eight, at times they felt more like eighty. They seemed to be on an endless quest to find rubbish on which to spend their money. At lunch time they sat around a pontoon of four tables and compared purchases. Little earthen jars of honey seemed the most popular items although models of the ubiquitous Alpujarran white chimneys came a close second. As they sat there in their new straw hats, munching locally made almond cakes and testing the licor de flores that one of them had just opened, I realised our plan might actually work.

José Felipe brought us drinks and tapas of tortilla and olives. "You can come back tomorrow," he said. "These people are leaving in the morning."

"Thanks, José, but we're okay at Juanita Antonia's place," I said. "And anyway, you're likely to be getting busier soon."

"What do you mean?"

"Just a guess."

He gave me a slightly concerned look and hurried back to the kitchen.

"What have you been up to?" Nikki asked.

"Just tweaking the tourist websites a bit. You know, adding a few places of interest they'd missed."

We finished lunch and headed up to the site. The place was busier than I'd ever seen it. Paint pots dripped their colours onto the grass as Ryan and Donny painted in the general direction of the shacks. Sean shouted periodic instructions which were mostly related to keeping the paint roughly within the confines of Andalucía and which were mainly ignored. Jason had reluctantly agreed to allow his wheeled monstrosity to be used as accommodation for the group and appeared to be trying to sandpaper away the rust from the bodywork. It was likely to be a pointless task as I had a feeling that rust was all that was holding the beast together.

Between shouting instructions towards Ryan and Donny, Sean was helping Bob drag several large wooden beams onto a section of paint free grass where they could be stripped of nails or screws leftover from previous usage. Sean intended these to become the remains of our trebuchet.

Nikki and I set to work inside one of the shacks and built a rustic shelf set from some old planks. It hadn't been intended to be quite as rustic as it turned out but carpentry was not one of my strong points. It would probably be okay provided we never trusted it with anything heavier than a pair of socks or anything capable of rolling.

I stood back to survey our work. "Well, I think it's beginning to look like a Visitor Centre already."

"It certainly looks better than the last Visitor Centre I saw," said Nikki.

"Where was that?"

"Palmyra."

As evening started to close, we all wandered back to the Casa de Pastores where José had prepared a huge salad for us. He returned with a couple of bottles of Cava and popped the corks.

"What's the occasion, José?" I asked.

"You were right." He filled each glass to exactly the same level with hardly a pause between them. "I have two new bookings from more tourists."

"That's great news, José. You'll be able to buy new bedding soon."

"My bedding is the best in the Alpujarras. My mother gave it to me when I took over the Casa de Pastores." He almost flounced as he headed back to the bar with a tray of empties.

"We could use some sheets for the caravan," said Donny. "It's got proper beds and everything."

"It's not a caravan," protested Jason. "It's an RV."

"What's the difference?"

"Caravans have to be towed, RVs drive themselves..." Jason's explanation tailed off as he began to realise the flaw in his argument.

"I rest my case." Donny emptied the last of his Cava and immediately replaced it with a bottle of San Miguel.

"José Martin thinks he's found an engine anyway," said Jason. "A Volvo D13 engine or something. It's currently in a truck at the bottom of the Poqueira Gorge after it came second in a chicken run with a German coach."

"A Volvo D13?" Donny said. "They're monsters. Cool."

Nikki and I finished our drinks and took a leisurely stroll back to the house.

I added a few more touches to the Virriatos Tourist website, including a picture of the remains of an ancient Roman trebuchet and a map of the battle.

Nikki handed me a glass of wine and we tried to watch Spanish television for a while until the relentless adverts defeated us and we took the bottle to the roof terrace to watch the evening gather. I lay back on one of the sunbeds and watched the night clouds stalk the darkening sky. Gradually the last stains of the departing sun disappeared below the mountain tops and in that magic moment between day and night, the air fell still.

"Well, I guess this is preferable to dragging around Bond Street guarding some despot's wife as she chooses her latest bit of bling." Nikki leaned against the balcony rail and the light breeze tugged at her silk wrap.

"Certainly less chance of getting shot at," I said.

She turned to face me, leaning back against the rail. "That's always a bonus. Although, I do miss the adrenaline rush." The wrap did little to conceal the fact that it was the only item she'd put on since her shower.

I reached to the little table for my wine glass and found it empty. "Any more in that bottle?"

Nikki leaned forward and topped up both glasses. The wrap shifted across her legs as she moved and the moonlight softened the normal firm tone of her muscles. I tried not to look as the flimsy cloth moved. I really tried.

She sat on the edge of my lounger and I shifted slightly to allow her space. The wrap fell open as she sat and her thigh slipped into the silver moonlight.

"You've been drinking a bit less lately," she said.

"Sorry, I'll try to keep up."

She pushed at my leg in a sign of gentle remonstration. "Stupid. You know what I meant." Her hand remained on my thigh, the warmth of the touch a soft island against the cooling night air.

"I guess my demons are suffering from the heat. I'm sure they'll be back as soon as we go home."

"And you've stopped smoking."

I reached into my pocket, pulled out the cigarette pack and dropped it on the table. "Not yet."

She opened the pack and looked at the one cigarette inside. "Okay." Her hand slid slightly on my thigh. It might have been just an involuntary movement. It might have been.

I slipped my hand on top of hers. "I sometimes get the feeling that this place is a step to the left of the rest of the world. Normality doesn't quite apply here. I think the ghosts are confused."

"Well, whatever it is, it seems to suit you."

"Now you're beginning to sound like a tailor."

She laughed and the moonlight caught the brightness in her eyes. I took a gentle grip on her hand and pulled, waiting for the resistance. None came. As she moved towards me, my other hand found the naked part of her thigh which had been tormenting me for the last five minutes. Her skin was soft but the muscles beneath were as solid as I knew they'd be. Both disconcerting and arousing in a very strange way. My hand continued upwards and snaked around her back. As I drew her closer, the wrap slipped away completely and fell to the floor, just at the moment our lips touched.

I felt her slight breasts brushing at me through my light cotton shirt and yearned for flesh to flesh contact. As we kissed, I fought free of my shirt and we pressed against each other breathing in the passion which had been simmering since the day we'd met. I felt her hand tugging at the button on my jeans and arched my back slightly to allow her hands to work. Another tug, a wriggle and a shuffle then I was as naked as she was. Our bodies entwined, searching and desperate. We became one just as the darkening night allowed the Milky Way to show itself as a jewelled trail across the sky. Marking out the way to eternity.

~ *C h a p t e r   S e v e n t e e n* ~

Casa de Pastores was already jostling in chaotic activity by the time Nikki and I arrived for our morning coffees and tostadas. José Felipe pulled another table into action for us and reappeared with our breakfast without us saying a word.

"More Yanks?" I asked Nikki.

"No, I think they're Brits this time."

"Why do you think that?"

"Teapots. There's teapots on the tables. I didn't even know José had any." Nikki refilled our coffee cups.

We watched the teapot trauma unfold as the breakfasteers attempted to jiggle more flavour from the little stringed teabags by repeated dunkings in the teapots. They jabbered noisily at José each time he passed but his increasing frustration was simply ensuring he gave the tables a wider berth with each passing.

"You look like you're having trouble?" I asked him as he brought a fresh coffee jug for us.

"I don't understand," he said, casting an eye to the three tables of teabag danglers. "I give them English tea like they ask but now they say the water is wrong. How can the water be wrong? It is the only water I have."

"I'll have a word with them."

I headed for the noisiest part of the Tea Club and pulled up a chair. "Hi, the owner says he's having a little trouble with his English, I wonder if I can help?"

A balding man with a red football shirt said, "Aye, lad. The fella himself is getting a reight monk on over the brew. Ta watter is reight nithered ain't it? You're not gonna mash a brew with nitherin watter. Wassa matter wi' the lad?"

I stared at the man for a moment while I tried to untangle the language. No wonder José was having trouble.

"I'm sorry," I said. "I got that there's something wrong with the tea, but… No, I lost the rest of it."

"I'm sorry," a young woman in a plain white T-shirt said. Her accent still spoke of Yorkshire but was at least accessible without recourse to Babel Fish. "It's the water. The waiter is trying to make tea with water that's not boiling."

"Ay, the wasak's no idea."

"Okay, Barry. You're not helping." The young woman turned to me. "Barry gets very upset if his tea's not right."

"I can see. He probably just drew it from the coffee machine. I'll ask him to boil some on the stove for you."

"T'at 'd be champion, lad."

I called over José and explained the problem. He seemed relieved to at least have a translation of the problem even if he wasn't overly impressed with the extra work.

"You guys up here for long?" I asked.

"Just overnight. We're here to see the Battle of Virriatos."

"Oh," I tried to remember exactly what I'd put about the battle on the Virriatos website. I was confident I'd never mentioned a battle actually taking place. But then, I had partaken of a few gins by the time I did that section so I wouldn't have been surprised if they'd said they were here to witness the moon landing. "You know there's no battle going on? I mean, not even a re-enactment. It's just an historic site."

"Oh aye. We kna' that. Wea'ar not gormless."

"We just wanted to see the place where it happened," said the woman. "The manager in our hotel said it's a very important site."

"I'll introduce you to Bo… Professor Carstairs. He's here doing a survey, he'll take you round." I waved an arm in the direction of our table. "Rupert! Rupert!" I called.

The table largely ignored me. I called again. "Rupert?"

Nikki glanced at me, her head tilted in momentary puzzlement then understanding broke, she nudged Bob and nodded towards me.

"Rupert," I called more loudly and Bob stared at me for a moment before receiving a less than subtle elbow in the ribs from Nikki. At last he twigged and came over to us.

"This is Professor Rupert Carstairs," I introduced. "He's an expert on the battle."

I slipped away, leaving Bob to the mercy of the visitors.

"You're not going to stay to translate?" Nikki grinned at me.

"I speak five languages and Geordie isn't one of them."

"Geordie is Newcastle, and Newcastle is in Tyne and Wear. They're Yorkshire."

"And geography, that was never a strong point of mine either." I sipped at my coffee. It was cold but still caffeine therefore a delicacy to be valued and not wasted.

We watched as Bob slipped comfortably into his latest personae. I hadn't yet worked out if he consciously created these roles or if he just happened on them and adopted them more by accident. The group seemed enthralled by whatever he was telling them. I just hoped that whatever is was, it wasn't too fanciful and that I wouldn't be involved in extricating him from another historical tangle.

We finished breakfast and headed up the track. I wanted to have a quick look round before Bob's group arrived.

Our 'Visitor Centre' sported some nice, albeit somewhat unusual, paintwork. The lack of any one colour in sufficient quantities had necessitated a degree of creativity which had resulted in a serendipitous camouflage effect. Not altogether out of keeping in the surroundings. Inside things were still somewhat sparse with a couple of trestle tables supporting the results of a quick raid of the antique stalls in the market and a few hasty posters of Romans and Moors with their weaponry.

Outside, Jason's immobile home still dominated the area but at least most of the moss and bird droppings had been cleaned off. I poked my head in the door and called.

"Come on in," returned Jason's voice. "Coffee's on."

The inside was decidedly more cluttered than last time I'd seen it but given the rapid upgrade from single occupancy to five-berth, it was still surprisingly roomy.

"Bob's bringing a group of Geordies up," I said.

"Yorkshire folk, not Geordies," I heard Nikki behind me.

Jason looked startled. "We're nowhere near ready," he said. "What's he thinking? We've got nothing for the gift shop."

"The gift shop? That's where you see the problem?"

"The gift shop is important," Jason said. "It sets the tone for the whole project. Where would the Coliseum be without a gift shop?"

"Well, it wasn't altogether planned. What about that box of random junk Sean brought back from Trevelez? There must be some old stuff in that lot."

"Mostly horsey stuff. Horseshoes, bits and pointy things."

"Pointy things?"

"Well, I don't know. I'm a banker; my only interaction with horses is usually from a box at Cheltenham."

"Well, see what you can do with that stuff while Bob's doing his tourist bit up at the ruin."

Nikki and I scanned the rest of the site. It would pass. It would have to. When we arrived at the ruin, I noticed Ryan was hastily surrounding his gardening patch with some Police Warning Tape.

"Where did you get that?" I asked.

He waved his arm towards the village. "You know that bit of road with the sharp bend and the sheer drop?"

"Yes."

"Somebody's crashed through the barrier again and the police put a load of this stuff across the gap."

"But you shouldn't have taken that. It's dangerous; cars could go through the gap."

He stared at me for a moment, then, "If a damn great metal barrier didn't stop them going over the edge then a little bit of plastic string's not going to make much difference." He went back to tying the tape around his garden.

The sound of approaching jabbering caught my ear and we turned to see Bob with his latest entourage marching up the slope. He stopped just short of the ruins to give his now well polished script about the battle between the Moors and Romans. As he finished, he led them over to the Viewing Circle and did his bit about Isabella watching Columbus set sail. He showed them the remains of the trebuchet and the remains of Castle Isabella whilst carefully avoiding Ryan's allotment or any mention of Royal Potpourri.

"Ah thowt t' Romans wor long gone afowa t' Moors arrived?" said the man in the red football shirt.

Bob stared at the man, blinking like a shell-shocked owl in a searchlight.

"Barry said he thought the Romans left many years before

the Moors arrived," said the young woman and now, official Yorkshire translator.

I'd come to realise that Bob's uncanny skills in character impersonation were only okay up until the point where he felt under threat. At which point he generally fell back on his goldfish impersonation. The mouth moved but words continued to remain unspoken.

I stepped over to try and help. "Yes, he's right," I said. "But this was the Twenty-Third Legion of Darmaticus. The lost legion, it was really famous. They settled here after the rest went back."

Barry's deep set eyes stared at me from under a set of heavily folded eyebrows but he said nothing. Instead he just grunted and pushed at an old brick with his boot.

Bob continued through the rest of his repertoire uninterrupted but we needed to prepare better. That's twice we've got away with our somewhat unusual versions of history but only just. We dropped by the field to warn Jason that they were on their way back then made our way to the Casa de Pastores where José Felipe greeted us as always like family and set us at our usual table.

I ordered coffees then turned to Nikki. "We need to button down this history business or we're going to get caught out before long."

"Well don't ask me," Nikki said. "My history education consisted of the Battle of Hastings and Dunkirk with not a lot in between."

I caught José's eye and he came over; he looked puzzled when he noticed our cups still contained coffee.

"Sorry," I said. "No more needed yet, I just want to find out some local history. Do you have a moment?"

José looked around the mostly empty tables then shrugged

and sat down. "There is much history here. Do you know about the Great Shepherd who came this way?"

"Yes, you mentioned it before. What about the Romans and Moors? Do you know anything about their battles?"

He thought for a moment then, "The Romans and Moors never met here," he said flatly.

That was a disappointment and if true, would necessitate a rethink of our site. "Maybe somewhere nearby?" I suggested. "Maybe they were fighting somewhere close and had a bit of a skirmish here?" I grasped.

"The Romans and Moors missed each other by..." He raised his eyes in thought. "By about... um... Three hundred years. More or less."

We fell silent for a moment while we thought about this information and the problems it presented our Visitor Centre.

Nikki finally broke the lull. "You didn't think to check this?" she asked me.

"To be fair," I replied. "I did mention this wasn't my period in history. I had a history teacher with a very narrow focus."

"Narrow focus? So, just what was your period in history?"

"Well, from around 1943 to... er..." I tried to recall my history lessons. "No, that was pretty much it."

"1943?" Nikki queried with a touch of incredulity.

"My history teacher had a thing about D-Day."

"You do realise that D-Day was in 1944?"

I thought for a moment. "You sure?"

"Absolutely, the Paras had a bit of a go at it. They're quite precious about their history."

I pondered this new revelation. "Well that makes a mockery of my History A-Level."

Nikki stared at me but said nothing.

I looked at José, "What about the old house on the ridge? I saw a brick which had Roman writing on it?"

"Ah, yes," he replied, after searching the sky for an answer. "The Old Mill. The Romans were there for a while. As were the Moors." He must have noticed my face light up because he hastily added, "Not at the same time you understand. Maybe 300 years later."

I thought for a moment how we could spin this then inspiration struck. "Windmills, great," I said to Nikki. "They're big in history. Maybe Don Quixote fought a battle here? He was quite keen on windmills, wasn't he?"

"Okay," said Nikki. "Just a couple of concerns. Firstly Don Quixote never actually fought any battles. That was the whole point of his story. And secondly, at the risk of further disturbing your faith in your education, Don Quixote wasn't real. He was a fictional character."

I turned back to José. "So, it was just a windmill?"

"No, it was not a windmill. It was a mill, a threshing floor for milling grain." My expression must have betrayed my lack of understanding because he added, "With horses, they pull threshing boards over the circle of stone to mill the grain."

I thought this through. The stone-paved circle, Isabella's viewing circle, was in fact just a flat area which farmers used to grind up grain.

"What about the house?" I asked José. "If it's that old, something must have happened there at some point?"

He smiled. "Of course, it is a very important place."

I brightened. "Go on," I encouraged. "What happened there?"

"The Great Shepherd," José said with an air of great import. "He once stood there." He turned to the sound of a table trying to attract his attention. "I must go."

I watched him as he left then turned to Nikki. "A shepherd stood there."

"Hmm," she said. "Not sure how we're going to big that up for a Visitor Centre exhibit. I suppose we could dress Ryan in an old sheet, give him a big stick and have him do a live re-enactment."

"Not helping," I said.

Nikki just laughed then said, "Come on, let's go see where Bob's got to. He's been a while."

We got up to leave but just then José intercepted me. "I need your help," he said, nodding towards a table near the bar entrance.

I followed his gaze and saw a pair of hippy types. All hair and ethnic shirts, it was difficult to tell from there if they were male, female or one of each. "What's up?" I asked.

"I do not understand them. You know my English is no good and they are trying to ask me things."

"Okay, I'll see if I can help."

I headed over to the table and the pair turned to me as I approached. The man was slim built but broad across the shoulders. His weathered face sported a week's worth of stubble and a small silver pin skewered his left eyebrow. His companion smiled as she spotted me. Her eyes were bright against the soft cappuccino tone of her skin and her build showed a strength which only comes from sustained physical activity.

There was nothing about them which would indicate their nationality so I defaulted to English. "Hi," I greeted. "Can I help? José said you were trying to ask him something."

"Oh, cool. It's our first time in Spain." The man's accent immediately set him in Western Australia, probably around Perth. "Sorry, my Spanish lessons only got as far as directions and menus."

"Even that doesn't seem to work very well," the girl said. "We just asked for beer and he brought food as well. We didn't order food."

"The Spanish round here is difficult," I said. "It's Andaluz, a heavy dialect. And the food, that comes free when you order drinks round here. It's called Tapas."

"Oh, that's cool. I was worried what we'd ordered," she said. "My name's Tania, this is Pete. We're from Margaret River, Oz."

"I'm Michael." I held my hand out; the man took it and did a complicated handshake which I tried to emulate with Tania.

"We were asking if there's any work round here," Pete said.

"We're Harmonious Travellers," Tania explained.

"We have to leave a positive spiritual footprint," Pete added. "So what we take out, we put back."

"I see," I said. I didn't.

"When we stop somewhere we have to replace the negative ripples we've caused with positive ones," Tania continued, as if that explained everything.

"We feel the harmonies here," Pete said.

"They're in frequencal harmony with our soul tunes," Tania said. "We want to help build the vibrational elements to raise this place to a higher plane."

No wonder José had struggled to understand them. "So you want work?" I tried.

"Yes," Pete said. "We can do Light Work or Rebirthing experiences. Tania's very gifted in chakra realignment."

I was beginning to feel my language skills were not up to this either.

"We also do Permaculture."

"What's that?" I asked. At least it sounded like something I stood a chance of understanding.

"It's living in line with natural ecosystems," explained Tania. "We observe the symbiotic harmonies in the earth before working with them and growing food in line with what the earth wants to offer us."

Nope. I didn't understand that one either. "There's not much work round here," I said. "Unemployment's around forty percent in parts."

"Oh dear," said Tania. She looked at Pete whose eyes had just taken the appearance of a sad puppy's.

"You could have more luck down on the coast," I offered. "You might get some bar work down there."

I was about to leave them to their spiritual footprints when I heard Nikki from behind me say, "You can come and stay up at our project. Just till you find something more suitable, you know."

I turned towards her and tried to silently transmit my displeasure at her suggestion by furrowing my eyebrows as fiercely as I could.

Nikki ignored my silent protests and a few minutes later we were trudging up the track to the field.

Nikki explained what we were doing there, which in listening to the explanation, actually seemed more complicated than spiritual permacultural footprints.

On the way, we passed Bob and his tourists coming down. They jabbered noisily as they passed and seemed in good spirits so I guessed things had gone reasonably well.

When we arrived at the field, Tania immediately ran to the woodline and opened her arms wide. I looked at Pete.

"She's feeling the energy of the trees," he said in reply to my unasked question. He went over to join her.

"What were you thinking?" I asked Nikki when they were out of earshot. "We can't give them work."

"They know how to work the land. Do you?"

"No, you know that. But we don't need to work the land; we've got the Casa de Pastores."

"If we can't make this Visitor Centre thing work, we're not going to be able to keep this up. Then you'll have to learn how to build a tree house and catch tofu."

I watched the pair moving between the trees, touching each one as they passed. "And you're sure these two know how to make vegetables?"

"Not entirely. But they certainly know more than all of us."

~ *C h a p t e r   E i g h t e e n* ~

Over the next few weeks Pete and Tania proved their worth
by building some highly effective huts from branches, leaves
and mud. They even turned out to be more waterproof than
Jason's monster RV during a freak thunderstorm.

I took lots of photographs of the huts and of the vegetable
patch they'd started and put them up on the site blog.

The Casa de Pastores kept busy with a steady flow of
tourists, even to the point of having to overflow to a couple of
nearby guesthouses on a couple of occasions. We adapted our
history profile as we went and had settled on a vague battle
between Moors and Christians and dropped all mention of
Romans. It was a bit of a shame as that had been the only
provable bit of history. But in the absence of anything
important we could attach to them, we felt it was generally
safer. We did keep the trebuchet although it was now a
Moorish weapon and proved very popular with many a
photograph of happy tourists sitting on the beam. We also
retained Queen Isabella's Viewing Circle as that always went
down well with the groups. Particularly after we found a huge
old chair in a junk sale that now served as the Royal Viewing
Throne. More magic photo moments at five euros a pop.

Our Visitor Centre improved day by day with each
additional artefact rummaged or scavenged from markets, junk

shops or forgotten sheds. Sean painted some realistic looking battle scenes of the area in the style of somebody called Diego Velázquez who, according to Sean, had a bit of a name for painting battles and royalty. These we had printed and framed locally and the visitors loved them.

José Felipe at the Casa de Pastores was more than generous in keeping us all fed and watered, his hospitality fuelled by the constant flow of new customers. With that, and the income from the Visitor Centre, we looked all set to coast through the next three months without ever having to catch a real rabbit.

For the briefest of moments, I felt at peace and this strange mountain, with its even stranger inhabitants, was beginning to feel like home. I'd had no flashbacks for several weeks now and much to José Felipe's concern, my alcohol consumption had dropped significantly. However, the demons of mischief were busy making their plans to screw up my life once more.

Nikki and I ambled up to the site in no particular hurry. The sun already held domain over the mountain and gave stark but beautiful contrast to the white snow caps against a blue which normally, only exists in travel brochures.

"I think I might even miss this place when I'm done," Nikki said. She stopped to shield the sun from her eyes as she stared up at the mountains.

"Never mind," I said. "They'll have you out there watching some spoilt brat offspring of a Russian Oligarch in no time. You'll soon forget us all."

"Hmm, somehow I doubt it. You lot have reminded me that there's a whole different level of crazy in this world beyond madmen chucking bombs at each other."

"Thank you," I said. "I think."

"What about you? It looks like this is going to work out. What've you got planned for your return home?"

I stared at the fringe of blue Mediterranean in the distance. "Don't know," I said after a while. "I lost my flat so I guess I'm free 'n easy. Blow with the wind, wherever the tide of fortune takes me. Or then again, I could always get a job as a security guard for Tesco's."

"With your record?" She grinned at me.

"Oh, no doubt I can make that disappear. That's first on the list. They'll want me as chairman by the time I've finished. Bentley, golf club and big house in the country. You going to come visit me? "

"Count on it." She turned to face me and planted the lightest of kisses on my lips.

I slipped my arm around her shoulder for a moment while we silently contemplated the horizon. The stomp of approaching footsteps and panting breath dragged me back to the moment.

"Give us a hand with this will ya?" Sean said and dropped a large cardboard box in my arms. "That feckin' hill's gonna be the death o' me."

"What is it?" I asked.

"Bunch of stuff I picked up in a car boot sale down in Órgiva. Traded it for an old CB radio set."

"CB radio? I didn't know we had a radio?"

"Just don't say anything to Jason. It came out of his mobile slum. I don't think he knew it was there anyway."

We took the box up to the budding Visitor Centre and emptied the contents on the table to begin sorting.

We chatted as we worked and the air was almost convivial. That was until the phone call.

I'd just finished helping set up our latest exhibit, an Inquisition torture device for crushing fingers. Sean had found it at a car boot sale in Trevélez and although he reckoned it was probably an old almond cracker or something, it still looked suitably evil and torturous and now held pride of place in our Inquisition Corner.

I glanced at my phone as it rang and the Newstart number coming up was a bit of a shock.

"Hello?" I answered tentatively. It had been so long since we'd had any contact, I was fully expecting it to be a wrong number.

Julie's voice dispelled that notion. "Hi, Michael. How're things going?"

That's always the opener to problems. If somebody's calling to give good news, they tend to get straight to the point. People only ring you up to ask how things are going when they know things are about to go very badly.

"All okay," I replied. "What's the problem?"

"Oh, no problem. Not really. Just a bit of news."

"Go on."

"There's been a bit of a problem in one of the Newstart project houses. Not the one you were attached to, the one in St. Pauls. Apparently, and you won't believe this, apparently Jimmy Watkins, don't know if you remember him? He's the guy with a bicycle tattooed on his forehead."

"A bicycle? Why a bicycle?"

"Oh, long story, mix up in a tattoo parlour in Bangkok. Never get a tattoo in Bangkok, I say."

"No, I don't remember him," I said.

"Are you sure? He's a lovely man."

"Positive, I think I'd remember a bicycle. What did he do?"

"Well, it seems he's been running girls from the house."

"Running girls? You mean in like running a brothel?"

"Well, we didn't want to actually call it that but yes, I suppose one could say it was a brothel."

"Enterprising, but what's that got to do with me?"

"Nothing really, except that the Department of Justice have got all excited about it and decided to do an audit on all the activities within the project group."

"I see."

"They've already been to the Yate house and shut down the printing workshop we had running there as part of a rehabilitation project."

"Why would they shut that down?" I asked.

"They found a few dodgy tenners in the Rose and Crown pub two doors up. Bit over the top if you ask me, I'm sure it was nothing to do with our house. Anyway, they also shut down the hydroponics project in the Clifton house and the film making club in Bedminster."

I could feel the knot in my throat tighten, just the way it used to when we were getting ready for an insertion somewhere dodgy.

"And now they want to know what's happening here?" I ventured.

"Yes, no, sort of. They're sending an inspector over to make sure it's all going in line with Department of Justice guidelines. Just a formality, I'm sure it's all hunky dory."

"Oh yes, it's all very… very hunky and dory." My eyes scanned the field with the Visitor Centre and Jason's RV. "All, just as it's supposed to be. When are they coming?"

"We don't know yet. I'll keep you posted. Love to everybody." The phone disconnected.

Nikki spotted my concern. "What's up?" she asked.

"The D.O.J. is sending an inspector over to check us out."

Nikki's gaze drifted slowly around the site. "Ah," she said, eventually.

"I think we need a team meeting," I said.

***

I looked around the table. "Where's Donny?"

"He's off with José Martin," said Sean. "He's been doing a bit of work for him recently."

"He never told me," I said. "What's he doing?"

"José Marin's picked up the contract with the Guardia Civil for collecting cars where owners haven't paid fines or finance. Donny helps bypass the immobilisers and locks. Nice little earner for him by all accounts."

"Hmm. And Ryan?" I asked.

Sean shrugged. "Don't know. He went off about ten with a bag of… Well, he didn't actually tell me what was in the bag."

"I can guess." I glanced around doing a quick headcount. The missing pair's places were currently being occupied by Pete and Tania, which was why it had taken me a moment to realise their absence.

"What's happening?" asked Bob. "Problems?"

"Potentially," I said. "The Department of Justice is sending over an inspector to see how we're doing."

"Oh, shit," said Bob.

"Well, that's screwed that," said Jason. "Might as well call it a day now and face the music."

"Not necessarily," I said. "I've had a bit of time to think. Thanks to Pete and Tania here, we have something which resembles self-sufficiency. It wouldn't be too much of a push to dress it up a bit more."

"But what about the Visitor Centre and the castle? Isadora's viewing circle?" Bob looked panicked as his eyes danced around the group.

"I think we can distance ourselves from that," I said. "We

just say it's nothing to do with us, all to do with the local tourist office. They're not to know. We just stop the tours until they've gone. I can't think they'll be here more than a day, maybe two. What's to inspect?"

"Could work," muttered Sean. "We just hide the real dodgy stuff. But what about Jason's bungalow, they're bound to notice that."

"It's not a bungalow," Jason protested.

"I thought about that too," I said. "Pete and Tania could stay in there for the duration; they could say they're travelling in it. We all live in the huts. Bit cramped, granted, but only one night, maybe two."

We sat still for a moment as we all processed the problem.

Nikki finally broke the silence. "They're going to expect some sort of food production which doesn't involve pizza," she said. "Not wishing to spread gloom and despondency but they're not going to believe we've survived all this time on those few sorry looking rabbits you sent them pictures of."

I hadn't thought of that.

"We could plant some vegetables," suggested Pete.

"Not much time for that," I said. "I don't know when they're coming but we won't have time to grow a vegetable patch."

"No, not from scratch," he said. "We talk to a local farmer and get some growing plants off him, carrots, potatoes and so on. Buy the whole plants and transplant them here. They probably won't survive the move but they'll look okay for a few days."

I pondered that idea for a moment. "That might just work. You know, we might get away with this yet."

***

For the next week we set about preparing for a rapid facelift for when the call came. We spoke to a couple of local farmers who, although completely mystified by our request, were quite happy to sell us growing plants. We persuaded Paco to bring his digger up and turn some earth ready for planting and we all made sure our personal stuff was ready to move at short notice.

José Martin was so pleased with his booming business that Jason was finally able to strike a deal over the Volvo engine and two days later, the monster was no longer a bungalow but an RV once more. Although, it did only do one circuit of the field before it ran out of petrol.

With everything ready for a quick change, we carried on as usual while we waited for the phone call. The call came a week later, just when we'd almost convinced ourselves that we'd been forgotten once more.

"Michael?" Julie's voice held a note of caution I learned to associate with bad news.

"Yes."

"There's been a teensy weensy development," she said.

"How teensy weensy?" I asked.

"Well, we thought the Department was going to send Clifford Postlethwaite over to you, he's a dear. Keeps tropical fish. Trouble is he's on suspension after taking a bribe from Jimmy Watkins. So, you're getting Anthea Perkins instead."

"Is that bad?" I asked.

"Well, she actually asked to go to your camp. Thought that was a bit strange but it turns out she's a bit of a history buff, you know the type, all tweed and Tony Robinson."

I was starting to feel the wheels of doom were once more rolling in my direction. "Why does she want to come here?" I asked, already feeling I knew the answer.

"When she read about your project, she did some research

on the area and discovered all the history there. Amazing coincidence or what?"

"Amazing."

"Turns out she has an interest in the Romans and the Moors who, apparently, were all over the bit where you are."

"They were? I can't say we've noticed."

"What? I don't understand." Julie sounded confused. "There's pictures of Bob all over YouTube and Travel Spy. I didn't know he did history. You can never tell can you, he didn't seem the history type. Must be terribly exciting for you all; just imagine discovering your camp is the site of an ancient battle. I bet there's ghosts. Have you seen any ghosts?"

"Not yet. When's she coming?"

"Um, hang on." I heard rustling paper. "The third."

"The third of what?"

"Next month, silly."

"But that's…" I did a mental calculation. "But that's only three weeks away."

"Uh? Mmm, yes, that sounds about right. Be a love and pick her up from Malaga, would you?"

"We haven't got a vehicle. You told us it wasn't allowed."

"Oh, yes. I suppose you'd better hire something. Don't be extravagant or they'll think we're spending government money on frippery."

"There's a local firm here who hires out cars. They do a little Suzuki, I think. Problem is they'll only take cash unless we're residents."

"Oh, okay but keep it cheap, I'm getting it in the ear about budgets again. I'll clear your card for a cash withdrawal. I'll let you have more details on email when I know. Bye for now." The phone clicked dead and I stared at the screen for a moment.

Nikki headed over to me. "Everything alright?"

I scanned the chaos in the field. "I think we need another meeting."

~ *Chapter Nineteen* ~

"What on earth were you thinking?" Jason moaned. "Have you never heard of keeping a low profile?"

"Well, I didn't know they were going to post the pictures all over the internet," Bob protested.

"They're Americans," said Ryan. "What did you think they were going to do? They'll post pictures of their toenail clippings on the internet. Pictures of their breakfast, new shoes, haircut, old shoes. Saw a picture of a possum somebody ran over once. Or that might have been a pizza."

"Well, if this all goes tits up, I'm just going to disappear on one of the Costas," Sean said. "Nobody'll find me there and there are plenty of expats happy to pay a hundred or two for an original Dali or Picasso."

"I think I'll stay up here," said Ryan. "Good growing country and it's legal."

"It's alright for you lot," said Jason. "I'll never survive inside. There's a lot of bad feeling towards bankers in prison. I saw a documentary with Ross Kemp."

"I saw that," said Donny. "Though I thought that was San Quentin?"

"They're all the same. They all have showers, I've seen it."

"Nobody's going anywhere," I said. "Don't you remember

the deal? One person goes native and the rest go straight to nick."

"Only if they can find me," said Ryan.

"We do this together or not at all." I caught José Felipe's attention and signalled another round. "How about we distance ourselves from the fake history? We can say we know nothing about it."

After a moment's silence, Nikki offered, "I'm not sure that will fly. There's a bit of a scam going on in a remote area in which a bunch of ex-cons just happen to be staying, yet coincidentally, they know absolutely nothing about it."

"Hmm," I pondered. "When you put it like that…"

"I say we all just 'ave it on our toes," suggested Donny. "I can line up some motors and we can be in a different country by teatime."

"Why don't we just find some real history," suggested Nikki. "This is Spain; there must be lots of history here."

"There was a Great Shepherd came this way," said Donny.

During the ensuing laughter my brain went into overdrive. "Right," I said. "Here's the plan, we have three weeks to find something real and then big it up enough to justify those photographs."

"And if we can't?" asked Jason.

"We can," I said. "Even if we have to rebuild the Visitor Centre in honour of the Great Shepherd, we can do this. We don't have a Plan B."

As the group dispersed, I called José Felipe over and persuaded him to sit with Nikki and I for a moment.

"History," I said. "We're still trying to find some history to make our publicity sort of legitimate. There must be more than a shepherd? Something? Anything? I mean, your bar is older than most of America. Something must have happened here?"

José thought for a moment then started to speak, "There was –"

"If you're going to tell me a Great Shepherd came by here, don't."

José fell back to silence for a moment then his eyes suddenly brightened. "You should talk to my cousin, José Antonio, he has the Virriatos Museum. He will know things."

"The Virriatos Museum?" I repeated. "There's a museum here? Why didn't you tell me?"

"You did not ask."

"How the hell could I ask when –" I felt Nikki's hand on my arm. "That's interesting. Where can I find José Antonio?"

***

The Virriatos Museum turned out to be José Antonio's house. Albeit a rambling and haphazard building jammed full of old stuff, it was still just a house.

José Antonio was a tall, proud man with thick bushy hair and matching beard. He showed us through the rooms pointing out great treasures as we followed a convoluted trek round the house.

"Here is the desk where my Great Uncle Manuel sat when he signed the papers to access the village water. And here, this is the axe head my great grandfather used to fell the great tree."

"The great tree?" I asked.

"Yes, it's gone now. My Great Uncle Pepe used this telescope when he was sailing to Cyprus and this is the portrait of Great Great Grandfather Antonio of San Sebastian. Ah, here is the linen napkin which Great Uncle Carlos took from the dining table when he met with General Franco."

And so we trailed round the house, bearing witness to the

collected possessions of this dynasty of wealthy, but ultimately, very boring people.

Eventually I paused him in the doorway of yet another roomful of random household goods.

"This is the Museum of Virriatos?" I questioned.

"Of course. You will like this room. It has my great grandmother's favourite chair. This is the one she used when she told her stories to my mother."

"Only, it all seems to be about your family. Not like that isn't absolutely fascinating, but I was expecting more of the town history."

He stopped and looked at me. "You are correct; the history of my family is entwined forever with the lifeblood of this great village. Come, let me show you the collection of envelopes made by my Great Uncle Francisco. It took him thirty years."

"Apart from your family, who were obviously a great and positive influence on the village, apart from them, did anything else happen here? Ever?"

José Antonio looked around as if searching for eavesdroppers, then, in an almost conspiratorial voice, "The Great Shepherd stood here."

I felt Nikki take my arm. "Come on, Michael. Maybe the Town Hall will have something."

I turned to her. "Have you ever tried to find *anything* in a Spanish Town Hall? That's where Russian spies keep their top secret papers. You want to know who killed Kennedy or whether the moon landings were faked? It's all being stored in a Spanish Town Hall somewhere because nobody and I mean nobody, will ever find them again. If you want the world to know something you tell MI6 but if you want to lose something forever, you give it to a Spanish Town Hall official and tell him it's urgent."

She touched my elbow. "I think we should go. We're not going to find anything here."

"In a minute." I turned back to José Antonio. "This Great Shepherd, did he stand in lots of different places or just one and everybody's confused as to where?" José Antonio drew a breath to speak but I was on a roll. "Or maybe there was more than one Great Shepherd?"

Nikki now tugged at my sleeve. "Michael, we really should go now."

José Antonio stared at me like I was a stupid child. "Only one Great Shepherd and this is where he stood. Virriatos, the town. He stood in Virriatos, this is why the town is named for him."

The clouds of confusion drew more dense and all I could manage was, "Uh?"

José Antonio shook his head. "Virriatos, known as the Great Shepherd. This is where his army stood when they faced the legions of Marcus Claudius Marcellus and a thousand of his men held ten thousand Romans at bay."

"Uh?"

***

We walked slowly back through the town towards our house. My mind sifted through the daze of new information.

"Why didn't somebody say something," I complained. "I mean, I've been asking about the history of the area since we got here."

"José Felipe did try," said Nikki. "He kept telling you about a Great Shepherd."

I stopped in the middle of the road and looked at her. "He might have mentioned that he was some huge warlord who defeated one of Rome's most important legions." I patted my pockets in search of my cigarettes and came up empty. "I mean, look at this place." I threw my arms wide to encompass the village. "It's hardly a major heritage site; you'd think there'd be a mention of something like that somewhere. Even just a little plaque on a wall, but nothing."

I heard a car horn sound from behind me and suddenly remembered we were still in the road.

"Come on," said Nikki. "Let's grab a coffee."

We stopped at a little bar and Nikki ordered coffees before I could stop her.

"I'd rather have a beer," I said.

"I know," she said.

"I mean, in England the National Trust will build a ticket kiosk and a gift shop at the point where the aunt of some obscure poet stopped off for a cup of tea. But here? A major battle takes place and everybody just shrugs their shoulders and carries on selling colourful rugs and walking sticks."

"So, what's the plan now?"

I stirred my coffee while I pondered. "We need research. And artefacts. There must be artefacts around; you can't have ten thousand soldiers charging through the area without dropping a sword or two."

"I think we might be a bit late on that one. I know history isn't your strong subject but it was two thousand years ago. That's a long time. Whatever was here is either crumbled away to nothing or sitting in an antique dealer's in Downtown Manhattan."

"Hmm, well we have three weeks to rustle up some Roman stuff, rebuild the Visitor Centre and create a battlefield."

We finished our coffees as we tried to hammer out some sort of plan then made our way up to the field to bring the others up to date.

We all gathered in the Visitor Centre and I ticked off the faces. Pete and Tania had joined in all our get-togethers now and eagerly helped where they could. We were still two down in our number though.

"Anybody seen Donny or Bob?" I asked. I always felt a slight impending sense of dread when Donny went missing. I half expected him to turn up with a Lamborghini one day.

Shaking heads and shrugging shoulders greeted my question so I just carried on. They would turn up eventually.

"Right," I started. "We have our history." I went on to explain our meeting with José Antonio in the Virriatos museum and then gave a precis of the research I'd done. "It seems that in around 150BC the Romans were having a bit of a problem with the Lusitanians –"

"I thought Lusitania was where Peter Sellers launched his moon rocket?" said Ryan. "What was the name of that film?"

"The Mouse on the Moon," offered Jason. "And that was Grand Fenwick, not Lusitania. Wasn't Lusitania where the Prisoner of Zenda lived?"

"No," I said. "I've been researching this and –"

Nikki cleared her throat loudly and I started again, "Nikki's been researching this and apparently Lusitania was a real country in Roman times, who'd have thought, huh? And it was sort of near here but a bit more over Portugal way." I waved my arm vaguely in Portugal's direction. "Now, the Romans wanted all this for themselves but the Lusitanians weren't having any of it so this character, Virriatos, stepped up and took them on. Anyway, he came up this way and at one point he had a thousand soldiers who were surrounded by a Roman Legion of ten thousand. The Romans got all overconfident and Virriatos gave them a good hiding."

"Just to clarify," Nikki said. "The places are all a bit vague as the only ones writing all this down were the Romans and as such they probably weren't too excited about recording such a spectacular defeat so nobody is exactly sure where this actually happened. But they did come through this way on their way to Murcia and they did have lots of battles and skirmishes on the way."

I picked up the thread again. "So, in the absence of absolute proof, we're going with local folklore and legend. If they say the battle happened here, then this is where it was. The Battle of Virriatos."

The group seemed oddly enthused with this new information as we made plans. Sean explained we could pick up cheap Roman trinkets in junk shops down on the coast especially if we weren't too worried about proof of authenticity. We agreed he should go down Bahia Blanco the next day to see what he could scrounge. I calculated I could arm him with enough cash from the card allocation for the hire car and still have plenty left.

Peter and Tania were tasked with the job of creating a realistic looking archaeological dig. It didn't need to be anything special, just an area of neatly dug earth with lots of stakes and string and the odd sieve lying around. I'd seen pictures of them on Time Team.

We were just wrapping up when the sound of approaching voices caught my attention. I stepped outside and froze. An army of people crested the brow of the hill and marched off towards the ruin.

"What the hell…" I heard Nikki breathe.

"There must be…" I did a quick calculation. "There must be at least fifty. What's happening?"

The trail of people threaded across the field, showing up their different capabilities as they went. The younger people had naturally gravitated towards the front of the group, leaving the more elderly and children trailing in the rear. Somebody waved to me but from there, I couldn't even make out if it was male or female. I waved back.

"Do you think we should follow them?" Nikki asked. "Find out what they're up to?"

"I think so. Although they don't seem hostile." I watched them straggle down the field towards the ruin. "Or official," I added.

Nikki and I set off to catch up with the mysterious group. As we approached, I managed to detect the languages, German mostly but with at least one voice in English. It sounded suspiciously like Bob.

We caught up with the group just as they came to a halt in front of the ruin.

Bob's voice now sounded clear of the general hubbub. "This is the remains of the Roman villa where Queen Isabella watched the departure of the Armada on its way to invade England." His now well-rehearsed commentary was being translated into German by a young, attractive, female who stood by his side. "And here are the remains of the trebuchet the Romans used to defend the coastline against the invading Moors. Which is why the Romans and the Moors never fought in Spain. Because they kept them away with trebuchets like this one."

I would need to have a chat with him about this.

From nowhere, Donny sidled up to me. "Great, uh?"

"Where the hell did all these people come from?" I asked. "There must be fifty."

"Fifty-three to be exact," Donny said. "Plus the guide."

"Okay, fifty-three. You just found them aimlessly wandering and decided to bring them up here?"

"No." He laughed. "Coach party in Pampeniera. Bunged the driver a fifty and he brought them up here."

"Fifty?" I asked. "How're we going to get that back?"

Donny smiled as he watched the German tourists then patted me on the shoulder. "You worry too much. We already have. José Felipe's bunged me a hundred to drop this lot in his bar after we've finished with 'em."

I stared at the scene in front of me. Bob giving his own unique account of Spanish history to a coachload of German tourists on the very spot reputed to have witnessed one of the major Roman defeats of the second century. It all felt slightly surreal.

"I think we're going to have to re-programme Bob," Nikki said.

I turned my ear to the group and caught Bob's talk. "…then the Romans swung their cannons out to sea and destroyed the Moor's landing boats…"

"Something wrong with that?" I asked. "Sounds like a perfectly reasonable military response to an invading army."

Nikki gave a great sigh. "It would be, had they had cannons."

"No cannons?"

"No, not for another thousand years or so."

"Ah, that would make it outside of my period."

"Your period of 1943?"

"That one."

We headed back to the Casa de Pastores ahead of the German group. The huge tourist coach dominated the scene and I wondered how it had actually threaded its way through the narrow streets.

"I kept you a table," José Felipe greeted. He aimed us at a makeshift folding table jammed up against the kitchen door.

"Sorry, this all I can do. I have many people today." He swept his arm around the room of tables, each with a hastily scrawled 'Reservado' sign prominent.

"I think we'll come back later," I said.

We went back to our little house for a relaxed beer, a bread and cheese supper and an early evening in.

~ *Chapter Twenty* ~

A week later and the new Visitor Centre was already showing signs of improvement. Sean's day trip to Bahia Blanco had turned out to be quite successful. The owner of one junk shop had agreed to swap a boxful of miscellaneous old stuff for one of Sean's El Greco's. Neither was inclined to question the provenance of the other's offering so the deal was quick and painless.

We sat outside the Casa de Pastores and Sean upended the box across the table. There were hundreds of bits and pieces. Rings, coins, belt buckles and general little bits of metal with no discernible purpose.

"Where did all this come from?" asked Nikki.

"Mostly metal detectors," Sean said. "They often can't be arsed to check out what the stuff is. They're looking for another Sutton Hoo, lost gold rings or coin hoard but beyond that, they just chuck it all in a box and when they get tired of moving it around they take it to a junk shop which pays them by the kilo."

"But doesn't the junk shop owner ever bother to sift them through?" I asked.

"Not really. There's so much of this stuff around that all they usually do is sift out the obvious bits, the gold and silver, add a bit more junk to the box and move it on."

"Sort of a junk shop version of a CDO," suggested Jason.

"CDO?" I queried.

"Collateralised debt obligations," said Jason. "The things which brought down the banking system in '08." Jason surveyed the puzzled faces in front of him. "Basically a sackful of securitised loan agreements that have been resold a dozen times and packaged up with some credit default swaps and Third World government bonds. Turned out to be wildly overvalued in the end and that's when everybody started shorting them."

Sean stared at Jason for a moment as if trying to understand some new language. Finally, "Yeah, what the man said. Just like that. You've hit the nail right on the head there, son. That's a far simpler explanation."

I picked through the little bits of metal. "This looks half decent," I said, holding up a bright gold coloured ring.

Sean took it from my fingers and gave it a cursory glance. "Came out of a Christmas cracker at a guess." He tossed it back on the table.

We sorted through the pile, removing obvious rubbish like modern badges and coins and nudging anything vaguely Roman towards Sean for a second opinion.

"I don't know why you think I'm the expert," he complained at one point.

"We don't," I said. "But you're the best option we've got and if it looks okay to you, it'll probably pass a casual glance by a tourist."

"Or an amateur historian?" asked Nikki.

"With luck," I said. "History all seems very subjective anyway. It's mostly just this person's opinion versus that person's."

"As quoted by your history teacher?"

After an hour, we had three piles. One made up of items which would pass reasonable scrutiny as being of the Roman era, another pile of obvious tat and a third of stuff that looked okay provided nobody got too close. We could put those bits at the backs of the shelves.

"Not a bad collection," Jason said. "I've seen worse on display in Blenheim Palace."

"Next step," I said. "I've been working on more of the history of this guy and he was quite something. Apparently he *was* a shepherd originally."

Ryan brightened. "Maybe that's why they called him the Great Shepherd?"

I looked at Ryan. "You think?"

"Well, might just be a coincidence but I'm not a real believer in coincidence," Ryan said. "Not since Bush ordered 911 at exactly the same time the Illuminati allowed The Lizard People to settle in Iraq. I mean, that shit just makes you think, don't it? It's Israel all over again."

I studied the rusty coin I was holding as I tried to untangle Ryan's steps of logic. Finally I tossed the coin back in the box and said, "You know, I'd never looked at it like that."

"That stuff happens all the time. You should look at the video of the *real* moon landings, not the fake ones put out by NASA. That'll mess with your head. It's on YouTube and everything."

"Anyway, back to Virriatos, I'm collecting info on him so we can put some fact sheet thingies up in the Visitor Centre. Like they have in all the proper museums. Did you know he gave the Romans the run-around for years and developed what is considered to be the very first Special Forces units?"

"Feeling a kinship, by any chance?" asked Nikki.

"Not in the slightest. Modern life may have its problems but it still has Netflix and pizza."

"They ought to make a film about him," suggested Nikki. "Sort of an olden day King Arthur."

"King Arthur was already olden days," said Ryan. "I saw the series with Merlin. It was proper olden days."

"And of course entirely fictional," said Jason.

"Bit like your Caramelised Debt… um… Objects," said Ryan, looking at his fingers as if the last word was amongst them somewhere.

"Collateralised Debt Obligations but nice try," corrected Jason.

I ignored this intellectual cul-de-sac and pulled a pile of printed A4 sheets from a carrier bag. "Here, I had these printed out." I tossed them on the table. "We'll call them Fact Slides. I'll get some picture frames to put them in and we can stick them around the Visitor Centre." I pulled another pile of paper from another bag. "And these are pictures of Romans fighting and stuff. We'll do the same with them. I couldn't find any pictures of the man himself though."

"They didn't have cameras in those days," Ryan said helpfully.

"I can knock something out," said Sean. "Quick sketch of ancient warlord? Five minute job."

The noise of a huge engine fighting its way up through the narrow village caused us to stop to watch. The huge tourist coach squeezed its nose out from the houses which crowded each side of the main street and slid towards us.

"Ah, that'll be Donny and Bob with another load," said Nikki. "Best get this stuff up to the Visitor Centre before they arrive there. Be a good chance to test it."

The coach pulled up alongside the Casa de Pastores and vomited its human cargo all over the patio area. The chattering which reached us as we retreated up the track indicated the predominant language of this particular group was English. At least that made life a little easier for Bob.

We reached the Visitor Centre a good ten minutes before the chattering group passed by on their way up to the ruin. We placed the gathered metal detectoring finds into the glass display cabinets, which in reality were just a collection of wooden crates with some old windows attached. I pinned the various Fact Slides to the walls; we'd not had time to frame them but they looked okay for now. I stepped back to survey the overall effect. Not bad. We had gradually created a passable exhibition and certainly more informative than anything else in the area, although, some of the history was still dubious. Sean's pencil sketches of battling roman soldiers were interspersed with the Fact Slides and the display cabinets. The gift shop was still sparse though and was primarily limited to a few framed prints of Sean's lost Masters or little plastic bags of Roman coins which we'd been assured by the guy in the market were original and genuine. Although, as we'd only paid twenty euros for a half a kilo of them, their provenance was probably doubtful.

The group arrived in the Visitor Centre in good humour, bought their prints and packets of coins, clucked at the Fact Slides, took photos of old metal and oohed over Sean's depictions of Roman soldiers. Although one person did comment that they didn't think Romans used throwing stars.

"I told you they didn't use those things," said Jason, once the tourists had gone.

"I'm an artist, not an armourer," complained Sean. "I keep telling you that and Ryan seemed convinced they had them."

"Jaime Lannister used them in Game of Thrones," said Ryan. "I saw them."

"Game of Thrones?" Sean stared at Ryan. "You didn't tell

me you were getting your historical information from Game of Thrones. You really are a new kind of stupid."

"It's not a problem," I tried to reassure Sean. "Just one tourist's comment. No damage."

"No problem? I have to throw out all the pictures that have throwing stars in them."

"Well, let's say we have a new rule, one where Ryan is no longer our Historical Consultant?"

"I'm tellin' you, if we all get our backsides tossed back in pokey, it ain't my fault. I'm wantin' that one on the record. Ninja throwing stars, pfhaff."

We followed back down to Casa de Pastores about half an hour after the tourists to find them all still drinking and eating. José Felipe pulled out a fold-up table for us and set us outside near the steps.

"They seem happy enough," said Nikki.

I watched as Bob posed for a series of selfies and wondered what new disaster would befall us when those images hit the internet. "Let's hope Anthea Perkins is also a Game of Thrones fan."

***

By the scheduled day of Anthea Perkins' arrival, our site was as good as it was going to get. The Visitor Centre looked almost real with the displays of old stuff, Fact Slides and gift shop selling prints, artefacts, plastic macs and postcards.

Outside, and with thanks to Pete and Tania, our encampment looked impressive. Mud and timber huts, vegetable patch, campfire, compost toilets. Bear Grylls would be proud.

I wanted to do a last minute inspection before heading off to Malaga Airport to collect our nemesis.

"It all looks very clinical," I said.

"What do you mean?" asked Nikki.

"There's no mess. If seven people have been living here for several months, you'd expect a bit of mess. You know, beer can ash trays, rubbish sacks, piles of paper for fire-starting, that sort of stuff."

Nikki glanced around. "Hmm, you're right. I'll get on to it. It'll all be fine by the time you get back. I'll make it look more like a Squaddie's camp and less like a Para's," she said with a smile.

I ignored the barb and headed the little Suzuki down the track and on to Malaga.

***

Ms Anthea Perkins was not difficult to spot among the arrivals at the airport. Firstly, she wore a grey tweed suit which, among the shorts and T-shirted holidaymakers, made her stand out like a tree in the desert. Secondly, she carried a big white board scrawled with the words, 'Ms Perkins for Mr Michael Purdey'.

I waved and she marched over to me, tailed by a small man in a brown suit who looked both bewildered by his surroundings and decidedly overheated.

"Are you Michael Purdey?" she demanded when she arrived in front of me.

"Yes, I assume you're Ms Perkins? I was only expecting one of you."

"There *is* only one of me. I am in the singular but this is Norman Timswick, he's the Departmental Field Accountant."

"Oh, a Field Accountant?" I studied the diminutive Norman Timswick. He was a symphony in brown. The light beige of his shirt nicely blending with the brown stripes on his tie and the dark brown socks just visible over the tops of the brown Hush Puppies. The only item which wasn't brown was the white handkerchief he was currently using to dab at the sweat on his forehead. "Did we need a Field Accountant? Only, we just have the one field."

Norman Timswick drew a breath to speak but it was wasted as Anthea Perkins beat him to the post.

"One field? What are you talking about? He's accompanying me to check your accounts. Now, where is your transport, we haven't got all day?"

I led them to the little Suzuki which was sandwiched between a Range Rover and a BMW. They stared at the car and gave off a slight air of disbelief.

"This?" was all Ms Perkins could manage.

"Budget restraints," I said with a sideways glance to the Field Accountant.

He gave a millisecond smile and dropped his trendy two-tone brown suitcase in the back as I held it open for him.

"Mind the er…" I pointed at something unpleasant in the corner. "Um… actually I'm not sure what that is but it's probably best if you don't put you bag on it."

Ms Anthea Perkins placed her Louis Vuitton case in the opposite corner.

"They do matching handbags to those in the local market." I closed the back. I didn't look at her expression but I could feel the scowl burning into my back.

The pair of them climbed into the back seat and waited. I suppressed my mischievous impulse to ask them to get out and bump start the vehicle but couldn't resist asking them to help me lean the opposite way as we go round corners.

Malaga traffic offered its usual midday chaos and I heard

the odd little whimper from the back seat as I dodged the lane-switchers and random braking. Although, I couldn't quite work out which one was whimpering.

I glanced in the mirror to see how they were doing and noticed that Ms Anthea Perkins had opened the jacket on her tweed suit. They must be feeling the heat.

"Sorry," I said. "There's no aircon in this. It's one of the budget range."

I heard some grumbles but couldn't make out what was being said above the rattle of aging Suzuki so I turned up the heating a notch and concentrated on avoiding a builder's van which came from nowhere.

"There's lots of history round here," I said over my shoulder once we'd finally cleared the melee. "They had Moors and Romans and the Armada and… Christopher Columbus." I suddenly remembered José Felipe's explanation and quickly added, "Not all at the same time of course."

As there was no response from the back I assumed they were either not in the mood for idle chitchat or they'd been rendered unconscious by the leaky exhaust pipe which I thought José Martin had fixed but clearly hadn't.

After an hour or so, we left the motorway and started our ascent into the Alpujarras. The whimpering resumed from the back seat as we twisted up the vertiginous roads and dodged little white vans.

"Don't forget to lean into the bends," I reminded them.

We reached the village at around three and I stopped outside the house we'd booked for them. It was actually a typical little Alpujarran house with wooden beams, leaky roof and scorpions. We'd purposefully booked something at the opposite end of the village from Casa de Pastores and the site to give us a bit more control. We figured they'd have to either ask for a lift or take the long walk. Either way, it would give us a bit more leeway when they were planning to visit. As it happened, that plan fell at first contact.

"What is this place?" Anthea Perkins demanded. "Why have you stopped here? Where's our hotel?"

"We thought you'd like it here, it's quaint. It's also the closest we could get you to the site. Thought it would make things easy for you."

She stared at the little house. "That's not quaint, it's positively Third World. There must be a hotel in this place."

"Not round here." I glanced up and down the road as if a hotel might suddenly appear. "Maybe in Trevelez, that's about twenty minutes that way." I pointed vaguely towards Trevélez.

"Well, what are you waiting for?"

I climbed back in the car, turned the heater up full and headed for Trevélez.

By the time we arrived outside the Hotel Mira Sierra, they were both showing signs of seasickness and heat exhaustion. They tumbled out of the car and stood panting by the steps of the hotel.

"You'll get used to the heat," I said. "Give it a few days."

"We have no intention of being here a few days," she said. "The sooner we can find out exactly what's going on here, the sooner we can return to civilisation."

I saw them to the reception desk and helped book their rooms then headed back to the car. I rang Nikki.

"How goes it?" she asked.

"We're in trouble," I said. "There's two of them and they're the evil-twin love-children of Ilse Koch and Joe Stalin. Only without the sense of humour. They seem to think they're only going to be here for a couple of days. Quick hatchet job and home in time for Downton Abbey."

"I'll warn the others. What time are they coming up?"

"Not till the morning. Apparently the journey was a little taxing and they've decided to make an early start tomorrow."

"Okay," she said. "I'll have a cold one waiting for you when you get here."

Nikki was good to her word and the beer was ready when I pulled up outside the Casa de Pastores.

I gave her a quick rundown of the journey and hotel fiasco.

"Any chance of winning her round?" Nikki asked.

"How are you at waterboarding?"

"Bit rusty I'm afraid. Though I have been told my singing can reduce people to madness so get me a karaoke machine and I'll give them a bit of Gloria Gaynor."

José Felipe brought a plate of cheese and olives out for us. "Why so sad, my friends?" he asked. "The sky is clear, we have the mountains and we have the wine and jamon."

I gave him a quick picture of the situation.

"Madre Mia," he said. "This is not so good. I could speak with my cousin, José Diego if you want."

"What can he do?"

"He is very good at solving these sorts of problems."

"Um, no thanks. We'll pass on that offer, appreciated as it is."

"Well, you let me know if you want me to ask him." José Felipe took the empty glasses and headed back inside.

"We'll just have to put on a really good show then," said Nikki. "If we can hook her with the history, we might win her round a bit. You never know."

"Have you ever tried to win round a rattlesnake?" I asked. "She doesn't want to be here, it's too hot, the roads have bumps, the hotel is not good enough and we're a bunch of cons who should be all locked up for the betterment of humanity."

"I thought it was her idea to be here?"

"It was, but she's only interested in the history crap and as far as Project Newhome is concerned, she's just looking for the opportunity to close the whole thing down. As soon as she figures out what we've been doing, she'll pull the plug."

Nikki swirled her beer in the glass, she looked captivated by the patterns. "I hope she doesn't shut it down," she said after a while. "It would be sad, not just for you guys, but for the locals. They've got behind this and ultimately, it's been good for the village."

"What about you?" I asked. "What happens if you get sent back before the contract's up?"

"I expect they'll reassign me. You never know, Brad Pitt might be looking for a bodyguard. Shame though, I was quite getting used to the lifestyle here. Sunshine, clean air, good food."

"And good company," I added.

Nikki stared at me and after a moment's thought she said, "Where?"

"Well…" I stroked my chin in mock contemplation. "There's Bob."

"Ah, yes. There's always Bob."

~ *C h a p t e r   T w e n t y - O n e* ~

We all gathered at the field early the next morning. The Visitor Centre looked almost business-like with its display cabinets and Fact Slides. Outside, the area actually resembled a proper natural living community. The huts had bits and pieces of daily living lying around, rubbish bags, firewood and even a couple of boxes of freshly dug potatoes. Although, I wasn't sure from where they'd been freshly dug and I wasn't about to ask.

My phone rang exactly on eight o'clock and Ms Anthea Perkins demanded to know why I wasn't waiting outside the hotel. I tried to explain I didn't realise that had been a standing order but she just talked over me then hung up.

"Well," I said, "the Evil Twins are awaiting and I have been summoned."

I pulled up outside of the Hotel Mira Sierra and they both climbed in the back without a word between them. I took a leisurely, and fairly circuitous, drive to the site on the basis that the less time they had for poking around, the less likelihood of them finding out what we'd been doing.

I stopped the car outside the Casa de Pastores. "We have to walk from here. The ground's too rough."

"But this is a four wheel drive vehicle," said Norman Timswick. "Surely it can manage the track?" That was the longest sentence I'd heard him say.

"It's to do with the insurance," I said. "The hire company demand a higher rental and special waiver indemnity whatsits if we want to take it off-road."

"That's unfortunate," he said.

"I can ask them to add it if you like?" I said. "That's if you're happy to okay the extra expense?"

"Hmm, no. We can walk."

Ms Anthea Perkins looked at the track as it disappeared up the hill. "We could still drive. They'd never know. How would they know?"

I studied her. "Wouldn't that be dishonest? I don't think I'd feel comfortable doing that."

Her expression darkened as a distinct cloud gathered across her brow, but she made no reply. I glanced at Norman Timswick and noticed the faintest of smiles flutter across his lips.

We set out up the hill at regulation yomping pace and it wasn't too long before the grumbling started.

"If I'd known we'd be doing hillwalking I'd have brought more sensible shoes," Ms Anthea Perkins said.

I looked at her shoes. I couldn't remember seeing anything any more sensible in my life. She wore a pair of sturdy women's brogues that wouldn't have looked out of place in an Enid Blyton book.

We had to take several rest stops on the way up the track, which was fine by me, less time for them to make a nuisance of themselves.

Finally, we crested the hill and the full vista of our very own Narnia was laid out in front of us.

Ms Anthea Perkins' tightly buttoned down chest pushed at its constraints as she struggled for breath. I wondered if it would harm or help our case if she keeled over about now.

"Is that it?" she said. "It looks like Glastonbury. Only not quite so noisy."

"Why is there a big vehicle there?" asked Norman Timswick. "Wasn't this supposed to be all about self-sufficiency?"

"That's where a couple of the maintenance crew live. The historical people's maintenance, not us. We don't need maintenance."

He gave me a slightly skewed look then took several photographs of Jason's RV before writing what looked like a fairly lengthy missive in his note book.

I led them down to the site and the others appeared out of the huts as we approached. I made the introductions while Ms Anthea Perkins made disapproving noises and Norman Timswick made notes.

The Evil Twins poked noses just inside the entrance to the first hut. Anthea Perkins sniffed like a dog with the scent of prey in its nose then turned to Timswick, "I can smell cannabis," she said.

Timswick made another entry in his notebook.

"It's Queen Isadora's Royal Potpourri," said Ryan. "It smells a bit like cannabis. I've been told. I don't know. How could I know? Why did you ask me?"

Two minutes. We lasted two minutes into first contact with the enemy before our defences crumpled.

Anthea Perkins studied Ryan. "Ah yes, you're Ryan Edwards. You're supposed to be doing two years for hiding two hundred potpourri plants in your loft."

"There were mitigating circumstances," he protested. "I was just minding them for a friend. Anyway, isn't that supposed to be secret information or something?"

The pair ignored his protestations and headed for the Visitor

Centre. "What's in here?" Anthea Perkins pushed the door open.

"It's the Visitor Centre for the... visitors," said Bob before I had chance to intervene. "For the history visitors who come to see the... um... history."

Anthea Perkins looked at Bob. "Who are you?"

Bob paddled his feet up and down as if that would help his words come together. "Professor... Doctor... Rupert. Hello, I'm Bob. Not a professor, just Bob."

"Hmm," she muttered and pushed her way into the shed.

Timswick made more notes.

This really wasn't going well. I caught Nikki's eye and she gave an exaggerated horrified expression to convey the air of disaster we both felt. I gave her the silent army signals to indicate we should kill these two and run. She wagged her finger at me like a scolding schoolmistress.

Perkins and Timswick stood in the middle of the shed-come-Visitor Centre and glanced around.

"Well," Ms Perkins finally said. "I have to say this is the strangest Visitor Centre I have ever seen. And I've been to many, including the one at Land's End."

"It seems sort of normal to me," I said. "I know it's not quite National Trust but then, this is Spain. Rural Spain."

"There's no green jumpers," Bob said.

"Green jumpers?" Ms Perkins asked.

"In all the real National Trust places like Dunster Castle or Stourhead they always sell green jumpers. And plastic macs, we've got those but we probably don't need them here. Plastic macs that is, the green jumpers might be useful in the winter."

"Hmm, I do realise this is Spain and not Wiltshire," Ms Perkins said. "However, even for Spain..." She looked at me.

"Even rural Spain, this is quite odd." She scanned the room. "It looks like a cross between somebody's shed and a car boot sale."

"I think it's still quite new," I suggested.

"And they don't have much money here," added Nikki. "It's quite a poor area."

"And what's this?" Ms Perkins tapped the glass case containing some of our Roman relics. "This is all rather eclectic."

"Eclectic?" I said.

"Well, it's not often one encounters a Neolithic arrowhead, a Roman coin and a modern beer bottle all in one display."

Ryan squinted and peered closely at the cabinet. "Oh, cool, I'd been wondering where that had got to." He lifted the lid and reached in to take out the bottle. "I thought Donny'd had it away." He shook the bottle near his ear, smiled then swigged the last drops as he headed for the door.

"He must have left it there when he was cleaning," I said.

Ms Perkins continued her tour of the exhibits, taking in the Fact Slides and peering closely at the items on display.

"What do we have here?" she said.

I studied the cabinet which had caught her interest, dreading what I would find but I couldn't, for the life of me, see anything untoward. No beer bottles, no Royal Potpourri, no pizza boxes. It all looked nicely antique to me.

"Look at this," she said. "It's a spur. In heaven's name, what's a spur doing here alongside these Roman belt buckles and brooches?" She stared at me as if I should know.

"I suppose it dropped off and got lost," Bob offered. "I lost a shoe once so I'm sure it's not difficult to lose a spur. I never did find it. Had to throw out the other one in the end. Pointless keeping one shoe, don't you think?"

She stared at him as if he were speaking in tongues. "It's a spur. Surely, every idiot knows the Romans never used spurs?"

"How did they make them go?" Bob asked.

"How did who make what go?" she asked.

"The Romans and the horses. How did the Romans make the horses go if they didn't have spurs?"

"They…" she started then shook her head and just walked away from him.

I turned to Sean, shrugged my shoulders, held my hands up and mimed 'WTF?'

Sean just raised his eyebrows and shook his head as if to say, 'How should I know?'

She studied the rest of the displays and finally turned to Nikki. "Who runs this place? There are no names of organisations anywhere, no official notices, not even a fire exit sign."

Nikki looked towards me. I heard the silent plea for help and said, "We don't really know. We think it's a sort of community project. We just help out a bit. Cleaning and stuff."

The sound of shouting from outside thankfully interrupted any more awkward questions. "Excuse me," I said and headed for the door.

My relief was short-lived. José Felipe stood at the head of a crocodile of people who straggled across the field behind him.

"Where is Professor Rupert? We have all these people." He waved his arm towards the gathering crowd just in case I hadn't noticed them.

"What's going on?" I asked as quietly as I could but still to be heard over the chattering throng.

"This coach comes now for a visit to the castle. Professor Rupert, he did not tell me."

"He's not here," I tried to whisper above the noise. "He's gone away. Why are they here?"

"The driver, Juan, he says he gets more payoff here than Pampeniera so he brings them here."

"Well, you'll have to tell him to come back when Professor Rupert's here."

José Felipe's eyes suddenly brightened as he looked across my shoulder. "Ah. Professor Rupert, you have a group to visit the castle."

I turned to see the others had followed me out. Bob stared at José Felipe, Nikki stared at me, Ms Perkins stared at the coach party, and Mr Timswick made notes in his little book.

"More helping out?" Ms Perkins finally said, raising one eyebrow.

"Yes, actually we –"

Ms Perkins ignored my struggle for a half believable answer and turned to Bob. "So, Professor Rupert. Tell me about this castle."

"It's not really –" I started but she held a hand up to stop me.

"Well?" she aimed her probe firmly at Bob, who looked ready to melt into the ground.

"It's a Roman castle…" Bob started, keeping an eye on her face for clues. He noticed her wince and said, "Not really a castle. More like a house… but broken."

"I think we should all go and see your broken Roman house then," she said. "We don't want to keep all your fans waiting. Do we, Bob? Or is it Professor Rupert?"

"That was just a misunderstanding," I tried. "It's because his real name was a bit difficult for the locals to pronounce."

"What, Bob?" she asked.

"No," I said. "It's Robert Cyrankiewicz. So everybody started calling him Prof."

"Prof? As a contraction for Robert Cyrankiewicz?"

"I know, but to a Spanish ear it makes sense."

"Mr Purdey, I speak fluent Spanish and Prof makes no sense to any ear."

It dawned on me that she had probably heard and understood my exchange with José Felipe.

"Come along then," she said. "Show me the way."

Bob looked at me and I raised my eyebrows and gave a slight shake of my head to indicate there was nothing else to do. I started walking and waved to the coach trippers that they should follow.

As we trailed up the slope Bob slid alongside me. "What do I say? I can't do this. You'll have to do it."

"You have to," I said. "They're expecting you. Just play it cool and don't say anything about spurs."

"No spurs."

"And it's Isabella, not Isadora, Isolde or even Esmerelda. Isabella."

"Right, Isabella."

"And don't mention the Royal Potpourri."

"No potpourri."

We waited by the ruin until the stragglers caught up. The brief pause also gave Bob a few minutes to prepare. Ms Perkins stood close to Bob as she surveyed the tumbledown building and paved circle. She spoke briefly with Norman Timswick and although I couldn't hear what was being said, the copious notes being scribbled in Timswick's notebook didn't look promising.

Everybody gathered expectantly and I nudged Bob.

"You're on," I said. "Keep calm and keep it brief."

He stood with eyes wide, staring at the people.

"Now would be good," I suggested.

"Here are the remains of the famous Roman castle where Queen Isa… Isa…" Bob looked at me.

"Bella," I whispered.

"…where Queen Bella stood when she waved off Columbus."

I glanced around. Ms Perkins and Timswick stood slightly behind Bob so he couldn't see her expression or Timswick's manic note taking. Fortunately, all Bob could see were the expectant faces of enthusiastic coach trippers.

He warmed to their appreciation and continued, "And here," he waved his arm towards our aged wooden beam. "We can see the remains of the trebuchet the Romans used to keep the invading Moors from landing on the beaches over there." He pointed into the distance where one could just see the sea between two peaks.

Perkins' expression blackened and Timswick's pencil threatened to burst into flames under the ferocity of his scribblings. It was then I recalled José Felipe telling me about the three hundred years which separated the Moors and the Romans.

I whispered to Bob, "No Moors. Tell them about Virriatos."

He stared at me. "Who?"

We'd been intending to rehearse this but had run out of time and figured the Evil Twins wouldn't be witnessing a coach party anyway. Clearly we'd figured wrong.

"The Great Shepherd. I'll do it." I stood forward and raised my voice. "Sorry, Professor Rupert…" I started then remembered Perkins and Timswick were there. "Professor Rupert couldn't be here today and would like to thank Bob here for standing in." I started clapping and a confusion of hesitant applause fluttered around the group. "Of course, there were no Moors here at the same time as the Romans. Bob was a bit confused. This is the site where Virriatos, known as the Great Shepherd, stood with his army of a thousand against Marcus Claudius Marcellus and ten thousand of Rome's finest legionnaires." I glanced at Ms Perkins. She was locked in heated conversation with Timswick. I raked my memory for more details of the battle and realised I didn't have any. That was it. I ran on the fly, "So, the Lusitanians knew they stood no chance against the Roman shield wall so they set out with a series of tactical interdictions that picked at the supply chain. A campaign of shoot and scoot coupled with running flanking manoeuvres gradually broke the lines, forcing the…" I stopped myself just before I said Taliban and realised I'd been describing a contact we'd had in Helmand. "Forcing the Romans to break lines and fall back." I saw the scene playing out in front of me. The Romans' disciplined troops being provoked out of their formations by vicious raiding parties which attacked with lightning speed before disappearing into the woods again. Virriatos must have been a military genius to win out against such odds. How had he remained so hidden in history? "Eventually, the Romans gave up their bridgehead leaving Virriatos to secure his position." I looked around the group, they seemed enthralled. I risked a glance towards Perkins and Timswick; they stared back at me as impassively as the heads on School Island. I wrapped up and handed control back to Bob to supervise photographs on the trebuchet then on to the gift shop. I braced for trouble and headed over to speak with the Evil Twins.

"There's your history," I said, getting my defence in first.

Ms Anthea Perkins stared at me for a moment then, "I have never heard so much rubbish in all my born days. Romans firing trebuchets over twenty miles. And at the Moors no less."

"That was just Bob, he's enthusiastic. The real bit, the bit about –"

"You do realise Rome never had trebuchets?" she interrupted. "No, I don't suppose you did. You're too busy trying to fleece the locals or whatever it is you're doing."

"But that bit's real," I said. "Virriatos was a real hero. He led –"

"Enough now," she said. "We've seen plenty of your shenanigans. Now if you'd be so good as to take us back to our hotel, we have reports to write up."

***

That evening, we gathered around our table in the Casa de Pastores. The air of defeat hung like a Beijing fog as we weighed the full impact of the day's events.

Even José Felipe broke with his usual manic rushing around to sit with us a while as we tried to deal with the inevitable consequences. "Maybe you can offer her some money," he suggested. "She works for the government, yes?"

"Yes, sort of," I said.

"Then money is the answer. Government officials, there are rarely problems that enough euros will not solve. They just like to know they are appreciated."

"Most times I would agree with you," I said. "But this woman, she is the worst. She thinks she is the keeper of the nation's morals."

"Then I will talk with my cousin, José Diego. He will solve this for you."

"No thank you, José. We'll plead our case back in England. Although, a few more of these might help." I held up my empty glass.

José gathered up the empty glasses and headed back inside.

"So, what chance do you think we stand back home?" asked Jason.

"About as much chance as getting Tony Blair to apologise for the mess in the Middle East," I said.

"There must be something we can do," said Nikki. "I can make a case for you all. It might have some weight."

I covered her hand. "I think you're probably going to be in nearly as much trouble as us. After all, you were supposed to be stopping us."

"Thank you for that," she said. "I needed this job."

"Well, I don't know about you lot," Donny said, "but I'm gonna 'ave it on me toes. They're not lockin' me up just 'cause some Lady Muck thinks she's better than us. Like to see her live in the woods. See how she'd get on then."

"I'll join you," said Ryan. "I can harvest the rest of the crop, you find us some wheels and we bugger off to Marbella. Place is full of rich people with boats. They'll pay top whack for this stuff." He patted his shirt pocket.

Conchita brought out the drinks and set them on the table.

"José gone to bed?" I asked.

"No, he had to go out," she said.

We sank a few more beers, nibbled unenthusiastically at the tapas and generally failed in our mission to drown our troubles.

By ten, I gave up. "I'm going for an early night," I said.

"Me too," said Nikki.

The usual wolf-whistles and ribald comments were only thrown out of habit and I couldn't even be bothered to engage in the traditional banter. We headed for the little house and fell into bed in a frenzy of lust which was more a search for oblivion than our usual passion for each other's bodies.

~ *C h a p t e r   T w e n t y - T w o* ~

We slept late into the morning. There seemed little point in racing up the hill to work on the site. We'd all be back in England soon, greeting our various fates, so we might as well kick back for however long we had.

It was my telephone ringing incessantly which finally dragged me into full consciousness.

I stared at the phone, 'Julie Calling'. I stabbed answer.

"Michael," her voice said. "What the hell's going on?"

I squinted at the time displayed on the phone. Just after eleven. Wow, hadn't slept like that for years. I turned to my left to see Nikki just stirring.

"Michael, Michael? Are you there?" my phone demanded.

"Huh, yes. Sorry, Julie. What's up?"

"What's up? You tell me. What's happening over there?"

I sat up and pulled at the yellow curtain. All looked normal outside. No earthquakes, meteor strikes or alien landing craft.

"Um, nothing," I said. "Just another fine day in paradise."

"Then would you like to explain to me why I've received a ransom demand for the release of two hostages?"

"Ransom? What? Who?"

"Who? Only Mssss Bloody Anthea Up-her-own-arse Perkins and Tonto. That's who."

"Perkins and Timswick? Ransom?"

"There we go, you're getting there. They've been kidnapped and some moron wants a ransom for them. Personally I'd pay to see the back of them."

"Who would kidnap them?"

"Yes, I know. I was the same. I'm like, who's going to pay to get those two back? And why contact us here? It's not like we've got any money. Well, not since the Yate House Project had its printing workshop shut down anyway."

I poked at Nikki. "Wake up. The Evil Twins have been kidnapped."

Nikki stirred and muttered 'huh?' from under the sheet.

"You've got to do something," Julie continued.

"Why me?" I asked. "This is a job for the authorities."

"You're S.A.S.," she said "This is what you guys do isn't it?"

"No," I said. "It's not what I do. I sat in a van and intercepted drones or internet connections. I keep telling you, I'm not Batman, I'm Vanman. If you want somebody to abseil through a window and blow up the bad guys, you're going to need to talk to Hereford yourself."

"I can't do that. We're hanging on by a pixie's whisker as it is," Julie said. "One more sniff of a problem with our setup here and they'll close us down for sure and I've still got two years left on my Peugeot."

"You expect to sort this out before the Department of Justice find out that two of their finest have been kidnapped halfway up a mountain in Spain?"

"Hmm, yes that's it."

"How much is the ransom?" I asked.

Nikki wriggled into a sitting position and rubbed her eyes open. "Ransom? Did I hear you say ransom?"

"Yes, the Evil Twins have been kidnapped," I repeated.

"Oh good."

"Thirty-two thousand seven hundred and fifty euros," said Julie.

"Thirty-two thousand euros? That's a very strange amount."

"And seven hundred and fifty. Don't forget the seven hundred and fifty. And yes, it is very strange but no stranger as to why anybody would kidnap those two in the first place."

"Any other clues? What did they sound like?"

"It was a text message. I'll forward it to you." The line went dead and I put the phone down.

"I wish she wouldn't do that," I muttered. "Dumps a problem then hangs up."

Nikki blinked at the clock. "Shit, eleven?"

"Just a question, hypothetically, is rescuing hostages the sort of thing your gang at Blacklance Security are any good at?"

"Probably, but how do I explain the fact that I was supposed to be the resident security here and not only have you lot set up a Potemkin Village of which even Stalin would be proud but I've managed to let two D.O.J. officers get kidnapped?"

"Okay, I see the problems in that line. Plan B then."

"Plan B?" Nikki slid out of bed and I became distracted by the sight of her naked body against the sunlight filtering through the curtains.

"Um, plan… oh yes, plan B. Rapid exfil to somewhere that doesn't have extradition arrangements with the U.K."

She shimmied into her jeans and pulled the oversized belt tight. "No. Plan A, we find them and get them back and we deal with the consequences."

My phone blipped and I glanced at the screen. "It's the ransom text. Julie's forwarded it to me." I read the text out, "32,750 euros in cash or we make the infidels disappear. I'm paraphrasing."

"Make the infidels disappear? Sounds a bit strange."

"Yes, it certainly doesn't sound like either Islamic terrorists or financially motivated kidnappers. Sounds more like complete amateurs." I pulled up the number embedded in the text header and hit dial. Dead tone. "Burner phone."

"So how are we supposed to negotiate even if we wanted to?" Nikki pulled open the curtains and squinted as the morning breached the window. "Ouch, that's bright."

"I think we start at the hotel, see if anything happened there."

***

Dolores behind the reception desk at the Hotel Mira Sierra remembered the Evil Twins leaving.

"A car came for them at eight in the morning," she said. "They seemed surprised but went with the man."

"What did the car look like?" I asked.

"A white van. Maybe a Berlingo? I don't know cars. If they had come on a horse I would remember, my father had horses and I could tell them apart from the other end of the field."

I turned to Nikki. "They went off with a man in a white van."

"Doesn't narrow it down much," Nikki said. "What about the man?"

I asked Dolores if she recognised the man.

"He had a hat, brown it was. Or grey. And a coat with a big collar pulled up like he was cold but he couldn't have been cold, we don't have the air conditioning on at eight in the morning. It saves electricity. And sunglasses. I thought the sunglasses were odd as the sun was only just up. Maybe he had just had cataract surgery. My husband had cataract surgery and had to wear sunglasses all day for a week, he kept bumping into things. I don't remember the man bumping into things though."

I translated the necessary parts for Nikki.

"Sounds like a bad spy movie," she said.

"That, or she knows exactly who it was and she's trying to spin us a line."

"What now?"

"If she knows who it was, I'm willing to bet so does José Felipe. Nothing much happens here without him knowing about it."

We drove back to the Casa de Pastores and found José Felipe preparing tables for what looked like it was going to be a large group.

"Expecting many customers?" I asked.

"Yes, Juan is bringing another coach up today. It's good, yes?"

"Yes… No. No it's not good. We agreed to keep things low key while the inspectors are here."

José tapped the side of his nose. "But they are not here, are they?"

"That's what I wanted to talk to you about. Would you happen to have any idea where they are?"

"No. Have they disappeared? It happens here sometimes. Sometimes people go walking and get lost in the mountains."

"José, this is the Alpujarras, not the north face of the Eiger. Those two would get out of breath climbing into bed; they're not likely to be up for a quick assault on the Mulhacén summit before breakfast. What do you know?"

"I know it is better if people do not interfere in things that do not concern them. We have visitors coming here, my rooms are full, the village shops are open all day again and my cousin José Martin's workshop is always full."

"Hmm." I watched him as he wiped the tables with an efficiency born of decades. "On a separate question, do you happen to know where I can find José Diego?"

"Who?" José asked without looking up.

"José Diego? Your cousin? You mentioned him the other day?"

"I do not know this José Diego. Now, I have kept your table, I will bring you beer and we have some special migas." He turned his back on me and continued preparing the tables.

We sat as instructed and a few minutes later, José brought beer and migas as promised.

"I'm thinking he has a hand in this?" Nikki asked once José had disappeared again.

"Hmm, more than a hand, I'd guess. The question is what do we do about it?"

"We force him to tell us or we get the police in," Nikki said. "I don't see an issue here."

"But wait a moment. José is right; the village has come alive since all this has been going on. Is it right to let them destroy all that?"

"So this was all for the good of the village, huh? Nothing to do with you lot just wanting an easy ride for six months? I should never have let this slide; I should have stopped you all from day one. You could have done your bit, caught the odd rabbit, grown some potatoes and all gone back with no problems. But no, you had to create your own warped version of Disney World and rearrange Spain's tourist industry for your own convenience."

"Well… I viewed it as a sort of win-win scenario. No harm done to anybody and the tourists got a better deal than just being dumped outside a gift shop every time."

Nikki shook her head. "You're irredeemable."

"Thank you."

"You can't just let these people kidnap two civil servants and get away with it."

"I know." I picked at the migas "I was thinking we could set up a yurt and do some glamping stays. That's a big thing now, glamping."

"This is not the Wild West you know. It may be rural Spain but there are still rules. We need to call the police."

"José may be right; they might have gone hiking after all. Perhaps we shouldn't get too hasty. Let's give them a week, see if they turn up." I supped slowly at my beer and let my eyes wander across the hills. "Or two."

Nikki stood. "Right, either you do something about this or I'm calling the police."

"Look –"

"Look nothing," she cut me off. "Just because we're sleeping together, that doesn't give you the right to screw up my career too."

I drew a breath, readying my argument then let it go again. She was right. The trouble was, so was José. "Okay," I relented. "But I actually have no idea where they are or how to find them."

She drew her face close to mine in a way I would normally find quite arousing but now, I felt distinctly threatened. "You're Special Forces, figure it out."

"But –"

"And don't give me that crap about you were only the Electronics Warfare Operative, aren't they the ones supposed to gather intelligence?"

"Yes, but –"

"Well, get gathering." She turned and headed off towards the village.

I watched her as she disappeared around the corner. Then I called José over.

"José Diego…" I started.

"Ah," he smiled. "No." He turned and headed back inside, picking up a couple of empty bottles from a nearby table as he went.

I pondered on what Nikki had said. Gathering intelligence is easy enough when all one has to do is to hack into the local area network and intercept the emails and WhatsApp messages of the bad guys. But here, whoever was holding the Evil Twins was certainly not going to be chattering about it on the internet. This was a tight community where everybody knows everybody else's business but nobody spills secrets to outsiders. Thirty-five years living under Franco had taught people to be wary about giving out secrets and that history takes a long time to change. So, where was the local intelligence centred? Who controls the information?

I had a thought and set off into the village.

The local pharmacy creaked under the strain of the morning exodus from the doctor's surgery as everybody gathered to collect their medicines. It seemed to be a ritual reproduced all over rural Spain. The womenfolk all turn up at the doctor's en masse, irrespective of their scheduled appointment time. They catch up on all the gossip, moan about their respective menfolk and discuss their ailments. Once the surgery closes, they all decamp to the farmacia to await their medicines where again, the noise of a dozen simultaneous conversations is enough to make one's ears bleed.

I stood in the middle of the sea of tight perms and nylon dresses and listened to the chatter. It took my ears a few minutes to tune in to the dialect and general melee of multilateral conversations before I could catch the threads of the discourse. Once I had tuned in, it wasn't unlike my previous experiences where I would have to listen to several conversations at once and often in different dialects or even languages. All the time my ears straining to catch the key words which would tell me which exchanges needed my attention, gradually filtering out the trivia and homing in on the critical.

I tried to become a non-person in the crowded pharmacy, which was not easy considering I stood about a foot higher than the bobbing waves of permed heads. I gradually filtered out the talk of bunions, grandchildren and feckless husbands and listened for the snatches of exchanges which might give the clues I needed. As the mundane blurred away, two conversations tripped my internal alert circuits. The name José Diego had of course been at the top of my keyword list and my ears caught a snatch of conversation about him having English guests who did nothing but complain about Spanish food. In the other one, José Felipe had been seen taking precooked meals down the Calle de Silencio and much speculation concerned the possibility of a fancy lady receiving his attentions.

My turn in the non-queue came round and I purchased a pack of aspirin and left.

***

Calle de Silencio was little more than an alley with terraced houses pressing in from both sides. The buildings all seemed to tip forwards slightly, giving a decidedly claustrophobic feel as I progressed down the ever steepening cobbled path. I scanned each house as I went, searching for clues. As was the custom, most houses hosted external letterboxes near their front doors, usually with the name of the occupants helpfully taped to the box. Sure enough, I soon found one which read, José Diego Garcia. Although I didn't know his surname, it seemed a fair bet that this was the house. Especially as it was the only detached house in the street and was set back from the rest with a small garden in front. Wrought iron pillars supported a first floor veranda where an aged grapevine wound its way up through the structure before continuing up the wall and over the roof.

I studied the building and wondered what to do next. I hadn't really progressed my plan beyond finding the house where José Diego lived. Making an entry, interrogating suspects, rescue missions, this was the point where I usually took to the back of the van and shut the door, leaving the showy stuff to the people who enjoyed it more than I.

I could just walk up to the door and demand their release, I supposed. But even in my most optimistic of moods, I doubted that would work. Even the assumption that this was where the Evil Twins were being held was a leap of optimism.

The front door opened and expelled a man in a battered brown leather bomber jacket and matching leather peaked cap. Both items seemed to have seen better days long before being thrown out then found again under the remains of a 1930's bomb ruin. At a touch under six feet, the man himself was quite big compared to most of the locals. His face showed several days growth which blended into the thick, wiry tangle emanating from under the cap.

I stepped back into the cover of the terraced houses and waited till I heard his footsteps hit the cobbles before moving. We passed each other with slight nods and the ubiquitous, "Buenas," before continuing in our opposite directions. I paused twenty paces deeper into the alley while I listened to his footsteps fading into the general background noise. Once I was sure he'd gone, I turned and headed back to the house. After a quick check to make sure nobody else was around, I slipped in to the garden. At least my training hadn't been completely wasted. The first window just offered a view of a small office with desk far too large for the room but little else. The second window I peered through was a small kitchen with traditional marble units and a huge oak table. The door in the opposite wall, however, afforded glimpses of another room just beyond. It was there that I caught a fleeting view of Ms Anthea Perkins. She walked past the open door with what appeared to be a cup in her hand. She certainly didn't show any signs of being under duress or restraint. For the briefest of moments, I contemplated forcing the door and charging in there on the rescue. But only the briefest of moments. My gallantry notions dispersed as quickly as a politician's promises when I noticed another woman sat in the corner of the room. She wore a once pink polyester apron and a scowl which would give a gargoyle a nasty shock. I guessed she was on point. I backed away from the window and out onto the street. I'd just started up the slope back to the village when the man I'd passed earlier appeared. He carried a plastic bag from the local shop with a baguette, a bottle of gin and what looked like a dozen or so packets of different teas. We grunted at each other once more as we passed and I carried on out onto the main road. I headed straight to our little house where I found Nikki at the table studying her laptop.

"How's the job hunting going?" I asked.

"Just freshening up my CV," she replied. "I have no intention of this fiasco taking me down. You called the police yet?"

"No." I filled the kettle and placed it on the hob.

"You'd be wise to." She turned to face me. "It's your best chance. I don't want to see you end up inside over this and I've been thinking that if you are the one who blows the whistle, you stand a chance of keeping out of the worst of the shit-storm that's coming."

"There might be another way. Tea?" I laid out two mugs.

"Thanks. What way? What are you up to now, Michael?"

"I think I might have found out where they're being held." I poured boiling water onto the teabags. "Not far from here actually."

She furrowed her eyebrows. "How did you find them?"

"Infiltrating local intelligence networks," I said. "Bit like Baghdad, only with little old ladies instead of drones and wiretaps."

"Hmm, so where are they?"

"Calle de Silencio, just down from the baker's. Getting them out might be tricky though."

"We could just try knocking on the door and suggesting they let them go? I mean, they're certainly not professionals and once they know the game's up they'll probably just roll over."

"You might be right but José Diego's not to be underestimated. He looks like he's been scrapping in these mountains since the Civil War. Same clothes as well, by the looks of it."

We finished our tea then made our way up to the site to bring the others up to speed. Unusually, everybody was there. They sat on logs and folding chairs with an air of expectant gloom. The bucket of empty cans told of the mood.

After I'd outlined the events and the options as we saw them, a morose silence fell on the group while each processed the information.

"Can we bribe them?" Donny suggested, breaking the silence.

"They're Department of Justice," said Nikki. "It's unlikely."

"Guy I used to supply motors for used to bribe border guards all the time. Most of 'em would turn a blind eye to anything for a wedge of euros. Could've slipped the queen's gold roller past them for enough folding. They don't care. All they're interested in is fags and illegals."

"Well, as we seem to lack sufficient quantities of the… um… folding stuff," Nikki said. "Or even insignificant amounts come to that, we're going to call that one Plan C."

"What happened to Plan B?" asked Ryan.

"That was Michael's original plan which involved significant amounts of C4 and a helicopter."

"I never said anything about a helicopter," I protested.

"Why don't we just knock on the door and pretend to be Jehovah's witnesses?" asked Bob. "Two of us could keep them talking while somebody sneaks round the back and gets them out."

"Or the Domino's Pizza man," suggested Ryan. "Everybody opens the door to the Domino's Pizza man."

"Even if you've not ordered a pizza?" I queried.

"Sure. Random pizza? Nobody turns down a random pizza."

"Okay," said Nikki. "If we've exhausted the impossible and the ridiculous, perhaps we can focus on a solution which at least has some basis in reality?"

"No, hang on," I said. "Ryan might have something."

"Really?" said Nikki.

"Really?" said Ryan. "But it's a Tuesday."

"Tuesday?" I queried.

"I never get my best ideas on a Tuesday. It's a well-known fact. I think it's something to do with earth rhythms."

I studied him for a moment. "But today's Wednesday."

"Really?"

I nodded.

"Oh, that'll explain it then."

"Right," I said. "Moving on, random food. Ryan's right."

"Those are words one never expects to hear together," said Jason.

"Bear with me," I said. "It's about causing confusion. Something so left-field that it couldn't possibly be seen as a threat."

We bounced ideas around, ridiculous, insane or just odd. By the time the evening closed in, we had a basic idea and the mood lifted slightly, even showing fleeting signs of optimism. We decamped to the Casa de Pastores for supper.

~ *Chapter Twenty-Three* ~

I spent the best part of the following morning tracking down the necessary items for our assault on the house in Calle de Silencio. Butter, flour, candles and party hats. I convinced José Felipe that we had a surprise party to set up, not a total lie, and he allowed us use of his kitchen. Bob got to work with the ingredients, an online recipe from the BBC website and a healthy dollop of optimism. By late afternoon, the plans were laid, the equipment checked and double checked, and the roles assigned. It felt like old times.

As Special Forces do the world over, we'd decided to time our breach for the time when the bad guys are in their deepest point of REM sleep. Here, in the Alpujarras, that meant three-thirty in the afternoon. Siesta time.

We moved our equipment silently into the Calle de Silencio and scoped the target. All seemed quiet. I crept up to the front window and peered inside. Nothing to be seen, the visible spaces were devoid of people. I wished I could have gained an obbo on the rear but a set of heavily padlocked iron gates made side access impossible without a set of industrial bolt cutters.

As my watch ticked closer to the scheduled entry time, we each took up our designated places around the front door. Our plan was to position each person for maximum impact on the target as the door was opened.

Nikki took the forward position as she was deemed to be the least threatening in appearance. Especially with her camouflage of pink frock, courtesy of the second-hand shop, party hat and plastic moustache.

"Nice knees," I said.

"I'm going to kill you for this," she hissed at me.

She held the birthday cake in her outstretched arms and I ignited the candles. I checked the others.

We'd decided that in the absence of smoke grenades, that Ryan should blow dope smoke at whoever opened the door. It should achieve the desired effect of disorientation and as nobody has ever used cannabis smoke as a precursor to violence, it should be immediately seen as a Non-Hostile Event. Donny held a carton of beer and Jason was ready with the confetti. To the sides of the door, Bob and Sean readied themselves with trays of cocktail sausages and bowls of crisps. I kept concealed in the deep flank ready to take advantage of the confusion and slip through unnoticed to secure the hostages.

My watch counted the final seconds and I tapped Nikki on the shoulder as an indicator to launch the breach. She wobbled the cake slightly as she briefly freed a hand to press the bell and re-connect with the tray before it fell.

The noise of the doorbell resounded through the whole village as our heightened senses strained for any signs of threat.

The silence took hold once more, punctuated solely by seven thumping heartbeats and the noise of Bob munching crisps.

The seconds ticked into mission time and still nothing happened. I was about to give Nikki the signal for a second execution of the doorbell when, without warning, the door creaked open. José Diego blinked at the light and took a backward step when he saw the group. His mouth dropped open and his eyes struggled ever wider as he tried to understand what he was seeing through the clouds of dope smoke.

He managed a brief, "Qué pasa?" before Donny dumped a freshly opened can of beer in his hand and our well-rehearsed rendition of 'Happy Birthday' sprang into action.

I slipped through the confusion and headed for the room at the back where I'd seen Ms Anthea Perkins. I risked a rearward glance as I went and noticed the others were commencing their ingress exactly as planned. They milled around José Diego, offering gifts of sausages and cake and at the same time, they slowly filtered into the house to follow me. I noticed that José Diego was wearing a party hat. That was a good sign and indicated compliance.

I cleared the door and positioned myself with my back to the wall where I could see both the door and the rest of the room. Ms. Anthea Perkins sat in an oversized Victorian style chair while Norman Timswick sat at a dining table nibbling neatly from a plate of biscuits. He brought to mind an OCD mouse. Just across the room from Ms Perkins sat another man. It took me a moment to place him then I realised it was José Antonio from the Virriatos Museum.

The rest of the squad came into the room and gathered around Ms Perkins while they continued their birthday song. A mystified looking José Diego trailed behind them. He wiped cake crumbs from his lips and took a sip of beer.

"Ah, Michael," Ms Perkins said. She let her gaze travel the room. "And… er… everybody."

"We've come to break you out," said Bob.

"That's very nice of you but I don't really need rescuing."

She placed a bone china cup on the table next to her. "Although, if you happen to have brought some English tea with you…?"

"Tea?" I asked, mostly for lack of something more relevant to say.

"Yes, José Diego has been an angel, to and fro the shop looking for suitable tea." She looked at José Diego. "Haven't you, dear?" She touched his arm. "There's a love."

José Diego grunted, "Si." The forced smile never reached his eyes.

"But all he could find were these herbal teas," she continued. "Now, don't get me wrong, herbal teas have their place, but not in the afternoon."

"So, you weren't kidnapped?" I asked.

"Oh yes. It was like something out of James Bond. Very exciting."

"I don't understand," said Nikki. "If you were kidnapped why… what…" she tailed off.

Ms Perkins took a sip from the tea cup and squinted in disapproval. "Oh, yes. I can see how you might find it somewhat confusing. You see, José Diego thought we were here to stop your tourist business."

I stared at her. "But –"

"Yes, I know. But that was when we thought you were all up to your old ways."

"But we tried –"

"Did you know José Diego's father fought against Franco in the Civil War? So brave." She touched his arm again and smiled up at him. "Well, once he knew I had a penchant for history, he introduced me to his cousin, José Antonio. He has a museum, would you believe it?"

"Yes, I think I mentioned –"

"José Antonio told me all about the Great Shepherd. Did you know a Great Shepherd came this way?"

"Actually –"

"This is quite possibly one of the most important historical sites in southern Spain."

"We only… What?"

"José Antonio told me how you researched the history of Virriatos and the battle. I have to say, I was quite surprised to learn about this. It's all very exciting; it's not every day one is fortunate enough to be so instrumental in bringing such a rich history to light. I could use this for my thesis."

I realised where this was going. "But it was –"

Nikki grabbed my upper arm and squeezed, cutting off both my intended outrage and the blood supply to my hand.

"But why the ransom?" Nikki asked, clearly trying to keep me diverted.

"Oh, that was José Diego. He thought if he could raise the money to buy the field he could keep the site open."

"Ah, hence the strange amount." I did a quick mental calculation. "Twenty-five thousand plus tax."

José Diego nodded.

"Are we still going to prison?" asked Bob.

I looked at Ms Perkins and raised a quizzical eyebrow.

"I think our recommendation will be that you remain here to see the project to an end." She looked at Timswick. "I think that's what we decided, is it not Mr Timswick?"

Timswick nodded. "Yes, you did."

She turned back to me. "I have to say, your methods of self-sufficiency have proved to be somewhat unusual but you did achieve the goal. Now, moving forwards, with my help and contacts we can really make the Perkins Alpujarras Historical Centre a great success."

"The Perkins Alpujarras Historical Centre?" I queried and instantly felt Nikki's iron fingers dig into triceps muscle. "Sounds... wonderful."

I felt a nudge on my other arm and turned towards José Diego.

"Do you want that I make her disappear?" he whispered.

***

The following morning, Perkins and Timswick joined us for morning coffee and tostadas at the Casa de Pastores.

"How are you feeling this morning, Ms Perkins, you know, after your ordeal?" Nikki asked.

"Oh, it was sort fun," she said. "And you must call me Anthea, dear. After all, we're going to be colleagues for a while."

My tostada slipped from my fingers and the tangly haired dog appeared from nowhere and took it before it hit the ground.

"Colleagues?" I queried. "How... um... how?"

"I've decided to use my holiday allowance to stay here for a while to ensure this site conforms to certain standards of historical authenticity," she said. "I've sent in my report saying how important it is that this project continues and requesting immediate leave."

"Oh," I said. "Are you sure? Only it seems a bit of a waste of a holiday? You could be sunbathing on a beach somewhere."

"Oh dear no. All that sand and sweaty men in tiny trunks? Heavens above. No, this place needs a firm leadership and a sense of direction. And those are my fortes, firm leadership and sense of direction. That's what got me where I am today."

I glanced at Mr Timswick. "Are you staying too?" I asked.

"No, he can't." Anthea intercepted Timswick before he could speak. "He hasn't any holiday allowance left. He has to go back tomorrow."

"Oh, dear," I said, with as much compassion as I could fake. "That's a shame."

Timswick said nothing but a flickering smile broke his lips before he could stop it.

"Well," I said. "We can't sit here all day, much as we would enjoy it. But we have to be…" I hadn't thought this bit through before starting to speak. "…um… over there." I pointed vaguely at the village. "One of the elderly ladies wants her television looking at and I promised to help. I like to help. It's all part of the new, reformed me. You coming, Nikki?"

"Oh yes, please," Nikki almost shouted the words. "I mean, I'm pleased to help if I can."

We headed off into the village leaving the Evil Twins to their breakfast.

"We need to do something about this," I said. "Maybe we should get José Diego to do whatever it is he does after all."

"You don't fancy being subject to her firm leadership and sense of direction then?" Nikki smiled at me.

"Whilst that may have a certain appeal to some, I'm prepared to pass up that little pleasure for the sake of the sanity of the rest of the people living in the Alpujarras."

We headed down to the Venta Pastor to find Donny and Ryan already there.

"You too?" Donny asked.

"Yes," I said. "She's driving me nuts, fortunately, I don't think she's discovered this place yet but it won't be long."

"Can't we take out a hit on her?" Ryan suggested. "She's

put her report in now, she said, so we can get rid of her. Right? You must know some people. Your lot were well hard, they might do it."

"You want me to get my old regiment to bump off a DOJ officer?" I said.

Ryan studied the sky for a moment. "Yeah," he said finally. "But can they make it look like an accident?"

"I don't believe we're having this conversation," I said.

"I'll take care of it," Donny said and sipped at an impossibly complicated cocktail. "Hey, these are quite good. Why didn't I get on to these before?"

"What do you mean, you'll take care of it?" Nikki leaned forwards and did her best fierce face.

"You know Jimmy? Jimmy Watkins?" Donny licked at the little plastic cocktail stick.

"Jimmy Watkins?" I queried. "The guy in the St Pauls house who was caught printing hooky money?"

"Allegedly," said Donny.

"Allegedly?"

"Yeah, they never did prove nothing, I think he was fitted up."

"So where does Jimmy Watkins figure in this?" asked Nikki.

"He can post a wedge of dodgy tenners to Ms Anthea's office."

"How does that help?" I asked.

"Well, somebody'll find it won't they? Then they'll think she's been up to naughties and she'll get the boot. Job done."

I noticed a figure I recognised walking up the road, José Diego. I waved and called, "Buenas dias."

He stopped. "Ah, Señor Miguel. How is your crazy lady?"

"Still crazy," I said. "Fancy a drink?"

He glanced up at the sun. "Si, it is just the right time for a brandy." He stepped over the small fence which separated the Venta Pastor's patio from the road and pulled up a chair.

"We were just discussing how to deal with the Crazy Lady," I said.

"Ah, no problem. I can make her go away if you like. It is not difficult."

"No thanks, I have an idea."

"You do?" queried Nikki. "Do tell."

"Would you believe that Ms Perkins used to be a professional dominatrix?"

Nikki thought for a moment, then said, "No."

"Okay, do you think the DOJ would believe it?"

"Unlikely, I think you're going to have to do better than that," Nikki said.

"What about if an old website of hers came to light? Do you think they'd believe it then?"

"Whatever it is you're thinking of doing, don't." She glared at me.

"But it wouldn't really do any harm. The Department of Justice would be obliged to investigate, they'd call her back and by the time they sorted it out everybody would have forgotten about us."

"And you don't think they're going to suspect you? Mr Expert Hacker with a prime motive? You'd be back in front of the judge so fast the ink wouldn't even be dry on your fake website."

"Ah, I hadn't thought of that," I confessed.

"I can make her go away," said José Diego.

"Really, thanks for the offer," Nikki said. "But we're just going to have to learn to deal with her. At least we're not being shut down."

"Let's just see what José Diego thinks," I said. "We can't keep her here indefinitely. It's not fair on Spain."

"Are you insane?" Nikki asked.

"No, I passed the tests, remember?"

"Hmmff."

I looked at José Diego. "What do you mean exactly? Making her go away? How does that work?"

"Michael," Nikki snapped.

I touched her arm in what I hoped was a soothing sign and continued to study José Diego.

"Is easy." José Diego threw his brandy down his throat in one and waved his glass towards the barman. "My cousin, José Ramon, he is the mayor of Virriatos. He can talk to her people in England. They will listen to him, he is an important man. You should see how big his desk is."

"So you're not... not..." Nikki tailed off.

"Not what?" asked José Diego.

"You're not going to... you know..."

"No, Señora, I do not know. What do you think?"

"She thought you were going to... make her disappear. Permanently."

"Oh, I see." José Diego laughed. "Of course not. What do you think I am? That will only happen if she doesn't go." He downed his second brandy, stood and patted me on the shoulder. "I will talk to José Ramon."

***

We spent the rest of the day trying to avoid the Evil Twins but come evening, the call of decent food without having to cook broke our will and we headed to the Casa de Pastores for supper.

The rest of the crew were there and by the looks of it, they had been for quite a while.

"Ah, we wondered where you'd got to," Jason greeted, his smile brighter than usual. "Have a drink." He pushed a bottle of Cava across the table.

"Bubbly?" I said. "What's happening? Ryan sold his stash or has the world just been introduced to another lost master?" I looked at Sean.

"You've not heard?" Sean said.

"Heard what?"

"The lady herself, she's on her way home. Did you not know that?"

"No, what happened?"

"Apparently she got a call from the fellas back home," Sean said.

"Yeah, all of a panic, like," said Ryan. "She turned up here couple of hours ago looking for you."

"I don't understand," I said. "What happened?"

"From what I can gather," said Jason. "The local mayor has been on the phone to London suggesting that her presence here is not conducive to the economy of Virriatos and that her continued stay breaches the conditions of the original agreements." He laughed.

"Yeah, right pissed off she was," said Donny. "Got a real cob on. Giving it all the blah blah about how these stupid Spanish wouldn't understand culture if it bit them on the arse." He took a deep pull on the joint Ryan had just slid into his hand. "She didn't say arse but that's what she meant." He blew smoke across the table and passed the joint on to Jason.

"So she's gone?" Nikki looked as puzzled as I felt.

"Seems like it," I said.

Nikki sat down at the table and snapped her fingers at

Donny. "Pass that bottle over here and Jason, I'm next with that joint."

***

The sun crested the mountain top and flooded the patio outside the Casa de Pastores in the orange glow of morning. It had been three weeks since the Evil Twins had returned to England and we still basked in the peace. Even though they had only lasted for three days, it had felt more like three months.

I stirred sugar into my coffee and stretched my legs into the expanding puddle of warming sunlight.

"We've not heard from them, do you think they'll ever come back?" I asked Nikki.

"Probably not." Nikki thoughtfully dipped the corner of her churro into the mug of drinking chocolate. "The locals didn't exactly make them feel welcome here and the mayor stepping in was probably the last assault on her dignity."

"That's about what I thought. What about you? You still not made up your mind?"

She stared at her cup and seemed to go somewhere else. The sound of chinking glasses as José Felipe readied the bar for the first of the day's coaches punctuated the good natured ribbing between Jason and Donny. They'd been debating whether we should all take Jason's RV out for an inaugural run to the coast now it had its new engine up and running.

Nikki lifted her head and watched the shadows move across the mountain face. "As much as this place infuriates me, somehow, it feels more like home than anywhere I've ever lived," she said.

"What about Blacklance Security? What are you going to tell them?"

"Already done it. I sent them an email yesterday asking them to cancel my contract."

I slid my hand across the table and took hers. I cast my gaze up the hill where the newly laid track now gave car access to the Visitor Centre and felt the warming sun seeping into my bones.

"That's good then."

The End

~ *Find my books and sign up for the newsletter* ~

If you would like to subscribe to my Newsletter, just enter your details below. I promise not to sell your email address to a Nigerian Prince or send you adverts for various biological enhancements.

I will however, at entirely random moments, send you a newsletter containing my writing updates, competitions, give-aways, general meanderings and thoughts on the latest Big Thing.

luddington.com/newsletter/

OTHER BOOKS FROM THE BEST SELLING AUTHOR...

Tony Ryan is bemused. He thought he understood the way the world worked, but now, as a sacrificial lamb of the credit crunch he finds himself drifting... drifting into the clutches of the ever resourceful Pete who could find the angle in a Fairy Liquid bubble... and into the arms of the enigmatic hippy girl, Astrid, who's about to introduce Tony to rabbits, magic caves and the joys of mushrooms.

THE MONEY
THAT NEVER WAS

David
Luddington

Charles Tremayne is a spy out of his time. After a long career spent rescuing prisoners from the KGB or helping defectors across the Berlin Wall the world has changed. The Wall has gone and no longer is there a need for a Russian speaking, ice-cold killer. The bad guys now all speak Arabic and state secrets are transmitted via satellite using blowfish algorithms impenetrable to anybody over the age of twelve. Counting down the days to his retirement by babysitting drunken visiting politicos he is seconded by MI6 for one last case. £250,000,000 of government money destined as a payoff for the dictator of a strategic African nation goes missing on its way to a remote Cornish airfield.

Tremayne is dispatched to retrieve the money and nothing is going to stand in his way. Armed with an IQ of 165 and a bewildering array of weaponry and gadgets he is not about to be outmanoeuvred by the inhabitants of a small Cornish fishing village. Or is he?

Schrodinger's Cottage

A Comedy of Quantum Proportions

David Luddington

Tinker's Cottage nestles in a forgotten corner of deepest Somerset. It also happens to sit on a weak point in the space time continuum. Which is somewhat unfortunate for Ian Faulkener, a graphic novelist from London, who was hoping for some peace and quiet in which to recuperate following a very messy breakdown.

It was the cats that first alerted Ian to the fact that something was not quite right with Tinker's Cottage. Not only was he never sure just how many of them there actually were, but the mysterious way they seemed to disappear and reappear defied logic. The cats, and of course the Pope, disappearing literary agents, mislaid handymen and the insanity of Cherie Blair World.

As Ian tries to untangle the mystery of the doors of Tinker's cottage he risks becoming lost forever in the myriad alternate universes predicted by Schrodinger. Not to mention his cats.

Schrodinger's Cottage is a playful romp through a variety of alternate worlds peopled by an array of wonderful comic characters that are the trademark of David Luddington's novels.

For fans of the sadly missed Douglas Adams, Schrodinger's Cottage will be a welcome addition to their library. A heart-warming comedy with touches of inspired lunacy that pays homage to The Hitchhiker's Guide whilst firmly treading its own path.

FOREVER ENGLAND

SPAIN

SPAIN

David Luddington

"...And there will be a corner of some foreign field that will be forever England."

Only these days it's more likely to be a half finished villa overlooking a championship golf course somewhere on one of The Costas.

Following an unfortunate encounter with Spanish gin measures and an enthusiastic estate agent, retired special effects engineer Terry England is the proud owner of a nearly completed villa in a new urbanisation in Southern Spain.

Not quite how he'd intended to spend his enforced early retirement Terry nevertheless tries to make the best of his new life. If only the local council can work out which house he's actually bought and the leaf blowers would please stop.

Terry finds himself being sucked in to the English Expat community with their endless garden parties and quests for real bacon and Tetley's Tea Bags. Of course, if it all gets too much he can always relax in the local English Bar with a nice pint of Guinness, a roast beef lunch and the Mail on Sunday.

With a growing feeling that he might have moved to the 'Wrong Spain', Terry sets out to explore and finds himself tangled in the affairs of a small rustic village in the Alpujarras. It is here where he finds a different Spain. A Spain of loves and passions, a Spain of new hopes and a simpler way of life. A place where a moped is an acceptable means of family transport and a place where if you let your guard down for just a moment this land will never let you go again.

Forever England is the tale of one man trying to redefine who he is and how he wants to live. It is a story of hope and humour with an array of eccentric characters and comic situations for which David Luddington is so well known and loved.

"Overall, this is a very warm and funny book. It is filled with wonderful characters and many laugh out loud moments."
book-reviewer.com

"Genuinely funny, with many laugh out loud moment..."
Matt Rothwell - author of Drunk In Charge Of A Foreign Language

Reading David Luddington is like "Like reading your favourite sitcom." – Nigel Planer

"The funniest book of the year." – Claire Ashton, Editor the Book Reviewer.

Retired stage magician turned professional mystic debunker, John Barker, finds his sceptical beliefs under fire when he encounters a strange man who claims to be Merlin. After several unsuccessful attempts to rid himself of his increasingly unpredictable companion, John finally relents and agrees to assist in the man's crazy mission, to find the true grave of the mythical King Arthur.

Following a hidden code contained within the text of a soft porn novel, they gather a growing entourage of hippies, mystic seekers and alien hunters as they leave a trail of chaos across the south west of England. When the group comes to the attention of a TV Reality Show producer looking to make a fast profit out of harmless eccentrics and fading celebrities, John decides it's time to take charge and prove one way or the other, the identity of this mysterious person who claims to be a fictional wizard.

"Whose reality is this anyway?" is a warm-hearted tale of what it means to be an individual and to follow one's dreams. With his trademark cast of oddball characters and absurd situations, David Luddington once more transports us into a world where who you are is more important than what you are.

"David Luddington epitomizes the elusive quality of writing that he perpetuates - the British Comedy." – Grady Harp

To Follow On Facebook:
www.facebook.com/DavidLuddingtonAuthor/

The Website: www.luddington.com

Twitter: @d_luddington

Printed in Poland
by Amazon Fulfillment
Poland Sp. z o.o., Wrocław